"A PENNY FOR YOUR THOUGHTS."

Raking a hand through his hair as he spoke, Seth rose and went toward her.

At the sound of his voice, Tess smiled, remembering how he'd said the same thing to her only a few weeks ago, on the bridge. She turned to look at him and her heart tripped over again at the sight of him, bare-chested and so recklessly handsome. A tremor of yearning shot through her. She tried not to let it show.

"Only a penny?" she responded lightly. "I'd have thought the price would've gone up by now. Or are you suggesting my thoughts are cheap?"

She'd meant it as a joke, but something in his eyes told Tess he wasn't taking it that way. There was pain on Seth's face, and when he spoke his voice held a strange, ragged note.

"No, Tess. Nothing about you has ever been cheap. From the first time I saw you, I knew you were like a rare jewel that wasn't for sale. And that I'd do anything I could . . . to get close to you."

ABOUT THE AUTHOR

Writing *Tess* was one of Katherine Burton's most
challenging experiences—as well as one of the
most rewarding. Together with her three closest
friends, Sandra Canfield, Terri Herrington and
Penny Richards, Katherine devoted many months
to the creation of Calloway Corners. The
birthplace of Tess, the heroine of Katherine's
second Superromance, is an imaginary place that
bears more than a passing resemblance to the
towns near the author's own home in Louisiana.
Married to her childhood sweetheart and the
proud mother of both a son and a daughter,
Katherine spends her time horseback riding
and painting ceramics when she is not busy
plotting books.

Books by Katherine Burton

HARLEQUIN SUPERROMANCE
292–SWEET SUMMER HEAT

Don't miss any of our special offers. Write to us at the
following address for information on our newest releases.

Harlequin Reader Service
901 Fuhrmann Blvd., P.O. Box 1397, Buffalo, NY 14240
Canadian address: P.O. Box 603,
Fort Erie, Ont. L2A 5X3

Katherine Burton
TESS

Harlequin Books

TORONTO • NEW YORK • LONDON
AMSTERDAM • PARIS • SYDNEY • HAMBURG
STOCKHOLM • ATHENS • TOKYO • MILAN

Published March 1989

First printing January 1989

ISBN 0-373-70346-5

Printed in U.S.A.

For my sisters in this project,
this book is dedicated to Sandra Canfield,
Terri Herrington and Penny Richards,
and to my editor, Nancy Roher.
Thank you all for giving me a chance.

CHAPTER ONE

SHE WAS TRYING to pick up the pieces.

It was the last day of June, and a dull shaft of evening sunlight filtered through the half-drawn blinds, swirling dust motes and casting hazy, barlike shadows on the paneled walls. In the seclusion of her bedroom, Tess Calloway Langford sat crouched on the floor, staring numbly at the bits of rose-colored glass lying broken at her feet.

She hadn't meant to let anything fall. One moment she had been carefully lifting the vanity tray from the dresser, intending only to dust underneath it. And then, before she'd realized it, and without so much as a wobbled hint of warning to alert her, the bottle of cologne had tipped over and fallen, crashing to the floor.

Lord, she thought, blinking back the swell of tears that seemed to fill her eyes too frequently and with too little provocation these days. Lately, it seemed she had developed some sort of compulsive affliction for bungling even the most menial of tasks. *I've got the Midas touch in reverse,* Tess noted ironically, *and it isn't gold I'm creating.*

Don't dwell on the negative, Tess told herself sternly as she leaned forward, her thick, light brown hair falling heavily over slim shoulders. Why dwell on anything beyond this moment? Surely any decision about the future could wait. It had *been* waiting, after all. What was a few more minutes—or days, for that matter?

The slender hand that reached for the first small shard of glass was strikingly bare and sensual, possessing an exotic tawny-skinned silkiness, that required no jewelry or other artifice to draw attention to the owner's quiet, sultry grace.

But Tess had never considered herself graceful or even particularly feminine. Instead, she had learned to pride herself, not on beauty, but in the perfection of accomplishment. And yet now, as she gingerly picked through the jagged bits of glass, her hazel-green eyes brooding and troubled, it was hard to imagine herself a practising perfectionist.

The bottle of cologne had been a gift from her ex-husband on their last wedding anniversary together. The scent was too heavy, too blatantly cloying for appeal, and in truth, Tess had never really liked it. Now the musky fragrance seemed almost overpowering. Yet she had treasured it, often worn it on special occasions to please Vance, and for the sentimentalities involved.

Now, with her divorce to Vance Langford final and six months past, Tess wondered why she hadn't already tossed the perfume out. Maybe it was an oversight. Or perhaps the token gift was just one more of those curiously self-torturing little keepsakes she'd held on to simply because there seemed nothing else left to hold.

Tess closed her eyes and held her breath until a blur of tears receded. But then she straightened her shoulders, and though her hands trembled with the soul-deep anguish of disillusionment and carelessly shattered dreams, she tossed the last of the glass into the bedroom waste can and mopped the spill with a handful of tissue.

It was over. *It's done, and you might as well accept it,* Tess told herself as she rose to her feet, struggling to banish the bleak thoughts from her mind. Picking up the wastebasket, she carried it with her as she made her way across the typically large, suburban house to its typically sterile, stainless-steel kitchen.

She emptied the can into a large bin under the sink, then set the small one on the back step to air. The breeze that rushed in through the open door was hot but not unbearably so, and with it came the distinctive, summer-time scent of charcoal smoldering in someone's grill.

The smell, though pleasant, did not make Tess feel hungry. In fact, she had almost given up food altogether these days. Telling herself to act in her own best inter-ests, Tess wandered to the pantry and looked inside. But the cupboard was virtually bare. Lately, it hadn't seemed important to grocery shop or to cook real meals any-more, when there was no one to look after but herself. She raised her eyes to the top shelf above a sparse offer-ing of dust-topped canned goods. Only the cooking wine, she thought facetiously, seemed to be holding under the strain. Impulsively, she reached for the bottle, noting that it was a tolerable Californian vintage. *Better wine than whine,* she thought, then laughed aloud at her own silly joke. Pouring herself a glass of the white liquid, Tess took a sip and then, thinking about her empty stomach, she decided to fix a spritzer.

Leaving the kitchen, Tess paused in the den and flicked on the stereo, just before sliding open the plate-glass doors and stepping out on the patio deck.

It was nearing sunset, and with the sun no more than a doomed ball of fire on the horizon, she thanked God for small favors, and for once, the presence of the ever-constant Texas wind, which she had so often cursed in the past.

Drink in hand, she settled herself in the sleek chaise longue and leaned her head against the nubby tan cushion. From the den, inside, she could hear the soft, soulful music drifting from the FM station that specialized in oldies hits.

Strange, she thought, how a certain old song could burst upon one's memory with such bright recall. Suddenly you could remember where you were, who you were with and exactly what you were feeling the first time you'd ever heard the music and lyrics.

The tune playing now was such a song. "My eyes adored you..." The singer was lamenting over a high-school love who had never really know he'd existed.

And suddenly, with her head fuzzy from the sun's heat and the wine's fire, Tess found her thoughts drifting back to her own high-school days, and a wild, pale-haired boy with blazing turquoise eyes—eyes that had always seemed to see everyone but her. *Seth Taylor.* How she had adored him... from afar.

He'd been cocky and reckless and had possessed a reputation for sullen belligerence and a fiery temper. She could see him now, as she remembered him: dressed in low, skin-tight jeans and a faded Levi's jacket, its rough collar turned up carelessly as if against the world, as he lounged in blatant negligence against a row of dingy gray lockers that lined the narrow halls.

She had always been a little afraid of him. He'd seemed so cynical and tough. And yet, there was something about him, something in the way he moved and stood—with a casual, though faintly derisive ease, which had seemed to her then so erotically and forbiddingly male, that she couldn't have ignored him, even if she'd wanted to.

Seth Taylor. Strange that she should think of him now, and wonder that she had never really understood him, or the two opposing sides of his nature.

Tess had seen him explode in a schoolyard brawl with an animal rage that had resulted in the dislocation of another boy's jaw, and two weeks' suspension for Seth.

But she had been present, too, on another occasion when a new boy—sickly and frail, his thin legs weighed down with heavy metal braces—had stumbled and fallen on the stairwell. Some had laughed, others had simply gawked then walked on. But it was Seth Taylor—the bad boy, the one they called "trash"—who had stopped and stooped down, lifting the boy into his arms, and had carried him effortlessly, his twisted legs forgotten, as they mastered the stairs together.

Seth Taylor. Oh, the girlish fantasies she had created around him, Tess thought now with a rueful smile. But fantasies were so safe. It was reality that was difficult. Reality and the realization that very soon she had to start making some firm decisions in her life. And, Tess promised herself by the last sparks of the fading sun, she would do just that—first thing in the morning.

TWO HUNDRED MILES AWAY, in a small town in Louisiana, Seth Taylor stood lounging in the shadows of a longleaf pine, and gazing westward toward the same fading sun.

The day had been a killer—over ninety in the shade—and Seth knew from experience that Lady Summer was only joshing around with the po' folks for now. It would be mid-August before she *really* got down to business, he mused. And by then, the noonday temperature in the heart of the Bible Belt would be nosing a hellfire-and-damnation one hundred, if it struck one nth of a degree.

Despite that not exactly chilling thought, and the fatigue of aching muscles and a sore back, Seth smiled as he gazed at the modest frame house, which was still under construction. The outer walls had just gone up, and the air was heavy with the exhilarating scent of fresh, dry sawdust and hard, seasoned pine.

Brown piles of dirt, gray sand rocky-clumped with dried bits of cement, and sawed-off shorts of lumber remnants, lay strewn around the grass-barren lot. Trees, however, were abundant: dogwood, pine and oak. And later, after the inside of the house was completed, grass runners of the St. Augustine variety could be sprigged into the fertile soil for the makings of a thick, green lawn.

It was going to be a fine house, a genuine *home*, he thought. And again, Seth Taylor smiled. Only this time the expression more closely resembled a lopsided grin. Proud and unabashed, it revealed a flash of straight white teeth and gave his angular, square-jawed face an irresistible boyish appeal. It was an expression he wore well, and given the incorrigible glitter of his deep turquoise eyes, it suggested a charming innocence—though he was anything but innocent. Still, this look alone might have had him passing easily for a rakish twenty-one, in spite of his true, hardened years of thirty-two.

"You've come a long way, baby." He spoke to himself as he reached in his pocket for a pack of cigarettes. There was a time when this town—Calloway Corners—had looked on him as God must have looked on Sodom and Gomorrah, just before the flood.

Or was that Noah? Seth frowned. He couldn't remember. He'd never been able to keep his Bible stories straight. He supposed now it was because he'd never been one much for church. At least, not until recently and all the trouble he'd been having with his son. Skipping school. Breaking curfew. And according to his ex-wife, Celia, there had also been a couple of minor, but concern-worthy incidents of fighting and vandalism.

And then, as if to pour salt on his own self-inflicted wounds, there had been Jason's complete and flat flunking of the eighth grade. An exclusive and at least marginally perverse achievement, which had landed the boy like a banished angel in the hellish underworld of summer school.

Leaning his back against the rough bark of the towering pine's trunk, Seth let his cigarette dangle from the corner of his mouth as he struck a match, one-handedly, with a thumbnail flick. The sulfur flame flared instantly, and he squinted his eyes against the smoke and the smell. Then, shaking it out, he flipped the match aside and settled back to take a long, satisfying drag from the filtered temptation.

He worried about Jason. Seth didn't want his son to grow up the way he'd had to—fighting, clawing, grasping only through gut, gall and his own blood, sweat and tears for every ounce of respect or success he'd managed to earn. Seth wanted Jason's life to be simpler. Though it was hard because Celia had custody, and Jason visited him only on holidays and two weekends a month. But in his heart, Seth loved Jason more than any human being on earth. And all he wanted was for *his* son to be close, to be proud of himself and of his father, the way Seth had never been able to be proud of his own dad.

It was for this . . . for Jason, that Seth had gotten himself involved in church and ventured the risk of expanding his carpentry contracting business into custom building.

The unfinished house was one of three he was building on his own, with only the help of a small but well-
trained crew. Not bad, he thought with deserving pride
and only a tinge of lingering bitterness—not bad for the
son of a thieving drunkard and the soft-spoken woman
who had been his father's common-law wife.

That he had been born and raised a bastard had
seemed to bother the good townsfolk of Calloway Corners far more than it had distressed either Seth or his
mother.

As for his father, Gage Taylor, he couldn't have given
a hoot or a care. Seth had been eleven years old when his
father was given a "one to three" sentence, to be served
at Angola State Prison, for the crime of theft and the at-
tempted resale of stolen goods.

Seth shook his head and sighed. Seven-foot tractor
tires, yet. You'd think if the man had to steal, he'd have
used the common sense to opt for something a little more
discreet.

However, it had never been the state of Seth's parent-
age that had caused him the most trouble in his formative years. The callous remarks concerning his
birthrights, or lack of them, had rolled right off his back.
It was the degrading verbal attacks against his mother
that Seth could not abide.

Why should it have mattered to anyone but her that she
had been only one of fifteen hapless products of a back-
woods family, too poor to furnish her with clothes, books
and supplies needed for school? She knew how to sew
and she knew how to cook and she could pop a squirrel
with a homemade slingshot straight in the head from
twenty paces back.

But Judy Rankin couldn't read, could barely print her
own name. And this, it seemed to her, to Gage Taylor and

to the charitable women who drove up in their fancy cars to leave their dirty laundry for Judy to do, was a cause for shame, and justification for calling her "trash."

Dropping his cigarette to the ground, Seth crushed the butt under the heel of his boot, a lazy action that came so naturally he didn't bother glancing down. Instead, his eyes were trained on the curving blacktop highway as he listened for what he thought was the sound of an approaching car, its tires singing on the sun-baked asphalt.

As the sleek, white sports car rounded the tree-lined curve, emerging from the shadows and into clearer view, Seth immediately recognized both the vehicle and the strikingly handsome couple inside.

Smiling, he straightened, pulling away from the broad pine trunk where he had been leaning, and stepped forward, lifting his hand in greeting.

"Hey, honey! Don't you ever go home?" a sexy platinum blond called out the passenger window. The man at the wheel, her husband, Ford Dunning, whirled the car into the graveled drive and braked to a crunching halt a few yards away.

Sauntering forward, yet tossing a tongue-in-cheek glance at Ford, who was already climbing out from behind the wheel of the low-slung car, Seth answered his friend's wife in a tone of grave exasperation. "Mariah Calloway, don't you ever mind your own business?"

Emerald-green eyes narrowed in a dangerously mocking display of an affronted feline squint. "Only when there is no other person's business to mind. And besides," Mariah added imperiously, "the name is *Dunning*, as you well know. I'm a legally and prominently married woman now. And I'll thank you, sir, to remember that in the future."

Seth laughed, and so did Mariah. Though they had never been particularly close in their growing-up years, Seth had known Mariah's family practically all his life. He knew her three sisters and had even worked for their father—the now-deceased Ben Calloway—at the family-owned lumber mill when Seth himself had been little more than a scared, tough-acting kid.

Now, he opened the car door and held it for Mariah Dunning as her husband, Ford—the somewhat unorthodox pastor of the church Seth attended, and perhaps his closest male friend—came around to take his wife's hand, helping her out of the low bucket seat.

"You know," Mariah said, looking up at her husband with undisguised adoration, "I could get used to this royal treatment. Two handsome men at my beck and call. No telling to what depths of iniquity I might be tempted to sink."

Despite Mariah's outrageous flirtations and Ford's subsequent swatting of her on the behind, it was apparent to Seth that here were two people, so different and yet so openly committed to each other and the strength of their love, that jealousy or other self-originated insecurities had no place in their relationship.

Theirs was the kind of love, Seth thought, one couldn't help but envy, even covet. Still, as he stood there watching them, Seth was reminded, with a dull ache in his chest, of the solitude, the loneliness and the sometimes overwhelmingly drowning sense of purposelessness in his own life.

"All right, you two. Break it up. This isn't any lover's lane," he said, then laughed, making a joke of it all because he didn't like being reminded that some people fit like perfect pieces in a puzzle. "What brings you lovebirds around here, anyway?" Seth asked.

"Well, two things really," Ford replied, as he removed Mariah's arms from around his neck and plastered them firmly to her sides. It did no good, for she simply moved to stand behind him, encircling his waist with her arms as she rested her chin on his shoulder.

"We wanted to see how things were moving along on the house. Looks like it won't be long now before we can start moving in."

Seth grinned. "Well, I wouldn't start packing just yet. There's still a lot of work to be done on the inside. In fact, all we've really got now is a shell. But I've been working at my shop on the cabinets, and the bookcases for the study are just about finished, except for the staining."

"Ah, well..." Ford cleared his throat, looking a bit uncomfortable, and Mariah's cheeks had suddenly taken on a color—if Seth had not known better, he could have sworn it was a blush—that caused her to hide her face in the square of her husband's back.

For one brief moment, panic—no, terror—struck Seth like a blunt object. Were they going to tell him that they were not going to buy the house after all? Ford's pastor's salary, Seth knew, was no bundle by any means. And though Mariah had been working, keeping books at the family lumber mill, he doubted if hers was much higher. If finances had suddenly evolved into the issue, he could surely understand. But at the moment Seth was thinking only of the money that *he* himself owed, and how much he'd been counting on the proceeds from the sale of this house.

While his stomach churned and his brain grew dizzy calculating construction-related expenses, Seth watched Ford and Mariah exchange one more coy glance.

And then, once again clearing his throat, Ford began solemnly, "About that study. I'm afraid there's been a change of plans. Do you think you could make it resemble a nursery, you know, for a baby, instead?"

Seth's mouth dropped open, and he stared first at a rather awkward but beaming Ford, then shifted his gaze to Mariah, who nodded a demure affirmative to the question that hovered, unspoken, around them.

"Well, I'll be the son of a bi— Oh, sorry, Ford." Seth sensed his own color rising at his near slip. But his recovery was quick in light of the occasion, and what followed next was a hearty round of pumping handshakes, silly grins and a big hug for Mariah.

Once the news was out in the open and the customary amenities observed, Seth explained without further prompting that it would be no problem at all to convert the planned library-study into an infant's bedroom instead.

The three stood talking for a few minutes longer discussing paint colors and wallpaper. As the sun began to fade and the twilight shadows turned the sky from lime to lavender, and then to a dim gray, all three of them knew it was time to be going.

It was Mariah who made the first move. Gently taking her husband's arm, she smiled warmly at Seth. "There is just one more favor we'd like to ask of you," she said, her voice tremulous.

"Sure." Seth shrugged, feeling suddenly a little uncertain about what he was agreeing to. "What is it?" he asked.

"I wish you wouldn't say anything. About the baby, I mean. Not just yet. We haven't told the family, and I don't want Eden to worry unnecessarily."

Seth didn't think of the request as a big favor. In fact, he thoroughly understood the Dunnings's desire for privacy, and he knew of Eden Calloway's tendency to worry, especially when it came to her youngest sister. "Okay. I'll keep it under my hat. Only . . ." Seth said, his eyes twinkling, "you'll have to name it after me, if its a boy."

"Out of the question!" Mariah shot back. "It's going to be a girl. I've already put in my order."

Seth laughed and stood aside as Ford opened the car door and Mariah slid in. With his wife settled, Ford turned around to shake hands with Seth.

"You know," he said, "we're going to announce the big event at Eden's house on the Fourth of July. Fireworks and barbecue are tops on the agenda, not to mention that the whole crew will be there. Eden, Mariah and myself, of course. Jo with her husband and the little child they're adopting. And as I heard it, even Tess is driving in from Dallas for the occasion."

At the mention of Tess's name, Seth was reverently thankful for the darkness that hid the hot rush of emotion he could feel burning like bee stings on his face. He had been about to reach down to the ground for a misplaced claw hammer that had caught his eye earlier. But now his hands trembled so badly that he shoved them into his back pockets.

"Sounds like fun," he remarked lamely to Ford. Deep in his gut, however, he knew what was coming, and his stomach churned in anguish at the thought.

"Why don't you join us," Ford suggested as Seth had guessed. "I know Eden would love for you to be there."

The thought was tempting, especially because he had imagined so often in the past how it would be to see her, to run into Tess Calloway again.

Would she be changed? he wondered. Or would she be as he remembered her—dark and dreamy and innocently seductive, like a sweet exotic flower. Magnolias in the shade. That was the way Seth remembered Tess.

"So? How about it? The invitation's open. The more the merrier, as Eden would say."

The sound of Ford's voice brought Seth back to their conversation, and the realization that his friends were anxious to get home.

With all the graciousness he could muster, Seth formulated a polite refusal. "Thanks, but, you see, I'll have my son on the Fourth of July and I was hoping to coax him into a fishing trip on Shadow Lake."

"Well, that sounds like fun, too. I wouldn't mind coming along myself, but..." He cast a gentle, sidelong glance at Mariah. "This is pretty special, too."

Seth nodded, smiling as he thought of his own son. "Yeah," he murmured, "kids can mean a lot in a person's life."

Minutes later, Seth stood alone, listening to the droning night sounds and watching as the red glow of the sports car's taillights faded into an infinite curtain of black.

Above him, a whimsical breeze quivered the treetops and whispered through pine needles before swooping down to tousle his dark blond hair. Sighing, Seth tipped back his head and looked up into the starlit sky.

June was almost over, he thought, feeling strangely nostalgic. Next would come tomorrow...and July, bearing more heat, more work, more...

He didn't allow himself to finish the thought, but reached in his pocket for another cigarette as he strode toward his battered blue work truck, parked now in the indigo shadows of a leafy cottonwood.

Swinging up into the cab, he cranked the ignition, flicked on the headlights and pulled out of the drive. Seconds later, a cigarette dangling from his lips, its red-hot ash only a pinpoint of light in the truck's dark cab, he leaned forward and fished an old Frankie Vallee cassette tape from the glove compartment. Then he eased back and let his mind drift to the music, back to another time and the woman who had been only a girl then . . . a girl his eyes had adored.

CHAPTER TWO

AT JUST AFTER SIX on the second morning of July, Tess Langford loaded her suitcases in the trunk of her small car and took highway I-20 eastbound out of Dallas. She had hoped to get a jump on the Independence Day weekend traffic. But even at this early hour dozens of vehicles, whose occupants had presumably had the same idea, sped and swapped lanes in a frenzy around her. Everyone seemed in a hurry to get out of the city.

Maintaining the speed limit, her hazel eyes narrowed against the rising sun, Tess tried to decide if she was in a hurry or not. She wanted to go home. No, she thought, that was putting it too mildly. She needed to go home; she had to. In her own mind, at least, the question of whether to spend the remainder of the summer alone in Dallas or to go back to her family home, near the small town of Haughton, Louisiana, had finally come down to a choice between saving face or salvaging her sanity. She had chosen the latter, but admittedly not without consequence.

Tess shifted restlessly in her seat. The sun was growing higher, and already its dazzling rays were beginning to hint at the grueling heat yet to come.

Reaching for her purse on the seat beside her, she kept her eyes on the road as she dug around in a blind search for her sunglasses. In the process, her hand brushed a carefully folded sheet of NCR paper, and Tess knew without looking that it was the real-estate contract she'd signed just yesterday morning—the agreement to list her house for sale.

In truth, Tess wasn't certain why she'd held on to the house this long. It was too big for one person, and now that she realized it had never been the house she'd wanted at all, but rather, the security of a home, she knew letting it go was the best thing to do.

When summer was over, Tess told herself, if the house had sold—as the realtor seemed convinced that it would—then she would look for a smaller place. An apartment, maybe. Just a few small rooms in an older building. A place with a feeling of warmth and coziness. A place like home. A place like Calloway Corners, where she had been raised.

At last locating her sunglasses, Tess slid the black, oversized rims on her small face, then adjusted the air-conditioner control to a cooler setting. She heard the compressor kick on, and the car seemed to lag in the surge. The temperature warning light flickered dimly on the dashboard, and Tess frowned. But then, just as suddenly as the red glow had appeared, it faded again. Tess shook her head and shrugged before settling back for the four-hour drive.

She knew it was probably ridiculous, definitely self-indulgent and more than likely a shade sadistic to keep dwelling on the failure of her marriage. After all, she'd tried reasoning with herself, worse things had happened to better people, and they had lived through it. And so she had at least established that she wasn't going to die from divorce. But she had determined that she couldn't go on trying to pretend as if nothing had happened, as if everything was okay, as if she wasn't scared to death of the changes taking place in her life.

A van cut in front of her, and Tess braked sharply, focusing her attention on the road until the traffic began to break up outside Terrell. Slowly, then, as she allowed herself to relax behind the wheel, her mind took up its activity again.

For the first few months after her divorce, she'd existed in a kind of stunned daze, drifting numbly through the performance of daily tasks with an ever-present feeling of heavy, stomach-wrenching dread. She went to school; she came home. She wrote her sister Eden, and occasionally spoke on the phone to one of her other sisters, Mariah or Jo.

Tess was known as the "good girl" in the Calloway family. The conventional one. The shy conformist with a gift for listening and empathizing with everybody else's troubles and complaints, without ever interrupting to burden them with her own. And not because she was so self-reliant or "had it all together," as even her notoriously skeptical fire-haired sister Jo had once remarked.

If Tess was a good listener, she privately admitted, it was because she had always been so anxious to please, to live up to her family's expectations of her. She had wanted them to believe, as they seemed to, that she was strong and unselfish, although she had never found one trace of those attributes inside herself. Still, she had gone on playing life by all the rules, aware yet never completely understanding why she felt compelled to seek approval from others, as if their opinions of her were more important than her own.

And maybe they were, Tess thought wearily. Of the four Calloway sisters, she, the second youngest at twenty-nine, had been the one the others had affectionately referred to as the one most likely to succeed. But now, because she no longer possessed either the will or the courage to struggle on in perpetuation of the family myth, she was here, traveling a bleached white stretch of interstate highway, the glaring sun beating down hotly through the windshield on her face. Defeated. Going home.

IN THE CITY OF SHREVEPORT, just across the Louisiana state line, the telephone in the home of Jason McKinsey Taylor rang seven times before Jason's mother rolled over in bed and made a fumbling attempt to answer it.

"Yes. What is it?" Celia McKinsey—rich man's daughter, perpetual prom queen and ineffectual adult—drawled into the receiver. Her dry, parchment voice sounded patently bored. The same way, Seth mused with a wry tightening of his lips, as the last time he'd spoken to his ex-wife.

"I need to speak to Jason," he said directly, without regard to morning pleasantries. Why set a new precedent with a woman who hadn't, in the twelve years since their divorce, had a kind word to say to him or about him to anyone else? Except, of course, when she was between jobs or boyfriends. He was the one she came running to when cash was low and she wanted to keep Daddy from discovering she had overdrawn her trust allowance . . . again.

"Who is it?" Seth heard a sleepy male voice inquire in the background.

"Nobody." Celia's voice rose an octave, lilting and syrupy. "Go back to sleep."

Seth's fingers tightened on the receiver. "Who was that?" In the brief second's pause, he could almost picture the careless shrug of her shoulders, the arrogant arching of one pencil-thin brow.

"None of your business," she returned icily. "I'm not married to you anymore."

"No kidding." Blue eyes narrowed with the menacing glint of a razor's edge. "Dammit! Celia, you know how I feel about you piling up in bed with some hard-leg jerk you picked up in a bar somewhere under the same roof where our son has to live!"

"I did not pick Ray up in a bar!" she started to protest, but Seth ignored her.

"I swear, every time I call over there, it's a new trick. Guys moving in, guys moving out. And how do you think Jason feels?" The hiss of his breath trailed into a curse as he lowered his tone. "Don't you have any decency, at all?"

"Decency?" Celia asked shrilly, then laughed. "And just who are you to talk about decency, considering where *you* came from?"

"I'm Jason's father and don't forget it."

She laughed again, her voice bitter and filled with spite. "How could I, when all you do is breathe down my neck about him? I have a life to lead, too, you know. And don't try to tell me that you don't sleep around every chance you get." Her voice dropped meaningfully as she taunted, speaking straight into the phone, "I'm the one who knows you, baby. I was the girl who had to pay for her mistake, remember?"

Winding his hand into a knot with the phone cord, Seth struggled to maintain control over his simmering temper. "There's always a way out, Celia. I've told you that. I'll take that mistake—as you so affectionately refer to him—off your hands, any time, any place. You name the date, and I'll be there."

"Oh, aren't we the big knight in shining armor?"

Seth thought he heard the creak of the headboard as Celia leaned back, propped up on pillows and smirking, no doubt. But surprisingly, her tone mellowed, making her sound almost sincere when she spoke again. "Of course you can't have Jason. I love him, and whether you can comprehend this or not, he loves me."

"Yeah," Seth said, unconvinced. "And your daddy would put a knot in the old purse strings if you were to let me raise him."

"Daddy has nothing to do with it," Celia shot back.

"Correction," Seth said. "Daddy has nothing to do with *Jason*. Might sully the family name, fraternizing with the son of a Taylor—which doesn't make jack to me. It's Jason's feelings I'm concerned about."

"That's absurd," Celia insisted. "And you're just jealous because you know Jason doesn't even like you and wouldn't live in that Bible-thumping, backwater town if you paid him by the week!"

Her words stung, but Seth was tired of arguing with her. Dragging a hand through his thick blond hair, he drew a breath and expelled his demand on the wind of a sigh. "I want to speak to my son."

"Well, I'm sorry, you can't," Celia snapped. "He's not here. He's off at school."

Seth had never wanted to slap anyone so badly in his life. "It's Saturday, Celia. Not even summer school is held on Saturday. Is he in the house? Do you even have an idea where he might be?"

"W—well, of course, I do. I, uh . . ." She was flustered, and Seth realized her sudden need to transfer the phone from ear to ear was only a tactic, designed to give her time to come up with something. "Oh, yes. I remember now. He went walking with some of his friends. Up to the convenience store, I think."

"You think!" he roared. "What you *mean* is you've been sacked out with your boyfriend there, and so you *guess* your son might be at the convenience store. But you don't really know, since he was gone when I woke you up with the phone. Isn't that it? Why do you think the boy stays in trouble all the time, when you don't even bother to keep up with him?" He heard Celia draw in her breath through the line.

"The boy," Celia said hatefully, "is thirteen years old. He isn't a baby, and he doesn't want or need me to follow him around with a diaper in one hand and jar of strained bananas in the other! So why don't you stop trying to act like I just turned an infant out in the streets?"

She was right, Seth realized, as much as he was loathe to admit it. Jason wasn't a baby, and he hardly needed a parental permission slip to walk four blocks from his house to the neighborhood store.

You'd think he'd learn by now, Seth thought, sighing wearily. Where Jason was concerned, his ex-wife would always have the ace in the hole.

"Would you tell him to call me, then? When he gets back. Could you at least do that?" His tone carried the heavy concession of defeat, and Celia laughed as if to acknowledge that she'd won.

"Sure thing, lover. And I'll be looking for that little ol' support check in my mailbox, just any day now. You take care. Bye."

When Seth slammed the phone down—his teeth gritted, his jaws clenched so tight they ached—it took every shred of control he could muster on a second's notice to keep from ripping the cord from the wall. Right now Seth felt like tearing up *something*.

That bitch! If it hadn't been for her, he wouldn't be saddled with this predicament either, having to practically beg her for a chance to even talk to his son.

And she was right! That was the killer. He hardly knew Jason, or Jason him. They were like strangers when they were together, and all because Celia wanted it that way. She wanted Jason to believe that Seth wasn't fit to be his father. After all, she'd told Seth that. Why wouldn't she tell Jason the same? Seth could almost hear her relating, in horrible detail, how he'd taken advantage of her and gotten her pregnant while they were still in high school. To hear her tell it, Seth would be willing to bet a month's pay, it was all his fault; he was a ruffian and she a vestal virgin, taken only through sheer brute force.

What a joke! If he wasn't so angry, Seth could almost laugh when he thought of the thrill-seeking rebel—the brazen temptress she truly had been.

Grabbing his truck keys off the kitchen counter, he stomped out of the house and slammed the door so hard behind him it rattled the window panes.

Outside, the midmorning sunlight assaulted his face like a blinding-hot flame, and he squinted his eyes in lingering fury.

Just once, he thought as he crossed the yard to his pickup truck, taking long, angry strides that struck the ground as solid as a quake, just once in his life, he'd like to slip his hands around that woman's throat and give a taut but thorough squeeze—not hard enough kill her, mind you. But just enough to cork her good and let her stew in the hot venom of her own juices for a while.

The thought became a highly visual one, and despite his anger and the suspicion that he could probably be arrested for the sheer entertainment of the notion, his eyes crinkled mischievously at the corners, and a wry grin tugged at his mouth.

In the end, however, Seth's amusement was short-lived. As he braked to a halt at the only red light in the heart of town, his mind doubled back to his prime concern, which was, of course, Jason. When Seth thought of his son now, realistically and perhaps a little sadly, he realized that Jason was no longer a child but a young man, struggling, fighting to discover himself, his worth and his place in this so often resistant and hostile world. Seth's own heart ached.

He thought of himself at thirteen, and wondered if others had seen in him, just as Seth had seen in Jason, the same fears and uncertainties that came with the inevitable approach of manhood.

As the light changed and Seth turned, heading east toward Calloway Corners and his job site, he wondered if Celia had ever thought to look beyond the defiance their son wielded, like a shield, and into the eyes of the frightened child hiding behind it.

What Jason needed, Seth thought, was a full-time father and a real mother. Someone who cared enough about him to stand behind him, to guide him, to consider his welfare above her own. But that, he knew, wasn't a need his son was likely to have fulfilled.

First, as Celia had already made abundantly clear, it would require an act of God to persuade her to relinquish custody of Jason to him. And second, since he had no prospective substitute mothers in mind, Seth supposed he had no choice but to accept things as they were.

But damn! He didn't have to like the situation any more than he liked this heat. Keeping one eye on the narrow, tree-lined road ahead, he stretched slightly to reach for the jug of ice water he kept on the seat beside him.

The pickup's windows were rolled down, and the heated wind that rushed in brought with it the pungent smell of scorched milkwood and pine needles parched by the sun.

Lounged back in the seat, careless of the wind that tore ragged wings at the sides of his sun-streaked hair, Seth draped one arm over the steering wheel and twisted the cap off the thermos. But he was just lifting the cold, sweating jug to his lips when, over the rim, he caught a glimpse of something—a car—sitting off the narrow road in the distance.

Seth tapped his brake, approaching cautiously. He squinted against a shaft of sunlight that shot through the treetops like a blazing bolt of fire, striking the road and reflecting back, bouncing painfully off his eyes.

But Seth didn't flinch. He knew the car; he knew it as well as he knew his own name, and long before his brain took note of the upraised hood or the steam rising up in lazy swirls from the engine, his gaze fixed on the Texas plates.

Then slowly, as he lowered the heavy thermos to the seat, feeling the blood drain from his face and a kind of sick anticipation welling up in the pit of his stomach, he knew, too, that the woman who owned it might very well be close by. Maybe just over that hill . . .

Strange, Seth thought. Why had his knee trembled just now, when he'd moved his foot from brake to accelerator?

He tried not to make much of it as he started up the hill. But his heart was pounding, and in his head a dark voice murmured like a chill wind. *Thirteen years is a long time. What if she doesn't even recognize you?*

And suddenly Seth felt an almost uncontrollable urge to whip his truck around and head in the other direction.

ORDINARILY, TESS THOUGHT, she wouldn't have minded the three-mile walk. But in this heat, with the stench of melting asphalt nearly suffocating her, and the gummy slicks of road tar sticking to the thin soles of her sandals, each step became a labored struggle for forward progress and breath.

Her lungs felt heavy, her chest was cramping, and with each winded beat of her heart, Tess was convinced that the other sound she heard was the slow boil of the blood in her veins.

She could have kicked herself. Why hadn't she paid more attention to the temperature warning light when it had first blinked on, over four hours ago, while she was still in Dallas?

And, she thought, pausing in a patch of shade to sweep the wide straw hat from her head, she could have kicked herself harder still for not pulling over somewhere in Haughton, when that miserable red light came on again and stayed on. But she had thought—she'd hoped—that she could make it home.

And blast it all!—she would, too, even if she had to crawl.

Ignoring the tears of exhaustion and disgust that burned in her eyes, right along with the gritty particles of tree pollen and dust, Tess fanned her face with the brim of her hat. The faint stirring of air did little beyond the wearing out of her arm, and served as a reminder of how dry her mouth was. Licking her lips to moisten them, she glanced toward home once more and mentally estimated her distance. She must have another mile left to go.

Damp strands of hair had worked themselves loose from her taut French braid and now clung wetly to the sides of her face and at the nape of her neck. She shoved at them irritably, trying to plaster the brown wisps close to her head, before coiling the length of her braid under her hat.

A beaded sheen of perspiration layered her skin, and when she turned to start off again, the folds of her thin muslin skirt stuck to her thighs, nearly causing her to trip. She swore, using an oath her sister Eden might have well expected from Mariah. She would have been both appalled and surprised to hear it coming from Tess.

But, since there was no one to hear her anyway, Tess cursed again, louder this time. Then, sighing, she took up her steps once more, making her way down the road, alternately swearing and plucking at the limp cotton that clung to her skin.

SHE WASN'T WEARING A SLIP.

It was the first thing Seth noticed as he topped the hill and saw the woman walking a hundred yards ahead. Her back was to him, and the yellow sunlight slanted through the pale gauze of her dress, revealing the dark, swaying curve of her slim hips and long, tanned legs that moved like shadows behind a dusty screen.

Seth touched the brake, and his stomach gave a strange little dip that had nothing to do with his up-and-over descent to the base of the hill.

He wanted to see her. He wanted her to see him, to see that he had changed, that he had made a success of himself, just as she had told him he would, long ago.

He wanted to tell her—he needed to say, "Thank you. Thank you, Tess. For believing in me. For giving me courage. For making me think that I . . ."

But then he was already there, easing his truck up alongside her, looking at her through the passenger window, and his mouth went so dry he wasn't certain he could speak at all.

Tess wasn't sure exactly when she first heard the sound of the vehicle, its slow approach behind her. She'd kept her eyes downcast, staring at the road, her face hidden, for the most part, under the shading brim of her hat and the great, dark glasses she wore.

The driver said nothing as the truck began to inch along beside her, but Tess knew intuitively that he was a man, and yet she was afraid to look, to confirm her hunch.

She had lived in the city too long to be anxious to encourage the attentions of a stranger, or to suggest, however inadvertently, through a glance or some other easily mistaken gesture, that she was interested in "taking a ride."

Maybe he'll take the hint and go on, she thought. But her heart was pounding, and she could feel his eyes upon her, and with desperation and fear mounting by the second, she decided that if he didn't say something or pass her up soon, she would simply run away into the woods up ahead.

Several seconds passed. The woods loomed closer; the truck inched closer. And then, just when Tess felt that first, hot rush of adrenaline flood her legs with lightness in preparation for flight, the man spoke—and the deep, resonant sound of his voice could have calmed a raging sea.

"I'm sorry to bother you, ma'am. But I saw your car back there, and I'd like to help you . . . if you'll let me."

Was it just his voice? Or had there been something else? Something in his words or in the way he said them that teased her memory and made her stop? Tess didn't turn around immediately, but she was aware that the truck had also drawn to a halt and that the man was still looking at her, willing her to look at him.

"Ma'am?" He spoke again, and this time there was no mistaking that familiar, deeply narcotizing drawl.

Feeling the pull of his gaze, and caught in the tender swell of memory, Tess reached up, removed her sunglasses and took off her hat, letting her long brown hair fall in its single braid down her back. Then she turned and looked into a pair of brilliant blue eyes, striking if for no other reason than the sheer purity of their color. Indian turquoise. Stunning against the dark bronze of his handsome face.

"Hello, Tess," Seth said softly.

"Hello, Seth," she whispered back.

CHAPTER THREE

IT WAS AWKWARD at first. Two strangers—and they were strangers now, after thirteen years—staring at each other through an open truck window, neither knowing quite what to say.

The silence, though it couldn't have lasted for more than a few seconds, was nonetheless unnerving. It seemed to throb against her, like the heat. And suddenly she wondered if maybe the the sun had gotten to her after all. *Seth Taylor.* She could almost believe he was a mirage.

She was more beautiful than he could have imagined, Seth thought. Caught in the moment, he noticed neither the silence nor the pulsing span of seconds it consumed. His eyes detailed her every feature: the delicate cheekbones, the sleek, richly brown hair, skin the shade of honey on roses. And the eyes....

"It's been a long time." Seth heard himself speak, but he couldn't be certain of what he had said. He looked in her eyes, and all he could think of was how abysmally his memory had failed in recollection of their tawny-green color, and the gentleness that shadowed their depths.

"Y—yes. It has been a long time." Tess smiled wanly and tried not to think of how bedraggled and wilted she must look.

While on the other hand, she thought, Seth looked... He really looked...

"You look really great," he said, capturing the essence of her thoughts, yet putting the words more succinctly than she would have been able to do.

"Thank you," she murmured, but it was an absent reply. Hardly noting the compliment he had paid her, Tess was thinking, instead, of how much he had changed. His hair was darker now, not the pale blond it had been when he was younger, but a color that made her think of warm river sand, sun-struck with burnished gold highlights.

He was older, of course, and though the same youthful appeal was still there, he look wiser and more tolerant—no longer a boy, but a man. And yet, contrary to the handiwork of time, the harsh lines of defiance and bitterness that had so marred his handsome features in younger years seemed less apparent. His appearance gave her the impression of a man, someone who was now more at ease with himself and his place in the world.

His was a confidence Tess couldn't help envying, even as she wondered what or who had happened along in Seth Taylor's life to bring about these changes in him.

Tess knew that Seth was divorced and had been for a long time. She didn't think he had remarried, but even so, her eyes drifted to his dark, tanned hands, still resting on the steering wheel. His left hand was in plain view. He wore no ring.

A sensation much akin to relief washed over her, but then as her brain consciously registered the emotion, and associated it with the idea that, perhaps, it mattered to her if Seth was married again, she mentally chastised herself for letting her eyes go astray.

This man was nothing to her, she told herself firmly. Only someone she had known briefly in high school. And that was a long time ago. Reluctantly then, she raised her gaze to Seth's again and found, to her chagrin, that his eyes had never left her face.

"Well, I . . . It's been really nice to see you, Seth. But I really need to try and make it on home now. Maybe I'll run into you again while I'm in town." She lifted her braid and coiled it under her hat.

Seth had been watching the play of emotions that had drifted like brooding shadows over her eyes, turning them with each twist of her thoughts from deep green to amber and back to hazel again. He had seen her gaze briefly touch his left hand, and he wondered if she had been looking for the presence of a gold band.

The thought that she might be even vaguely interested to know if he was married again or not pleased him. And so Seth let his own gaze move to that tiny brown mole on the left side of her mouth, just above her full upper lip. Sweet memory filled him like a subtle shift of warmth in his bloodstream. And he remembered that he had always been fascinated by that mole. But he had touched it only once . . . first with his finger, and then with his lips.

The warmth turned to fire, and the memory burned him suddenly, jolting him back to reality. What was the matter with him? Couldn't he see that she was still standing in the blazing sun? And now she was getting ready to leave . . .

"Hey, wait a minute!" Seth crouched down a little deeper in his seat for a better view of Tess through the truck's narrow window. "Surely you don't think I just stopped by to say hello. Come on. I'll give you a lift."

She considered taking him up on his offer. It certainly beat walking, but then he grinned, and it wasn't just that crazy, lopsided smile of his, but a full, teeth-flashing, dimple-denting grin. Her stomach floated up with a sensation that sent warm shivers from her neck to her toes.

Caution took the better of her. "No...no, it's all right, really. I don't have very far to go now. And I need the exercise. Honest." *Like I need five more blisters on my heels.*

Seth's eyes held hers for a moment and then, drawing a long, slow breath, he turned his head and looked down the road toward Calloway Corners, a thoughtful expression on his face.

Long seconds passed, and Tess was beginning to get the feeling that it might be best if she just slipped away quietly. But it was too late. She watched as Seth licked his lips, and very slowly his eyes slid back to her again.

"I'll tell you what," he said in a tone that was as intriguing as it was grave. "I'll admit this ol' truck ain't much to look at. Her valves clatter, her tires are slick and the only way to get any air conditioning is to stick your head out the window. So..." His lips tightened grimly. "I can't blame you if you decide you don't want to be seen in a heap like this one. But at least it runs." He slipped that one past. "And I'll tell you something else. If you won't let me drive you home, then I'll park this ol' heap and walk you there. Either way, I'm not leaving you here, stranded in the heat."

By the time he'd finished his pitch, Tess couldn't help the wry grin that twitched at her lips, itching to become a soft giggle. It had been a long time since she'd felt like laughing, and the sensation left her warm, but there was still some distrust of her own emotions lingering inside. And she had never been the type to throw caution to the wind. Maybe he was just bluffing.

"Well, I don't know," she hedged, eyeing him sideways, half kidding, half serious. "I'm not certain I trust this truck—or her driver—to get me any place, besides in deep trouble."

Seth squinted his eyes, tipping his head to one side, speaking once more in his deepest southern drawl. "All right, ma'am. This is your last chance to name your pleasure. Do we ride in the shade, or walk in the sun?"

Tess told herself later that she'd finally agreed only because she didn't want him to feel that he had to walk with her, or to leave him thinking that she was ashamed of his transportation.

Still, it was difficult to convince herself that these were her sole reasons for accepting the ride. Her stomach fluttered with the sense of his nearness throughout the three-minute drive, and she couldn't seem to stop herself from stealing glances at him, sometimes catching him doing the same.

To mask the discomfort they both felt in being confined together in such small and smoldering quarters, it was amazing the things they found to talk about. At Seth's inquiry, Tess told him about the private school where she had been teaching remedial reading to junior and senior high students for almost five years.

At Tess's insistence, Seth explained that he was still doing remodeling and repair work on the side, but that he was building houses now, too. "And one of them," he announced with a proud smile, "is going to be the home of Reverend Ford Dunning and his new bride, Mariah."

"What?" Tess turned to him in utter surprise. "I didn't know that. When was all this decided?" Though she was happy for Mariah and Ford, Tess wondered why no one in the family had bothered to mention the news to her. Heaven knew, Ford and Mariah needed a larger place to live. His small trailer was fine for one person, but two made it more than cramped. But why hadn't anybody told her that Seth was building the house?

Sensing her upset, although not the reason for it, Seth tried to explain. "Well, actually, the house they chose was one I was building on speculation. They just decided on it a few weeks ago. Maybe Mariah just forgot to tell you, and besides," he added offhandedly, "it's been nearly a month since you were home last. You've probably missed a lot of the news."

It took a moment for the underlying implications of his words to fully sink in, and then Tess still wasn't certain she'd heard him correctly. "What did you say?" She sounded bewildered and suspicious at the same time. "How do you know when I was home last?"

She saw the color seep almost imperceptibly into his face, and if she'd thought there could have been any possible reason for it, she would have sworn his expression was one of blatant guilt.

"Oh, I don't know. Maybe I heard Ford mention it. Or...saw your car in the drive. You know." Seth shrugged, and his tone seemed suspiciously casual. "I pass this way to the job site at least twice a day. That's probably it. I probably saw your car at the house last month."

Last month? Tess thought he sounded like he was trying to convince himself as much as her, but before she had time to ponder the issue further, they'd reached the Calloway house, and she was home. At last!

"Eden!" Tess called out the window, as they pulled in the drive, and she saw her oldest sister rounding the corner of the house. Eden held a long-handled hoe in one hand and a pair of garden shears in the other. Her shorts revealed long legs, tanned by all the hours of working in the yard, legs that Tess had always envied and the men of Calloway Corners—men Eden had hardly even noticed in all her thirty-three years—admired from afar. Her hair was slipping out of the ponytail she'd tied on top of her head, the strawberry-blond wisps sticking to her face. She shoved it back neglectfully with a dirt-crusted work glove.

"Tess?" Eden squinted her eyes against the now past-noonday sun. "Is that you? What on earth are you doing in that junker?"

Embarrassed by Eden's blunt assessment of Seth's truck, Tess turned to apologize. But Seth was laughing, as if Eden's teasing was a standard joke between them. "Now, Eden," he began, climbing out from the driver's side of the truck, his blue eyes riveted to hers in a mock scowl. "If I've told you once, I've told you a thousand times. I don't like you bad-mouthin' my trusty work-horse. And Matilda doesn't like it, either. Do ya, gal?" He patted a battered fender with sincere affection as he skirted the hood of the truck and met Tess midway in the yard.

"Seth, you crazy fool!" Eden laughed and cut her eyes in humorous speculation at Tess. "You two better tell me what's going on."

Tess wished she knew. She had never seen Eden so affectionately familiar with any male outside the family, and with their dad gone now, that left only Ford Dunning and Jo's husband, Ellis.

Did Eden have designs on Seth? No, Tess thought. She just couldn't see it. And yet, they seemed so...

"Ya'll come in," Eden was saying, and Tess watched as Seth hastened to the porch to open the screen for her entrance.

His expression was warm and easy as he watched Eden through, and though he remained at the door until Tess had also entered, his face seemed to change subtly as she passed. He was still smiling, but his eyes seemed to darken just a shade, and when he closed the door, his steps falling in behind hers, his manner was stiffer, almost wary, not as relaxed as before.

"Come on in the kitchen," Eden instructed, leading the way. "I've just brewed some tea, and I've been working up a thirst in the garden." She turned to Seth then and asked, "How do you like your iced tea? With sugar or without?"

"Three scoops," he answered blandly.

Eden reached to the cupboard for the glasses. "Why don't I just drop a speck of tea in the sugar bowl, there, and you can drink that," she teased, fetching a tray of ice from the refrigerator.

"You know me." He was speaking to Eden, but his eyes turned to Tess, who was seated across the table from him. "I'll take sugar any way I can get it."

Eden laughed and set two glasses of iced tea on the table, then turned again to the countertop before returning with her own.

Pale with shock, Tess sat watching this friendly exchange, too stricken to even comment until now. "I didn't realize you two knew each other so well."

She had meant for her tone to sound casual and conversational, but when the words came out of her mouth there was a barb to every syllable, and even she could hardly believe the distinctive ring of jealousy in her voice.

Both Seth and Eden turned to look at her, their own expressions reflecting mutual shock.

"Why, Tess," Eden said patiently. "You know Seth and I have known each other for years. But since Daddy died, he's been coming around and helping me out if I need handiwork done around the house. And since he's building the new place for Mariah and Ford now, well…" She glanced at Seth and gave a bewildered shake of her head, as if to indicate she didn't understand what all the fuss was about.

Seth wasn't sure he understood Tess's attitude, either, but his face was filled with concern and honesty as he turned to her with a smile. "I thought a lot of your father, Tess, and now Eden lives here all alone. My coming around here is just my way of paying off an old debt. If it bothers you, I won't come back." His eyes narrowed and hardened with a more subdued but familiar glint of defensive belligerence. "I can assure you, your sister's reputation and welfare are safe with me."

His eyes continued to pin hers for several seconds before Tess looked away and blushed with guilty shame. "I never meant to imply..."

She left the sentence unfinished. The plain truth was that she had been jealous. Not especially worried that Seth was trying to cuddle up to her sister and thereby ruin her forever. But simply because just being around men and women who seemed easy together and had fun, enjoying themselves in each other's company, made her feel more isolated and lonelier than ever. She longed to have the same kind of teasing affection in her life again. But she was afraid, and it seemed to her now that the divorce had left her with more bitter scars than she had already encountered. Jealousy, suspicion and distrust had never been a part of her nature before.

Tess felt that she needed to apologize to both Seth and Eden, but she didn't quite know how to go about it or the right way to explain, and so she placed the blame on fatigue. "I guess I'm just tired and hot. I'm really sorry if I sounded sharp or judgmental in any way."

"Well, of course you're tired." Eden was always quick to forgive. It was one of the things Tess loved most about the sister who had raised her. "That long drive, and then trouble with your car. Isn't that what you said, Seth?"

At the mention of his name, Tess stole a glance at him and was relieved to see that his features had softened and he was smiling at her now. "Yeah. That's what I said."

Strange, Tess didn't remember anyone saying anything about her car. Maybe she had been too caught up in her own thoughts to listen.

"What you need is a cool shower and a change of clothes to make you feel better," Eden said. "Seth, why don't you go out to the truck and bring in Tess's suitcases.

"Suitcases!" they said in unison, and then Tess groaned. "Oh, heavens. I left them in the car. I couldn't carry them, and when you came along I didn't even think to ask you to go back and get them for me."

"Don't worry about it," Seth said. "I'll go get 'em for you now."

"No, Seth," Tess protested. "You've done enough already. Eden can take me to get them later."

"And what about your car? Were you planning on just leaving it there?"

Tess shook her head. "No. I don't know. I guess I need to call a tow truck or something."

This time it was Seth who shook his head. "The cost of a wrecker would be ten times what it'd take to fix your car. If it's just a radiator hose, which I'm pretty sure that's all it is."

"Well, I've got to get it somewhere..."

"Look, I'll go get your suitcases and bring them by on my way home from work tonight. If you can wait that long."

Tess nodded. She had three sisters, after all. Surely she could manage to find a top and a pair of slacks.

"Okay, then, I'll go by tomorrow and have a look at your car. If it's a hose or something simple, I'll go buy the parts and fix it right there. If it's something I can't handle, I'll hook a chain on it and tow it to the garage in town myself."

Tess refused. "No. I can't put you through all that trouble. You've got work of your own and—"

He reached over and pressed two fingers to her lips, halting her protest and the beat of her heart with his touch. "You did a favor for me once, remember?" His voice was barely a whisper, and something in his eyes held her as still as if she had lost all power of motion. "Let me do this for you," he murmured. "I want to."

His fingers fell away from her lips, leaving them feeling strangely cold, but she stood slowly and reached into the pocket of her skirt for her keys. Then just as slowly she stretched out her arm and held them out to him in her open palm.

Their hands touched and their eyes held for long moments, as if both were remembering another similar moment.

"I really appreciate this," Tess said, her eyes looking straight into his, and yet her voice sounded trancelike, abstracted, as if she were thinking of something other than what she was saying.

"I'll, uh... I'll get your car back as soon as I can." Seth's tone held the same mesmerized quality.

"No hurry."

Seth smiled. "Then I'll call you, okay?"

"Okay," Tess whispered.

Turning then, Seth crossed the room, but when he reached the front door, he paused and glanced over his shoulder. "It really is good to see you again," he said huskily. And then he was out the door.

CHAPTER FOUR

THE OLD COUNTRY HOUSE where Tess was raised had changed so little over the years that sometimes she could hardly believe she had changed so much. The ceilings were high, and the rustic hardwood floors supported the memories of a lifetime, old-fashioned furnishings, family photographs and trinkets whose value exceeded money.

Her father had built the ground-floor section over fifty years ago, before he had met and married his young wife, Grace. The upstairs portion, which consisted of two loftlike bedrooms separated by a small bath, had been added later when the children had started to come along, Eden first, followed by Jo, then Tess, who had been only three years old when their mother had died giving birth to Mariah.

Now, as Tess climbed the narrow staircase, she noted with a wry smile that the fifth tread from the bottom still creaked, just a little, when struck just right. The pine handrail was worn smooth by years of trailing hands—and the seats of little girls' pants.

At the head of the stairs, Tess paused and drew a deep breath before turning down the short hall that led to the bedroom she had shared with her younger sister throughout their formative years.

Though it had been only a month since Tess had been home last, she felt as if it had been years. When she eased

open the door and stepped into the little room, bright
with its eyelet curtains and wallpaper with tiny yellow
flowers, nostalgia misted her eyes, and a warm rush of
emotion filled her heart. Slowly, she let her gaze con-
sume every detail. And, as always, she could have
laughed when she spotted the strip of black tape that ran
from the ceiling down the length of two walls and across
the floor.

Dividing the room in half with tape was a measure their
father had taken out of sheer exasperation and as a final
means of compromise between Tess, the dark-haired
dreamer who could not bear upheaval or disorganiza-
tion, and Mariah, the blond adventuress who thrived on
both.

Tess smiled, remembering how Jo had teased them
mercilessly, calling the tape "the Continental Divide"
until their father had informed her it was cheaper than
building a firewall. Which was what he'd have had to do,
had Jo been sharing *her* room with Mariah.

But the truth remained that Tess and Mariah had been,
and were still, very different, almost continents apart. Yet
Tess had always felt that in some strange way, she and
Mariah served to balance each other in the family circle.
Just as, in their old room, Mariah's bulletin board with
its clutter of notes and travel brochures served to balance Tess's black and white etching of John Lennon with
a single word, "imagine," printed in the corner.

Imagine, she thought. Imagine all the people she could
have run into today. Why had it been Seth Taylor?

"I'll call you," he'd said. She was afraid to trust his
words. And she wondered, with a peculiar twist of her
heart, if he even remembered he'd made that very same
promise over thirteen years ago....

Tess had uncertain feelings about men in general. Having been raised in a houseful of females, the only male she had ever really spent time with had been her father. And, though he had always been good to his daughters, he was not the kind of man one could easily get close to. He was dark and remote, and unless it was to scold one of them for some misadventure, Ben Calloway had little to say to his daughters. He worked hard, and was gone from the house most of the time. Even when he was home, Tess remembered thinking, he never really seemed to be there. And she had wondered why he'd always looked as if he longed to be somewhere else, far away.

But if Tess had found something unapproachable about her father, she had discovered something much more disturbing in Seth. She could barely stand to pass him in the halls at school, but scampered past him, her head ducked, not daring to meet his eyes if he happened to be looking in her direction, for fear that her own eyes would reflect the unsettling sensations his nearness created inside her. A nice girl wasn't supposed to feel those kinds of things, especially if the girl wasn't even sixteen, and the boy was someone like Seth Taylor.

Besides, Tess remembered believing, he didn't know she was alive. Or so she'd thought, until the day he'd approached her in the schoolyard.

It had been one of those brisk February days. School had just been dismissed, and she was standing under the covered walkway in front of the gym, waiting her turn to climb into the bus. She remembered that she had been holding her books clutched to her breast to ward off the chill when she'd heard someone call her name.

"Tess? Tess Calloway?"

Not only she, but everyone in line, had turned around
to see who was calling her. And Tess nearly died when her
eyes collided with Seth's. She didn't even answer him, for
at that moment she didn't think she was capable of
speech. She'd stood frozen, her eyes wide yet oblivious
to the curious glances of the other students as they de-
toured around her, mounting the bus in single file behind her.

"I, uh . . . I'd like to talk to you," Seth said, and she'd
noticed him glance, rather uncomfortably she thought,
at the people surrounding them, before he added,
"Uh . . . privately. If it's okay?"

She lifted a shoulder, intending to shrug, hoping to
appear nonchalant as though his approaching her was a
common occurrence and she was not about to hyperven-
tilate. But her voice had betrayed her. "Sure," she'd
chirped, and to her own ears, at least, that was exactly
how it sounded, like a strangled chirp.

Her face had caught fire, and she'd wondered if it
wasn't bad enough that she had to look like a common
sparrow. Did she have to sound like one, too?

But in spite of her self-consciousness, Seth didn't seem
to notice anything except that she had agreed to speak to
him in private. About what, she had no idea, but she
hadn't protested when he slid his hand to the back of her
waist and propelled her toward a small alcove, formed by
a recessed doorway, around the corner of the building.
Even now, she could remember how she'd shivered when
he'd turned to face her, bracing the palm of his hand
above her head and leaning so close that she'd almost
flinched as she pressed her back to the cold metal door.

"I'm failing English," Seth announced flatly and
without preamble, as if his confession was supposed to

be not only something she had expected, but was connected with somehow.

Then he looked at her as if she were supposed to make some profound comment, and so Tess had tried not to look too stupefied as her brows lifted and her lips formed a simple, "Oh?"

But for Seth, that one word was apparently profound enough. "Oh, yeah," he growled disgustedly, pushing his weight off the door and turning, in one motion, to fling his back against it with a force so strong it rattled her teeth.

But it wasn't her teeth—it was her arm she was concerned with, and the electric sensations that were charging through her as if she'd grazed a hot wire instead of a hard-muscled shoulder.

Somewhere in the back of her mind, Tess thought she had registered the sound of the buses pulling away from the school grounds. But it was one of those subliminal, inconsequential things one hears but doesn't really notice, like a plane passing overhead. And later, Tess thought, even if she had consciously realized that her bus had left without her, she wouldn't have been able to make a move to stop it. For by then, she was too headily aware of the tall, blond youth wedged beside her in the doorway, his thigh pressed against her hip, her slim shoulder molded to the muscled contour of his upper arm.

Her heart had begun to beat in a crazed rhythm, fluttering high in her chest and quivering there like a rabbit's, before plummeting down with a painful thud, striking somewhere near her stomach.

"You know, if I don't pass that stupid composition class, I won't graduate. I'll be flunked for the year."

It was the sound of Seth's voice and the dejection in his tone that jarred Tess out of her daze. Turning her head, she raised her eyes to his. "You could go to summer school," she suggested softly.

"The hell I can," he muttered bitterly, almost inaudibly. "Do you know how much it costs to take a summer course?"

Tess shook her head.

"Too much." His pale eyes darkened with inner shadows. "Besides, it's not just the money. It's the time. I need to work full-time this summer, and I can't do that if I'm hung up in summer school."

Tess remembered thinking how surprised she had been to discover that Seth was even the least bit interested in whether he graduated or not. He certainly didn't give the impression of someone pressed with intellectual concerns. But she didn't think his parents gave him much motivation, either. She knew that he came from a poor family, and that his father drank and couldn't keep a job.

And maybe, because she knew these things, it was then that Tess first began to suspect that there was more to Seth Taylor than he would have people believe. Maybe he wasn't half as rough and tough as he seemed. And she, for one, was willing to give him the benefit of the doubt.

But his image wasn't the issue. Graduation was. Pulling herself away from the door, Tess turned to stand in front of him. "How can I help?" She wasn't certain, but somehow she felt that was the right question to ask. And she was right on target.

Seth straightened slowly and slipped his hands into his jean pockets, an odd, almost sheepish expression crossing his face. "I, uh . . . I don't suppose—since you're so smart and all—that you'd be willing to . . . well, you know, tutor me, sorta?"

Tess's eyes widened. "Why, it's . . . it's not that I wouldn't want to," she admitted honestly. "It's just that

I'm not sure I'd be qualified. You're a senior. I'm just a sophom—"

"But you're taking some accelerated courses, aren't you?"

"Well, yes. But—"

"And this is a special project, anyway. A term paper. It's going to count triple against our semester grade, and if I can manage a B, or better..." He grinned. "I'll have it in the bag."

His grin was contagious, and Tess felt a wry smile tugging at her own lips. "What's the subject?"

"Thomas Wolfe." He made a face as if he'd just tasted something sour. "Mini-bio, report and commentary on a major work."

Tess shook her head and pressed her lips together to keep from laughing at his expression. "Well, then I guess you're in luck. Although I almost hate to admit it now. Thomas Wolfe happens to be one of my favorite authors."

"Yeah, I know," he said. "I saw you carrying one of his books the other day. That's why I asked you."

Tess's smile had faded, but the joy in her heart had only escalated. Had he really noticed the book she was carrying, when she would have bet money that he hadn't even known her name before that day? Was it possible that he'd been the slightest bit interested before he'd needed a tutor?

Looking back now, with the objectivity of years on her side, she thought maybe there *had* been some interest there on his part, and that it explained, in part, why he'd asked a sophomore to tutor him in a senior-level course. If she'd only understood it then, maybe she wouldn't have gone and gotten her heart broken. And maybe this second failure in her life wouldn't have hit her so hard.

Trying to shake the memories out of her head, Tess eased her legs up on the bed and leaned back against the pillows, closing her eyes. She was tired; the heat had really taken its toll on her this afternoon, and all she wanted to do was fall asleep. But her mind refused to halt its busy parade of memories, and almost against her will, she was reminded of how she and Seth had argued about the fee for her services.

Seth had vehemently insisted on paying her an hourly wage in a reasonable range, which he described as "somewhere above the going rate for a dependable baby-sitter and somewhat below that of a professional tutor." But Tess had just as vehemently refused to accept his money.

"Then you can forget it!" Seth roared. "I won't let you do this for nothing. I'm not a charity case, and I won't have you treating me like one."

"Fine with me." Tess refused to let his show of temper dissuade her. "I'm not the one working two jobs and trying to *save* money. Besides, if you're too prideful to let a person do a favor for you, then I don't think I want to study with you, anyway."

He had relented finally, sighing in exasperation, but not without vowing that he would "do a favor for her someday."

The book they chose was *Look Homeward Angel*, because it was Tess's favorite of Wolfe's novels. Somehow it seemed the most complete, and something in her nature responded to the repetition of the theme of loss.

And so the pattern was set. Three nights a week, from the middle of February until early May, Seth came to her house and they would go out to the little apartment her father had built above the garage and read the book together.

Sometimes they read in silence. Other times they would read aloud to each other, pausing often to discuss interesting phrases or points that seemed glaringly autobiographical. And sometimes they talked of other things . . .

"What do you want to do with your life when you get out of school, Seth?" Tess had asked him one night after a long study session. He was sitting on the floor, leaning back against the old coffee table, which was cluttered with books and notes. Tess sat facing him on the floor, relaxed against the couch. Their calves lay next to each other, barely touching.

"I want to build things," he'd said, and a starry glint came to his eyes. "If I had the money, I'd go to college and study architecture. But I can't afford it, and my grades aren't good enough for a scholarship." He'd issued a sigh that lacked the defeat Tess would have expected. "I guess I'll have to be satisfied with taking a few courses at the vocational center and getting my o.j.t." A grin pulled at the corners of his lips, and he'd looked, at that moment, as if he could conquer any adversity fate set before him. "And then I'll show those college boys how to build a house," he'd said.

She had smiled thoughtfully at him for a moment, imagining the architectural marvels he could create if he only had the chance. But Seth, she knew, wouldn't wait for chances. He would go out there and get it. She was proud of him for that.

Finally, he had leaned forward, crossing his legs Indian-style. "What about you, Tess?" he'd asked, his voice dropping to an intimate rumble. "What are you gonna do when you get out?"

Tess shrugged, for she'd never really given it much thought before now. "I don't know," she'd said. "College, I guess. I haven't really decided what field I want to go into yet. Teaching, maybe."

"You'd be good at that." He'd smiled and lifted a lock of her hair from her shoulders, brushed it back with the tips of his fingers. "You *are* good at it."

The intensity of his gaze flustered her for a moment, and she looked away. "The truth is, it scares me sometimes to think about life after high school. Up until now, it seems like my life has been pretty well mapped out for me. I haven't had to make very many decisions."

"And you don't like making decisions?" Seth asked softly.

She met his gaze steadily. "I don't like taking risks."

He smiled a lazy smile and his eyes grew dark, shaded with bemusement and something else, something that looked almost like a secret challenge. "Don't you know that life is a risk, and the person who shies from risks shies from life?"

"And is that what you think I do? Do you think I shy from life?"

"It isn't important what I think. It's what you think that matters. But I'll tell you this, because I've learned it firsthand: only a person who risks is free. The person who doesn't will live in bondage all his life, trapped inside himself instead of being a part of the world."

His words had hit a little too close to home, and Tess remembered how restless and unsettled his nearness had suddenly made her.

With her back to him, she'd spoken in sharp self-defense. "Well, I know of one thing I want from this life, and I'm not afraid to take my chances trying to go after it."

"And what is that?"

Tess heard the slight lowering of his voice as he rose to his feet and came to stand behind her. But when she turned, she hadn't expected to find him standing so close, his bright blue eyes glittering down at her.

She had to swallow before she could speak. "I...I want a family. A husband...and children. I think that's all I really care about. Making someone happy and finding a place to belong."

"Is that all you want? Are you sure?" His voice took on a strange husky note, and she saw his gaze drift to her lips.

She didn't know how to answer, or if he ever expected her to. The way he was looking at her...Tess licked her lips, and his mouth crooked into a faint smile.

"Come out of your shell sometime, little Tess," he invited seductively. "And maybe you'll be surprised to find out where you belong."

If she had been older, Tess reflected, looking back on it all now, perhaps she wouldn't have fallen so hard, so fast, for Seth Taylor. But she'd been only a girl then, and terribly naive about men.

Night after night of that sultry spring leading into her sixteenth year, she'd dreamed of Seth. Fancying herself in love with him, she would lie awake in bed for hours, replaying each word he'd said, reliving every touch—no matter how seemingly insignificant. And sometimes, she even took the liberty of recasting his lines and rearranging his gestures so that, in her fantasies at least, he loved her just as desperately and as fiercely as she loved him.

But time was running out. Their work was almost finished. And one night in mid-May, Tess made up her mind that she was going to have to do something. She couldn't let Seth just walk out of her life. She was going to tell him she loved him. Deep down, of course, the idea was terrifying. What if he laughed at her or made light of her confession, because she was only fifteen and nothing like the sophisticated kind of girls she knew he dated?

He arrived at six as always, and they went directly to the garage apartment. The term paper was finished, except for some last-minute polishing. Seth had come prepared to work, but Tess couldn't keep her mind on their studies. She'd been gazing off in the distance, wondering what to say and how to say it, unaware of how she'd been chewing on her nails, until Seth reached over unexpectedly, his large hand closing over her smaller one as he drew it away from her mouth.

"You shouldn't do that, you know."

"What?"

"You shouldn't bite your nails like that. You have beautiful hands, so small and delicate, and your skin is just like satin. Smooth, tawny satin." His eyes raised to meet hers as he began to gently rub the pad of his thumb back and forth over her knuckles. "Don't bite your nails anymore, Tess. Don't ever distract from the loveliness of these hands."

She remembered watching, mesmerized, as he'd lifted her fingertips to his lips and kissed them, long and slow, one by one. All the while, his eyes held hers with a curious wariness, as if he feared she'd pull away should he give her the slightest chance.

But Tess had no intention of pulling her hand away from Seth's tender hold. His lips, his fingers, moved over her hand, massaging, relaxing, working a dizzy magic through her skin and into her bloodstream, until her head buzzed and her eyes felt as heavy as lead.

When he finally released her hand, he reached out to touch her hair, running his hand from the top of her head to her jaw. And then he cupped his hand to her chin and drew her closer.

Her lips parted, and his thumb moved to caress the tiny mole at the left side of her mouth. He murmured her name, and his voice was like his touch, a spellbinder's magic, weaving a web of sweet seduction that was as inescapable as any trance.

She braced her hand on his chest and felt his muscles constrict. The heat of his skin permeated the loose weave of his shirt and radiated through her palm and up her arm with the subtle warmth of a sun-baked rock.

She saw the shutter of his eyelids begin to droop lazily, half-closed as the light pressure of his fingers spread to her jaw. Gently, he urged her lips closer . . . closer, until each breath she took was drawn from him.

"Oh, Seth," she sighed. And then there had been only the slow, sweet coming together of their lips.

It was all so innocent, Tess thought now, she could almost laugh at the poignancy of it, for they had done nothing more than kiss—though they'd kissed that whole night long.

She recalled that the window was open, and a sweet spring breeze had wafted inside as they sat on the floor, staring out at the stars, her head on Seth's shoulder, his arms around her, one hand idly stroking her hair.

"It's getting late. I'd better go," Seth finally said.

"No—" she'd started to protest, but he'd kissed her into silence. And when, at last, he'd lifted his head, smiling down into her face, his eyes had crinkled as he asked, "You don't want your daddy coming out here with a shotgun, do you?"

She'd laughed at that, but realized that he was right. It was getting late, after midnight, and her father would be upset and might come looking—though not with a gun—

if she stayed out any longer. Seth rose to his feet, and she took his hand, reluctant to let it go even after he'd helped her up.

He walked her across the yard to the back door and kissed her once more under the dim amber light. "I'll call you," he had whispered, and she had to bite her lip to keep from shouting and whirling around like a child in giddy elation.

She watched him walk around the corner of the house, the moonlight glinting off his pale hair. And when she could no longer see him, she snatched open the screen door and ran through the kitchen to the living room, pulling back the drapes on the front window so she could watch him sliding into his car.

"Tess? Is that you?" her father called from his bedroom down the hall.

"Yes, Daddy. It's me."

"Is the boy gone?"

"Yes, Daddy." *But he's going to call me. And when he comes back it won't be just to study.*

"Well, you'd better get on upstairs then. Tonight's a school night, and six o'clock comes mighty early."

"Yes, Daddy," she'd said, but it had been all Tess could do to keep from running up the stairs as fast as her feet would take her, and she didn't sleep a wink all night long. She was too excited, thinking of seeing Seth at school the next day.

But Seth hadn't been at school that next day. Nor did he call her over the weekend, as he had promised. She worried, she wondered, she thought that surely something terrible must have happened. Was he sick? Had he been in an accident? She'd tried asking around discreetly, but no one seemed to know...or care. She had even worked up the nerve to call his house, but when his fa-

ther answered she had lost her courage and hung up. But
then Monday came, and when he was again not present
at school, depression began to settle over her. Though she
was crushed, she wasn't surprised when he didn't show up
for what was to have been their final study session.

Still, Tess told herself stubbornly, she would not give
up hope. She would give him until the end of the week,
and then, if he hadn't called or returned to school, she
would try to persuade her father to let her borrow the
family car—she had had her license for only a few
months—and she would drive over to Seth's house and
find out what had happened.

As it turned out, however, she hadn't had to resort to
those measures. She was in the girls' locker room, dressing for gym class the next day, when she accidentally
overheard two of the school's more popular girls talking.

"Did you hear about Celia?"

Tess recognized the voice of Mandy Sandridge, a ju-
nior-year cheerleader and homecoming maiden.

"No, what?" Norene Carroll had replied. It hadn't
been Tess's intention to eavesdrop, but the girls were
standing just across from her, and Tess knew without
having to be included in their conversation that they were
talking about Celia McKinsey, Haughton High's head
cheerleader, the prettiest and the richest girl in school.

"Well, honey...you won't believe it. She's pregnant."

"Oh, good grief! Are you sure?"

Tess heard Norene gasp, and then the sound of muffled giggles.

"Well, I wasn't there to witness it firsthand, if that's
what you mean. But according to my source, she's not
only pregnant, but the guy is dying to marry her."

"Eric? I can't imagine him wanting to marry anyone unless it was himself." More giggles.

They were talking of Eric Randolf, the captain of the football team and senior-class president, who had been Celia's steady for over a year.

"Ah, but Nori, honey. That's the best part. Eric's not the daddy."

"You mean—"

"That's right," Mandy sing-songed. "Looks like Daddy's girl sneaked out her window one too many times. Can you imagine the look on ol' man McKinsey's face when he found out his Baby Doll not only got herself knocked up... but by Seth Taylor no less? *Can* you believe?"

The two girls went on talking as the bell rang and they headed out of the dressing room. But Tess could not move. She felt as if she had been suddenly turned into a cold statue of granite, unable to think, too numb with pain and shock to even function. He never told her! He never told her he'd been seeing Celia McKinsey. Her heart hammered in feeble protest and denial. Maybe it wasn't true. She tried to believe that; she tried to convince herself that Seth wouldn't have led her on—he wouldn't have kissed her, he wouldn't have told her all those things, that she was beautiful and that he would call her, if he hadn't meant them.

She had tried to tell herself all these things. But deep down, she knew she was only hurting herself more by refusing to face the truth: that everyone else in school seemed to have known of Seth's and Celia's relationship. Everyone, that was, except Eric Randolf...and her.

Tess was never quite sure how she had managed to drag herself through the rest of that day, and in fact those last two weeks of school. As was the custom, the seniors were dismissed a week ahead of the other students, and since Tess elected not to attend the graduation ceremonies, she only saw Seth Taylor once more after the night he'd kissed her. But by then, he was already married, and was the father of an infant son.

Jason. Strange, Tess thought, that she should still recall the child's name, after all this time. And as for his father, Tess didn't know why she had reacted so strongly to seeing Seth Taylor again. It was silly. It was absurd. They didn't even know each other now. But in the back of her mind, a cautious voice warned her that once Seth had finished with her car, she'd be better off to avoid him.

IT WAS AFTER NINE in the evening when Seth swung by and dropped Tess's suitcases off at the Calloway house. Eden had met him at the door, explaining that Tess was exhausted and had already gone up to bed. Seth wasn't certain if he felt relief or disappointment.

Maybe a little of both, he admitted to himself as he climbed back into the truck. Maybe it was better that he hadn't been offered the opportunity to see her again. At least, not until he'd had a chance to examine his reactions to the old feelings she'd stirred up inside him.

"Where to now?" Jim Spier asked from the passenger side of the truck as Seth got in. Jim was a big man in his middle forties, a journeyman carpenter, whom Seth had trained under during his apprenticeship years. Now Jim worked for Seth.

"Back to her car," Seth replied, pulling out of the driveway and heading for the blacktop highway. "I fixed the hose this afternoon, but I need to put some coolant in the radiator. And, since I can't drive them both, I need you to follow me back to my house in the truck."

Jim shrugged and gave the bill of his baseball cap a brief tug as he lounged back against the seat. "Okay by me. My ol' lady's been in a bitch of a mood lately. And I don't mind telling you, I'm in no hurry to get home."

Seth slid his friend a sidelong glance. "If I was Wanda and I had to wake up with you in my bed every morning, I think I'd be on the moody side, too."

"Thanks, buddy," Jim replied dryly. "You're a real pal."

Seth laughed, and minutes later he pulled his truck off on the shoulder of the road, leaving his headlights to shine on the hood of Tess's car. "Sit tight and let me see if this thing will start."

Climbing out of the pickup, Seth followed the beam of the headlights until he reached the little green Audi. The keys glimmered in the same light as he unlocked the door and swung it open, sliding in behind the wheel.

In the car's dark interior, the faint, sweet scent of Tess's perfume assailed his senses, seducing him like a Gypsy's potion. He cranked the engine, then gave Jim the signal to turn the truck around, but all the while his thoughts were on Tess. And later that night, as he lay in bed, smoking and staring into the darkness, he wondered what she would think if she knew how much he wanted to see her again.

THE CALL CAME in the wee hours, jarring Seth from a dead sleep. Rolling over in the bed, he reached for the phone on the nightstand.

"Hello?" He glanced at the clock. It was three o'clock.

"Seth?" His ex-wife's voice trembled over the line, and panic shot through him suddenly, jolting him wide awake.

"Celia, what is it? What's happened? Where's Jason?" He couldn't receive the answers fast enough to halt his mind's split-second conjuring of at least a dozen horrible possibilities.

"He's right here. And I'll tell you what's happened. He's tried his best to ruin my life—and after everything I've done for him. I don't know how he could pull a stunt like this!"

Realizing his son had not been hurt or killed or maimed, Seth sighed with relief and dropped his head in his hand. "Celia, you scared me to death. Do you know what time it is?"

"Yes," she snapped. "As a matter of fact, there's a great big clock sitting right here on this officer's desk at juvenile hall. And I think you'd better get down here."

"I'm on my way." Seth slammed down the phone and grabbed his pants off the back of a chair. Minutes later, he was tucking in his shirttails and on his way out the front door, when it dawned on him that he needed to make another call.

CHAPTER FIVE

SUNDAY MORNING SUNSHINE filtered through the open window bedside Tess's bed, caressing her face and coaxing her from the depths of sleep. With a faint smile, she rolled over on her back but kept her eyes closed, content to savor the impressions of home: line-dried sheets against her skin; the vague, sweet scent of vanilla candles and a whimsical breeze that carried the warm smell of summer grass newly kissed by the dew.

Far in the distance, Tess thought she heard the sound of children laughing. And, as she lingered, reluctant to abandon the last remnants of a dream, she could almost imagine the voices were those of her sisters, Jo and Mariah, playing games of tag or chase in the wide meadow beside the house, while they waited for her to come out to join them.

A tender lump of nostalgia rose in Tess's throat, and just for a moment, she longed more than anything else in the world for the power to defy the barriers that separated past and present. Sweet heaven, what she wouldn't give to be a child again! To go back to the innocence and the dreams of her youth, when the world had seemed so bright and nothing was impossible. Oh, how she wished she didn't know now all the things she hadn't known then.

A light tapping on the door distracted Tess from her wistful reflections, and she opened her eyes, sitting up and reaching for her housecoat as Eden stuck her head through the door.

"Good morning." Her sister greeted her with a smile as bright as the sunlight pouring into the little yellow room. "I wasn't certain you'd be awake yet," Eden said as she stepped inside. "Did you sleep well?"

Tess's eyes returned Eden's warm expression. "Yes. Very well," she answered, smiling almost gratefully as she realized nothing could have been closer to the truth. For the first time in weeks, she could honestly say she felt well rested and relaxed. For the first time in months, she felt . . . secure.

"Are you hungry?" Eden asked lightly as she moved to the window to adjust a tie-back the morning breeze had caused to slip down from its proper position, securing starched eyelet curtains.

Tess shook her head and stood to slip her arms into the velveteen sleeves of the emerald-colored robe Eden had loaned her. "No," she answered. "I seem to have gotten out of the habit of eating breakfast."

Knowing that her sister would worry, Tess didn't bother to add that living alone this past year had, in fact, turned mealtimes into such depressingly solitary events that, with the exception of occasional binges of impulsive snacking, she had almost given up food altogether.

Eden turned away from the window, her jade-green gaze meeting Tess's green-fired hazel with a beguiling glint. "I've got your favorite," she tempted, her lilting voice full of mischief. "Home-baked cinnamon rolls *with* confection icing. And real butter."

She added the last remark as if the mere mention of her home-churned specialty, as opposed to any greasy, supermarket substitute, was in itself enough to convert even a devout anorexic—which Tess was not—into a salivating calorie addict.

And maybe it was, as Tess's stomach chose that very moment to growl a loud protestation of its emptiness. Eden laughed and Tess, blushing despite herself, pressed her hands to her rumbling middle. "All right, all right! I give up!" She grinned at her older sister. "Cinnamon rolls and real butter. How can I refuse? But of course, you realize this constitutes domestic blackmail."

Both women were smiling as Eden, who was already dressed in casual slacks and a white cotton blouse, started across the room toward the door. Following close behind, Tess glanced down as she knotted the belt of her housecoat, securing it around her slim waist.

"Aren't you going to church today?" she asked curiously, knowing that Eden was one of the regular nursery workers and seldom missed a service at the small church where Mariah's husband, Ford, was pastor.

"No doubt, I probably need to," Eden tossed back over her shoulder. "But it's been so long since you and I've had a chance to really talk, I thought I'd stay home and take advantage of your company this morning, before the house fills up for the holiday tomorrow."

A tender swell of emotion unfolded in Tess's heart, and she smiled. Eden always seemed to know instinctively when someone needed her. It was one of the things Tess had long admired about her oldest sister. But today admiration gave way to a deeper sense of appreciation. Too much time alone had left Tess hungry for companionship, and she was grateful for Eden's presence.

As they left the bedroom and headed into the hall, Tess reached around to the back of her neck and lifted her hair to free a brown swathe that had been caught under the heavy collar of her robe. Momentarily occupied, she wasn't paying too much attention to where she was going and didn't notice the suitcases, which hadn't been there last night, until she nearly stumbled over them.

The designer pieces—two large Pullmans, a hefty garment bag and a small tote, packed to bulging—stood now against the wall just outside the bedroom door.

Frowning, Tess glanced at Eden. "Did *you* bring these up?" The two largest ones, she knew, were quite unwieldy, and Tess hadn't intended for her sister to have to lug them upstairs without help.

But Eden shook her head, sending bright wisps of hair that appeared more red than blond in the morning sunlight dancing over her forehead. "No. When Seth came by last night, I told him it would be all right just to set your things in the dining room, that one of us would tackle them later. But he insisted they were too heavy and would hear of nothing until I let him carry them up. You were already asleep, so he left them for you here in the hall."

A gently persuasive but strictly unwanted touch of warmth curled around Tess's heart and strained against her firm resolution to keep her thoughts and reactions regarding Seth Taylor within the safe boundaries of polite but casual reserve.

"That was...very thoughtful," she murmured, and her voice was steady. But her mind betrayed her with a sudden, vivid flash of imagination—a vision of Seth, standing at her bedroom door, his hands at his sides, his blue eyes dark and shaded with remembrance, watching her as she slept, unaware.

Stop it! Tess shook her head to clear it of such nonsense. What good were daydreams and silly fantasies?

"I was surprised, though," Eden was saying as Tess snapped out of her mental fog. "I couldn't believe there

were so many. You usually travel so light. And I told
Seth, if I didn't know better I'd think you'd dragged
along your entire wardrobe this time!'' She laughed.

They had just descended the stairs and were turning the
corner into the kitchen, and Tess was glad that Eden, still
walking ahead with her back to her, couldn't see the
guilty flush that stung her cheeks.

Tell her! a small voice urged from the back of her
mind. And Tess knew she'd been given the perfect opening to confide in Eden. Tess wanted her sister to understand that though she had managed to survive the worst
of her marital breakup—Vance's betrayal, their separation and the final divorce—something had happened to
her in the process.

Her image of herself had changed. It was as if everything she'd ever believed about herself had been shaken
to the core. And once the layers had begun to crumble
and fall, like false walls around her, she had discovered
an utter stranger living inside her body. How quietly self-
contained she'd always felt herself to be! But now she
knew how easy it was to regard oneself as independent
when there was always someone to depend on.

Before Tess could find the words to explain to Eden
that she wasn't planning to go back to Dallas—that for a
while, at least, she needed desperately to stay here, to be
near her family, Eden was shoving a mug of steaming
black coffee into her hands and sitting her down to a
platter of delectable, oven-warm pastries and real butter.

When breakfast was over and the dishes done, the remainder of the morning progressed in typical lazy Sunday fashion. While Eden set about washing and chopping
fresh greens for the midday meal, Tess went upstairs to
bathe and dress.

It was already growing hot, and the house was beginning to harbor some of the warmth from the outside. Eden, who had always been something of a naturalist at heart, had never acquired even a passing fancy for air conditioning and preferred to keep the ceiling and window fans swirling constantly.

With her body still damp from her shower, the gentle stirring of air felt good on her skin as Tess donned a pair of beige shorts and a crisp, khaki-colored blouse that was only a shade or two darker than the natural olive of her complexion. She didn't bother braiding her hair as she had done yesterday, but brushed it until it shone like a thick, glossy shawl of brown sable, spilling over her shoulders and shimmering down her back.

Several times during the morning, she thought she heard the telephone ringing, and jumped at the sound, only to realize it was merely the bell-like music of an occasional breeze moving restlessly through the wind chimes on the porch.

Ridiculous! she chided herself. *Why am I so edgy all of a sudden?* Seth said he would call, and of course he would. He had her car; he wasn't going to keep it! For heaven's sake, why was she acting as if she were expecting him to phone her for a date rather than to report on the condition of her car?

At just after noon, Tess was sitting on the front porch swing, trying to occupy her fanciful thoughts with the more practical task of shelling field peas from Eden's garden.

There was a neat trick to shelling peas, but unfortunately, Tess mused wryly, she had never quite gotten the hang of it. She knew that once she stripped away the little green string that held the pod together, she was supposed to be able to wedge her thumb inside the top and glide right down until the peas tumbled out, like small, round buttons popping off a shirt.

But no matter how hard or patiently she worked, the task did not go so simply for her. The string would break halfway down, forcing her to use her nails to dig out the tiny green treasures. Or else the pressure of her thumb proved too great, and she'd end up with a seven-pea pile-up and a glob of mush that looked a lot like mud.

"Darn it!" Tess gritted her teeth as she was forced to discard yet another ruined pod into the brown sack at her feet. But she persevered until, thirty minutes later, with her impatience mounting, Tess was seriously contemplating dumping hulls, peas and all, in the garbage barrel at the back fence. The sound of an approaching car distracted her from her plan.

Standing up from the swing, Tess narrowed her eyes and watched as the driver slowed on the narrow dirt road to maneuver the turn on the winding drive that circled in front of the house. As the dust clouds settled and the car drew closer, she immediately recognized the little green Audi as her own. She caught a glimpse of a blond-haired driver and her heart did an unexpected pirouette. Seconds later, she was damning herself for the reaction and the fool she was, as the car halted, the door was flung open and the willowy driver slid out.

Mariah Calloway Dunning grinned as she slammed the door behind her. "We missed you at church," she called to Eden, who was just stepping out on the porch to join them. Then, turning to Tess, Mariah greeted her childhood "cellmate" affectionately. "Hey, Sis. It's good to see you. We brought your car along, by the way."

"So I see." Tess couldn't suppress the tinge of dryness that crept into her voice, anymore than she could have denied her suddenly lucid realization. Seth wasn't going to call her, after all. With a harsh little laugh, she wondered why that should surprise her. History, after all, always repeated itself.

"Afternoon, ladies." Ford Dunning greeted his sisters-in-law as he skirted the fender of the white sports car he'd driven in behind his wife.

The sleek vehicle was not exactly the kind of car most small-town folk expected to see their preacher tooling around in. And, not for the first time, Tess recalled Eden's mentioning that there had been some controversy regarding Ford's seemingly laid-back life-style and rather unorthodox approach to his faith when he'd first arrived in Calloway Corners. But over the months, it seemed, the people had come to know and respect Ford for the hardworking and sincerely dedicated man he was. He'd been a true godsend to Mariah, and a comfort to them all, when their father had passed away suddenly last December.

But at the moment, Tess wasn't concerned with her brother-in-law's innumerable contributions to their family's welfare. Instead, she was wondering why he and Mariah had been elected to deliver her car.

"Here's your keys," Mariah said blithely, dropping them into Tess's hand as she headed into the house and was followed inside by Eden. "Mmm! Something smells delicious!"

Tess heard her younger sister's comment from the kitchen just as Ford stepped up on the porch and reached out to hold the door open for Tess.

"I don't understand," she said as they crossed the living room to the kitchen. "I thought Seth Taylor was supposed to be taking care of my car. What happened? How did you get it?"

"Long story," Mariah answered before Ford could. Then, lifting the lid on a pot of something boiling briskly on the stove, she turned to Eden. "What is this? Turnip greens?"

"Mustards," Eden clarified.

"Oh, good! Give me a spoon," she wailed, and the other three turned simultaneously to stare at her, their expressions registering various shades of disbelief.

"Mariah, honey, are you sick?" Eden asked, half jokingly pressing a hand to her sister's forehead, as if checking for a raging fever. "You don't even like mustard greens. Remember? You've hated them all your life. And turnips, too."

"Well..." Mariah shrugged as she picked up a wooden spoon and proceeded to eat directly from the pot. "I guess my taste buds are craving something new."

Eden tossed Ford a look that was frankly perplexed. But he only lifted his shoulders and shook his head, feigning bewilderment. Tess, however, didn't miss the suspicious grin that played on his lips for just an instant as his gaze connected with that of his wife's. Mariah giggled for reasons that seemed apparent only to the two of them, then turned back to the stove and her leafy feast.

"Well, Mariah, if you're *that* hungry—" As Eden reached into the cupboard to get her sister a bowl, Ford managed to drag his attention back to Tess.

"I'm sorry," he said. "Weren't you trying to ask me something a minute ago?"

Sighing, Tess spoke again, her tone drawn with exasperation. "My car. I was just trying to figure out how you came by it. And whether it's fixed now, or if I need to see about getting it to the garage."

"No, I don't think that's going to be necessary. It seems to be running fine now," Ford assured her, before going on to explain. "I got a call from Seth sometime around three this morning, saying that he'd gotten it fixed, but that he wasn't going to be able to bring it back, as he had originally planned. He—"

"But I don't understand," Tess interrupted, frowning in confusion. "Why did he bother you? Wouldn't it have been easier for him to have phoned me? If there was a problem, Eden and I could've gone after the car."

"It was late," Ford pointed out reasonably. "I don't think he wanted to disturb or frighten you or Eden with a call in the middle of the night. He asked me if I'd mind swinging by his place after church and picking up the car, in case you needed it before he made it back to town."

Tess blinked. "Back to town?" she echoed, and then the import of Ford's words dawned on her. Something must have happened, some kind of emergency, some entirely unanticipated development, for Seth to have been carried away in the wee hours. Otherwise, he would have . . .

She didn't finish the thought, for slowly a cold feeling of déjà vu crept over her like a sickness, and as if in programmed response to another time, another "unanticipated development," dread gripped her with a leaden chill.

"His child," she choked out, not knowing how or why she knew her feeling had something to do with Seth's son. Ford stared at her, but she forced the words from her mouth. "Did something happen? Is the boy all right?"

He looked at her strangely, his expression at once puzzled and hesitant. But then, as if he had seen something in her eyes, something in the emerald fires that leaped from their darker hazel depths to explain her perceptiveness and her concern, Tess saw Ford's features relax.

"There has been some trouble with Jason," he confirmed. "I don't think it's anything too serious—Seth didn't have time to go into lengthy detail. But from what I gather, the boy doesn't get along with his mother's new boyfriend, and last night, their latest skirmish resulted in a minor scrape with the law."

"Oh, no. Really?" Picking up on the tail end of Tess and Ford's conversation, Eden rose from the kitchen table where she and Mariah had been sitting, quietly discussing another matter—a problem concerning the family's lumber-mill business.

As Eden crossed the room to where the other two stood near the dining-room entryway, Mariah rose also, and went to set her bowl in the sink before joining Ford and her sisters.

"I guess it's no secret that Jason has problems," Ford was saying as Mariah walked up, and he slipped an arm around her shoulders. "He doesn't seem like a bad boy, really. But he's sure a tough one to reach. Believe me, I thought that—"

"What do you mean he has problems?" Tess interjected, her voice full of concern. She didn't recall anyone ever mentioning Seth's son as being anything other than normal. But then, why would they? It wasn't as if she'd been keeping tabs on the boy. Yet now she couldn't help wondering if Ford meant that Jason possessed some kind of handicap or emotional disturbance. Dear heaven, she hoped not.

Her vision blurred suddenly with a vivid image from the past, and as if it had been only yesterday, Tess could still see the pride that had been so apparent on Seth's face that day in the corner store. Had it really been thirteen years ago? She had run into him one day, purely by accident, and he had shown her a picture of his infant son.

Strange, she thought, how that tiny memory still carried with it a particularly poignant power to hurt.

Tess had directed her question to Ford, but it was Eden who responded, speaking to them all in general. "Well, if you ask me," she began, her tone assuming that certain, opinionated quality Tess had always thought of as her "voice of maternal authority." "There's nothing wrong with that boy a little love and a stable home life couldn't fix. Everyone knows that mother of his has done nothing but drag him from pillow to bedpost since the day he was born. It's no wonder the child stays in trouble."

"I think you're right," Mariah agreed. "I don't know Jason well. I've only been around him a few times. But I believe what he needs, more than anything else, is a firm hand and the assurance that somebody really loves him."

"But what about his father?" Tess protested. Surely, anyone who had ever seen or heard Seth speak of Jason couldn't deny the man's obvious affection for his son.

Tess saw the strained look on Ford's face as he sighed and shifted his weight—wearily, she thought. And in a neutral voice she heard herself calmly ask, "Don't you believe Seth loves his son?"

Ford's mouth hardened slightly. "On the contrary. I believe Seth loves his son very much. But I have a notion Seth's ex-wife would like Jason to believe otherwise."

Tess's eyes widened. "But why? For what purpose?"

In high school Tess had been well enough acquainted with Celia McKinsey to know the girl could be catty, even vindictive if she felt the situation warranted it. But Celia was a grown woman now, and a mother. Why would she want to turn her own son against his father?

As if he'd read her thoughts, Ford answered her with a grim twist of his lips. "War game," he stated suc-

cinctly. "I've seen it happen time and again in families
I've worked with in counseling. Some parents—and not
just the divorced ones or those on the brink of it—use
their children as a means to manipulate each other.
Sometimes it's intentional. Sometimes, I believe, it's an
unconscious thing. But the results are the same in the
long run. The kids get caught in the middle, and finally
they become so confused they can't decide which parent
to trust—if either."

"Then what you're saying is that the child doesn't appear mentally disturbed or deficient in any way? That
you see his problems as more behaviorally related?"

Almost without her being aware of it, Tess's voice and
manner had become more confident as her inquiries
shifted, subtly becoming, through force of habit, those
of a trained educator assessing the facts.

Ford, a trained educator himself, smiled in appreciation of his sister-in-law's swift analytical skills. "I'd say
that's a fair assumption. The boy seems bright enough."

"But he has been having trouble in school," Eden
pointed out.

"Yes, but some of that may just go with the territory," Ford maintained. "According to what little Seth
has confided in me, the boy's been in and out of more
schools than a college football recruiter. And it's been
only in the past few years that Jason's mother has settled down in one place long enough for Seth to take advantage of his visitation rights on any kind of regular
basis. Still..." Ford's voice grew suddenly low and his
mood reflective. "I imagine it must be difficult for a father to build a close relationship with a half-grown boy
he sees only twice a month."

No one seemed to have anything appropriate to add, and a short while later, Mariah suggested that it was time she and Ford were headed back to their own home.

As they said their goodbyes on the porch, Tess gave her tall, platinum-haired sister a brief hug and thanked her for getting her car back to her safely. A feat that was, Tess mused wryly, considering Mariah's rather madcap style of handling a vehicle, a minor miracle in itself.

Behind her, Eden and Ford were engaged in their own teasing form of conversation. And seconds later, when Ford moved forward, reaching for his wife's hand to guide her down the wooden steps, Tess smiled as he reassured Eden, with an incorrigible grin tossed over his shoulder, that nothing short of an act of God—"and a disastrous one at that!"—could keep the couple from the family's traditional Fourth of July celebration, to be held on the back lawn of the Calloway house the following day.

The remainder of the afternoon passed quietly and without event. And even Tess, the relentlessly perfectionist Tess, who had been thoroughly disgusted with the mess she'd made of the pea shelling earlier, was gratified to discover the vegetables were not ruined after all.

At Eden's insistence, however, and despite her eager offer to assist with the evening meal, Tess found herself suspiciously at leisure. With the evening sun slanting in a red blaze through the gingham-draped window above the sink, she sat at the kitchen table, sipping a cup of spice tea and watching her sister at the business of blanching and bagging the peas for the freezer.

The scene was a familiar one, for it seemed to Tess that in all her years of growing up in this house, she'd never known her eldest sister to be idle, had never seen her when she wasn't busy with one task or another. Gardening. Canning. Running errands. Baby-sitting for the neighbors' children. Forever, Eden Calloway seemed involved in doing for somebody else. Always wrapping herself in other people's lives.

Tess supposed the caretaker instinct had become habit with her sister by now. But sometimes she wondered if Eden had ever resented or grown tired of the responsibilities of "practicing motherhood"—a burden that had been thrust upon her when their mother had died mere hours after Mariah's birth.

Tess had been only three years old then. Jo was five, Eden seven. And though their father had hired a live-in housekeeper, Aunt Martha, as she was affectionately called, had stayed with them only a few years, residing in the garage apartment behind the house, until Mariah had started school. But by then, Eden had just turned fourteen, and was old enough, Ben Calloway had said, to care for her sisters and run the house.

Now, as Tess raised her cup to her lips, her eyes narrowed. Shadows swept their brooding green depths. She studied her sister closely, and wondered if Eden was really as happy as she seemed. Did she want nothing more than to spend her life in the service of others, never having a family of her own? Or where there times when she, too, like Tess, was plagued with feelings of emptiness and despair?

They were different, Tess mused, she and Eden. But then, Tess had always considered herself vastly different from her sisters. She was not tall and blonde and daring, like Mariah, or fire-haired and fierce-natured, like Jo.

Instead, she was almost painfully shy, dark and intense, a dreamer who possessed a tendency to hold herself apart from others, sometimes even from the people who loved her most.

Often, Tess realized, her reticence was mistaken for aloofness, but deep down she knew that her quiet demeanor was only a cover for her insecurity. For reasons that had never become completely clear to her, Tess had always felt that if she didn't try harder, work faster, do better and more of what was expected of her—and flawlessly, besides—then something terrible might happen. She would become a terrible person. A failure. A nonentity, whom nobody wanted and wouldn't miss were she to simply disappear, fading away like a flaw in the woodwork.

It was crazy. Tess knew it. And yet the fear was there. Insecurity. Unworthiness. Feelings that Vance's leaving and her subsequent divorce had, not surprisingly, served only to intensify.

Tess thought, as she let her gaze drift back to her oldest sister, how Eden was more outgoing and preferred to surround herself with people. Always eager to help out someone else in time of need, Eden appeared to be perfectly secure of who she was and what she wanted out of life.

But now, possibly because Tess had had so much time alone to think in these past few months—or maybe because she'd grown weary of carrying her feelings inside and needed a link, some connecting sense of common ground, she found herself wondering if she and Eden were actually so different. Wasn't self-sacrifice merely another way of coping with insecurity? Was the quiet dreamer any more of an escapist than the dutiful caretaker, who hid her real self behind the dust clouds of activity? Tess wondered . . .

"Eden?" she called softly and watched her sister turn, a faint smile hovering on her lips.

"Yes, honey. What can I get for you? More tea?"

In the face of an expression that couldn't have been more serene, Tess was seized with uncertainty. Words clumped in her throat, and swallowing became an effort as she shook her head, refusing Eden's offer.

Okay, she reasoned, so maybe she was wrong about her sister. Maybe Eden was perfectly happy. But Tess herself was not. She felt alone and desperate and somehow, she needed someone to understand. Tess had never been very good at expressing her feelings. Communication. Hadn't that been one of the things Vance had complained their union lacked? Communication and children. The two big *C*s that had swept her marriage away and left her in a flood of confusion. Now Vance had both. And she had...

Her sister's attention.

Tess's stomach knotted. Self-consciously, she stared at the brown liquid in her cup. The tea she'd hardly touched had grown cold and cloudy; sediment darkened the bottom. Tess drew a deep breath. "Have you ever been lonely, Eden?" she asked, her throat constricting. She strained against the aching cords. "I mean *really* lonely? With Mariah and Jo married now, and Dad—" Tess paused to swallow "—and Dad gone. Do you ever get tired of living here with ... with nobody?"

Trying desperately to reach out in her own way, Tess slowly raised beseeching eyes to Eden's just in time to see the benign expression her sister had worn minutes before melt into pale oblivion.

"I'm ... I'm sure everyone gets lonely sometimes," Eden replied with a careless shrug, leaving Tess to wonder if she had only imagined the vague edge of defensiveness in her sister's tone.

But did she only imagine, too, the stiffness that caused her sister to move with the jerkiness of a wind-up doll as she crossed the kitchen and sat down in the chair at the head of the table?

"I try not to think about it," Eden said, matter-of-factly. "I stay busy with my baby-sitting, and though it's true I probably feel at a loss more often, now, since Dad died, I still have you and our sisters. Married or not," she insisted, "we're still family. And now we have little Carmen to think about."

Eden's face softened and the smile she'd worn earlier crept back to her lips as she spoke of the little two-year-old girl Jo and her husband, E.Z. Ellis, were in the process of adopting. "And who knows," Eden continued, beginning to sound more like herself again, "with the way our family is growing, no telling how many other little ones we'll have running around here before long. Why, I wouldn't be surprised if..."

Tess was no longer listening. As fond as she was of little Carmen, and in spite of the genuine gladness she felt for Jo and Mariah and the happiness they'd found with the men they loved, she didn't feel much like rejoicing in their successes at the moment. And she supposed it was selfish, but considering the mess she'd made of her own marriage, she didn't feel much like hearing Eden talk about them, either. There were more important things to say just now.

"I can't go back to Dallas," Tess blurted suddenly, startling herself as much as Eden when her thoughts seemed to explode into words.

"Wh—what?" Eden stared at her sister, her eyes wide and bright with confusion. "What are you talking about?"

Shocked at her outburst, Tess sprang from her chair, spearing a hand agitatedly through her hair and flinching when her nails grazed the scalp. "Oh, Eden, I've been trying to tell you all day!'' Her voice was filled with desperation. She walked to the back door and stood, staring out through the wire-mesh screen at the evening shadows falling heavily over the vine-thick arbor, where she used to play as a child. Hide-and-seek, Tess mused wryly. The game hadn't changed so much. Only back then, there had always been someone to come and find her.

Sighing, she reached out and touched the barrier of the screen. ''I can't go back to Dallas,'' she murmured softly, her tone sounding as weary and as spiritually drained as she felt. ''I've put the house up for sale. I haven't gotten up the nerve to quit my job yet. But I've been thinking about it, and I suppose that's something.'' But she gave a harsh, self-deprecating little laugh, then closed her eyes, drawing in a ragged breath.

Her head ached. It was hard for her, hard to express her feelings aloud, to admit that she wasn't as strong as her family had always believed her to be. For as long as Tess could remember, her sisters' faith in her had been both her pride and her burden. She wanted them to think the best of her. And yet, in spite of her innate need to share with them only her triumphs—never her trials— there were times when she longed less for her family's approval of her strength than for their acceptance of her weakness.

Eden said nothing more, but Tess knew her sister was watching her. She could feel the troubled, searching gaze at her back, and her stomach churned with uncertainty as she forced herself to turn around and face Eden across the room that had grown hot and dim in the smoky gray of twilight.

''I don't know what I want to do with the rest of my life,'' Tess admitted. ''But what I do know is that I need some time to sort some things through. To make some decisions about . . .''

Her eyes filled suddenly with tears, and her lips twisted, growing white and quivering with strain. She lowered her head. A wave of brown hair fell over her shoulder and hid half her face. She took refuge in the cover, and stared down at her tightly clenched hands.

"I'm so lonely, Eden." Her voice dwindled to a rasping whisper. "I just don't know what to do anymore—what's right, what's wrong. But if I could stay here, just for the rest of summer. If I can be home with...with you and Jo and Mariah, then maybe I can figure out where my life got off the track...and how to start over again."

She lifted her head, and her throat muscles clenched, cutting her breath and making it difficult to force further words beyond the pain. But she knew she had to. She had made it this far. "Eden..." Tess's eyes grew dark and pleading. "Can I stay—in my old room? Would it be all right with you?"

Eden Calloway rose very slowly from her chair. The pearl glow of her white blouse contrasted against the shadows that obscured any emotion in her face. "I can't believe you," she was saying as she started towards her younger sister.

Tears stiffened instinctively, and she all but tuned out Eden's next words. "So much pride . . ."

Eden stood in front of her now, and the look on her sister's face was one that brought a fresh rush of tears to Tess's eyes.

"We've always been so very much alike in that way, you know," Eden said tenderly, smiling as she lifted her hand and lightly caressed her sister's face. "Too much pride. And too much carried on the inside. You and I. We'll never be like Jo or Mariah. Not as assertive, not as adventurous, maybe never quite as sure of ourselves. But while the other two may have inherited the guts in this family—we got the heart. And that's something special.'' Eden's eyes misted. "Of course, you can stay, honey. This is your home. I can't believe you even thought you had to ask.''

CHAPTER SIX

THE NIGHT WAS THICK with humidity and so choked with
heat it seemed to throb, pounding against Seth Taylor's
ears with a pulsating rhythm that gave him a dull headache.

Even the air, and the occasional tepid breeze that normally attested to its existence, seemed to have suffered
and died, leaving behind not a final, gasping breath that
might be recycled through the desperate lungs of the living.

But the mosquitoes, which had to be the worst practical joke nature had played on mankind since the evolu-
tion of cockroaches, were out in flying form. *Damned
insects!* Seth thought irritably, as he slapped at one of the
worrisome creatures. He'd just as soon have it bite him
as listen to its maddening buzz around his ear.

In the shadows of his porch, he slouched in a ladder-
back chair, his spine pressed to the flat rungs and reared
back against the wall. His white dress shirt was sweat-
blotched and hanging open, the limp tails swept away
from the damp waist of the Levi's that clung uncomfortably to the sticky, perspiring sheen of his skin.

But it wasn't the mosquitoes or the pressing heat that
weighed heavily on Seth's thoughts. Easing his chair to
the floor, he pulled in the last drag of his cigarette and
leaned forward, resting his forearms on the spread of his
muscular thighs. His shoulders slumped slightly as he

stared down at the glowing red tip for several seconds. Then, sighing wearily, he exhaled the smoke and straightened, flinging the butt away.

This wasn't going to get any easier, Seth thought, his gaze shifting to the edge of the porch and the sight of his son, his flaxen hair the only bright spot in the darkness.

"You wanna tell me what happened?" Seth asked softly.

He'd been patient, he told himself. Through the nerve-rending hours of raging quarrel and uproar at his ex-wife's house. And then later, during the silent and tension-wrought drive back to his own house, his son had hugged the passenger door so closely Seth had been afraid that if he didn't keep a cautious watch each time he forced the truck into a turn, the boy would either jump or be slung out accidentally. Yes, he'd been more than patient. But now, with Jason simmered down and settled into his room, Seth decided, it was about time for some answers.

Jason Taylor, however, had nothing to say. Feet on the ground, hands firmly clenched to the porch ledge on either side of him, he offered his father little more than the shadowy view of his slim, rigid spine. His head was ducked and his neck craned forward, lending his body the crouched appearance of a runner positioned for propulsion into a long-distance heat.

Seth drew a breath, inhaling deeply, as if the stagnant air, so solid it felt almost like mud, could possibly revive his thinning patience. He spoke to his son again. This time, however, his tone betrayed his draining tolerance.

"Jason, son, I'm trying to talk to you, and I'd appreciate it if you'd at least turn around and look at me when I speak."

With all the drama and belligerence of a hardened criminal meeting death, Jason turned his head to the side and glanced over his almost ridiculously thin and unintimidating shoulder, presenting his father with that special, known-to-teenagers-the-world-over look. Translated, the expression read: *Get off my back, man. And while you're at it . . . go to hell.*

Despite his expression, however, the words that came out of Jason's mouth were not—and fortunately for him, Seth conveyed—quite that daring. Instead the boy asked, in a mumbling tone as bland and devoid of interest as was humanly possible, "Just what is it that you want me to say?"

Exasperated, Seth set his teeth, drawing his lips back tight against them as he rolled his eyes and sighed. "Look, Jason—I know you don't like your mother's boyfriend, and I can't say I blame you. He's rich, he's a pretty boy, he's a smart aleck, and he's twenty-two years old. That's not much older than you, Jase, is it?"

Refusing to commit himself to the conversation, Jason offered no comment, but merely continued to regard his father, his young face set, his dark eyes flat and blank in the dead cast of the moon.

Seth stared at his son, his own eyes glittering; aqua fires, standing out like brilliant lights from his face and becoming his only distinguishable feature as the others blended into the black shadows of the porch.

"Jason," Seth began again, his tone solemn, weary. "I know you took your scout knife and punctured the tires on Ray's Corvette. And your mother made sure I saw, too, the little number you did on the man's custom chrome guards. Now I understand how you might get angry sometimes, and want to do something about it. Everybody feels like that once in a while. But Jason,

son . . ." Seth shook his head, as if he still couldn't believe the boy capable of the willful destruction that had been done. "*Slashing* up the man's leather *seats*?" he rasped. "Surely, that's not your style."

"My *style!*" Jason cried. And suddenly it was as if he were a man, burst free from the brutal chains of repressed emotion and trembling, wild with the force. Fury blazed from Jason's eyes, and he lunged off the porch, spinning around violently, facing his father with fists clenched at his sides. "How would *you* know anything about my style?" he sneered. "Did you ask me? Does anybody ever ask me what I want? How *I* feel? Who gives a damn about my style!"

The boy's features twisted almost grotesquely, and even in the distorting pale moonlight Seth could see the stark defiance on his son's face, the furious rise and fall of his narrow chest.

Anger, compassion, regret, guilt erupted like fires in Seth's gut and coalesced instantly to form a piercing stone of anguish in his heart. He rose up slowly, aware of the rigid pull of tension tearing at every muscle and sinew of his body as he straightened. Standing then, he looked at his son, and though he spoke quietly, his tone was as unyielding as his stance.

"First off, let's get a few things straight. If there's any swearing to be done around this house, I'll be the one to do it. Second, I want you to know that while I don't approve of what you've done, I do care, Jason. I care about you and your style, how you feel and what you think. You're my son. And though we may not have always been close, I want you to be happy, now that you're here. And . . . I'd like to try and help you, but I can only do that if you'll talk to me and let me try to understand you."

"Oh, yeah? That's really great, Dad. Understand me? Sure. Why not? Everybody wants to understand me now. Now that I've gone and messed up, all right. But nobody wanted to understand before. So I figure—hey! You wanna get somebody to listen to you? You want them to understand? Then you set a fire under their rear end and maybe then, by God, you'll get their attention."

"That's enough!"

Jason glared at his father. "No, it ain't. You said you wanted to understand, so I'm letting you understand. I hate it here. I hate this stupid hick town. There's nothing to do. I don't have any friends, and if you think I'm gonna be happy here, you're crazy!"

In three angry strides Seth crossed the porch and grabbed his son by the shoulders. "Stop it, Jason. Stop it right now or I'll—"

"What? Beat me up? Go ahead. It won't be the first hard lick I ever got. Like father, like son, right? And if you could take it from your ol' man, well, I guess I can take it from you."

Seth turned white. How could Jason know about his past? He'd never told him. He had never wanted his son to know of the beatings Seth's own father had . . .

Celia. In a raging explosion of blind fury, her name blared across his mind and staggered his stunned brain with disbelief. How could she? What had he ever done to make her despise him so? He'd never hurt her. He'd never laid a hand on her. All he'd ever done was . . . marry her.

Almost as if he had forgotten he was still holding his son, Seth became aware of the pressure he was exerting. Oh, Lord, was he hurting him? As if in a daze, Seth felt his fingers unfurl as his grip loosened, his hands going weak and limp.

"Jason, I . . ." Where were the words? What could he say? He was sorry. He didn't want to hurt his son, and yet he knew the boy needed discipline. But where were the lines between just discipline and angry punishment? He couldn't remember, suddenly.

There was a strange look on Jason's face as Seth dropped his hands to his sides and took a step back. He was staring at the boy and yet not really seeming to see his son. He was looking beyond him, or was it into him? The defiance suddenly drained from his face, Jason backed away from his father, still watching him warily. And then in a matter of seconds, he spun on his heel and dashed into the house, leaving the screen door banging behind him.

It wasn't until Jason was gone that Seth felt himself breathing normally and his thoughts touching base with reality and the present again. He felt drained, he felt confused. Nothing like that confrontation had ever happened between Jason and him before, and yet for a split second, it was as if Seth had been caught in some kind of time warp. He was the victim of a flashback to a private war zone in another time in his life, when he had been involved in a similar battle. Only this time, in the present just moments ago, the roles had been reversed. Just for a second, Seth had seen himself as his own father, and Jason as Seth, the vulnerable boy.

Stumbling back to his chair, Seth slumped into it and buried his face in his hands. All these years. All these years, he'd thought if only he could have had Jason, if only Celia had let him have custody from the beginning he would have been capable of raising the boy right, able to give him all the love and guidance he'd ever need to grow up strong and healthy—physically and emotionally well. But now, when Celia had at last relented and

Seth had exactly what he'd always wanted, what was he going to do? Was he going to discover that deep down inside him ran a seed of violence he had not been aware of, the pod his father had planted and was incapable of controlling?

No. No, Seth knew himself too well for that. He had been in a few scuffles, even a brawl or two, in his lifetime, but always with males who were equal or better than himself in maturity and strength. No. Seth knew he wasn't by nature or habit a violent man. But what about Jason? What did Jason think? And, Seth wondered, how was he going to find a way to get through to his son? To convince him that he loved him. To discipline him without force, while at the same time not allowing himself to become intimidated by his own son, for fear that there would be times when he'd lose his temper, as he had tonight.

Damn, he thought. Not only had he placed more of a wedge between them than had already existed, he had allowed it to happen on the night before the Fourth of July. The day he'd set aside for a fishing trip with Jason. The day he'd planned to get closer to his son.

Well, they were close, all right. Right here together in the same house…with nothing but the bedroom door and Jason's blaring rock music between them. It wasn't Jason's choice to be here with Seth. If he'd had the choice, Seth feared, this was the last place he'd be.

Seth rubbed his eyes with a rugged hand, and decided tomorrow was one Fourth of July he'd be glad to have over with.

IN THE CALLOWAY HOUSEHOLD the Fourth of July holiday had always been associated with the word "cookout." Just as Jo Calloway, alias Mrs. E.Z. Ellis, had always been associated with the word "rush."

"Hurry, Carmen," the redhead called over her shoulder as she slid out of the shiny new Astro van, a large brown grocery bag in her arms. Her small daughter, glad to be free of her car-seat restraints, scrambled out behind her. Crossing the yard as if it had been a bed of hot coals she'd been forced to conquer barefoot, Jo made her way toward the house. "E.Z., get the other stuff, would you? And watch the baby."

"Watch the baby," E.Z. mimicked good-naturedly and wisely under his breath, admiring the sexy sway of his wife's hips. With her flame-red hair and liquid green eyes, Jo Ellis possessed a number of admirable attributes. Beauty was one. Intelligence and the willingness to commit herself wholeheartedly to any goal, any cause, for the betterment of mankind were also qualities of her innately humanitarian nature.

Unfortunately, however, there were other aspects of her personality that were in need of improvement—her sense of humor, for one. According to her husband, Jo took herself and life a little too seriously. And, along with the red hair, she had a temper. But the strange thing was, in her husband's eyes, her crazy temper was one of the reasons he loved her.

"Come on, little bit," E.Z. said as he lifted Carmen from the van's step. "You're not a baby, are you? You're a big girl. But let's don't tell Mom, okay?" He wrinkled his nose and the little girl grinned, wrapping her arms around her adoptive father's neck.

"Okay," she agreed, then giggled as E.Z. gave her pug nose a little tweak.

Mariah and Ford had already arrived, and Mariah was in the kitchen with Tess, peeling potatoes for a salad, when Jo came bustling in.

"Where's the fire?" Tess asked. Paring knife in hand, she glanced up from the sink with a warm smile for her second-oldest sister.

Jo grinned. "With all the meat in this sack," she said, depositing the load of chicken and ground chuck on the kitchen table, "the fire better be in the grill."

"Meat?" Mariah exclaimed, looking scandalized. "Did you say meat? Don't tell me married life has corrupted you already? I thought you only ate bean sprouts, raw oats and hay."

Jo glared at her youngest sister while Tess turned her head and bit her lip to keep from laughing out loud. She had never been quite sure when Jo had given up meat in favor of a vegetarian diet. But ever since, Mariah hadn't let the redhead have a moment's peace. "Can you believe it, Tess?" Mariah teased. "Our Lady of the Causes eats the same stuff most people feed their cows."

This time Tess couldn't hold her mirth in and she burst out laughing, also earning her share of the evil eye from Jo.

"I eat wheat germ, not oats. And alfalfa comes in other forms besides hay."

"Oh, yeah?" Mariah feigned interest. "What do they do? Put it in tea bags? Or do you roll it up in those funny little papers and smoke it?"

"You are disgusting."

"I know it. But just think how boring your life would be if you didn't have me as a cross to bear."

Just then, E.Z. came in, carrying Carmen on his shoulders. He had a small travel bag with extra clothes and training pants hung over one arm. A set of badminton rackets was tucked under the other. Three brightly packaged Roman candles protruded from his hip pocket.

"How's it goin', ladies?"

"Fine," Tess and Mariah chimed simultaneously. But Jo frowned when she spotted the fireworks.

"E.Z., those things are dangerous. I thought we agreed..."

"We did." He grinned incorrigibly. "We agreed that you don't like them, but I do."

"E.Z...." Jo began warningly, as her husband unloaded his goods on the table beside the food and shifted Carmen to his hip.

"Aw, come on, Red. Don't be a spoilsport. What's the Fourth of July without a few fireworks?"

"Safe," she answered in a word, to which E.Z. responded by grabbing her by the waist with his free hand and pulling her to him.

"Woman, when are you ever gonna learn? You're never going to be safe from me." E.Z. growled and, baring his teeth, made a pretense of biting her neck in vampire fashion.

Carmen giggled. "Silly Daddy," she said, while Jo tried to shove her husband away.

"Stop it, you nut!" she insisted, but a blushing grin destroyed her attempt at a stern expression, and it became apparent that the two newlyweds were enjoying themselves thoroughly.

Feeling awkward suddenly, as a witness to this rather intimate scene, Tess glanced at Mariah, but she, too, was smiling. A dull pain twisted in Tess's chest, and she looked away quickly, feeling suddenly isolated. Alienated in a world that had been from the beginning of time founded on the love of man and woman. Suddenly a vision of Seth Taylor sprang into Tess's mind, but she forced his image away, turning her attention to Carmen.

"Hey, how about a kiss for Aunt Tess," she asked the little girl, who reached out her small arms and quickly obliged. "Thanks," she said, pulling back when Carmen began to squirm. "I'm afraid I don't get many hugs around my house any more."

Tess hadn't meant to say that, and her cheeks burned as a result. Still, she smiled wanly and pretended not to notice the concerned looks Jo and E.Z. exchanged with each other and Mariah.

"Well..." E.Z. said, breaking the tense silence. "I, uh...guess I'll go and see about putting the coals on."

"Too late," Eden said, stepping into the kitchen from the backyard, where she had been scouring the grill racks. "Ford's already got the fire going, but I'm sure he'll be glad for the moral support."

As E.Z. started out the door, Mariah called after him. "Hey, boy. You did bring your guitar, so you can entertain us later, didn't you?"

E.Z. tossed her one of his famous magazine-cover grins. "Haven't you heard? I'm a family man now. I don't do live concerts anymore."

"No problem," Mariah offered with a shrug. "I'll just get my tape recorder, we'll all go into the bathroom and you can pretend it's a recording studio. Believe me, the acoustics aren't bad. I've been singing in there for years."

E.Z. laughed and glanced at the dark-haired two-year-old still riding his hip. "Come on, sugar bear," he said, addressing the child. "We better get out of here. These women are not well."

The four women looked at each other and burst out laughing. When the phone rang, Jo snatched it up as if she'd never stopped living in the old house with her three sisters. "Hello?" she said.

Eden turned from the barbecue sauce she was stirring to see if the call was for her.

A look of downright dread passed over Jo's face, and she turned despairing eyes on her husband. "Max, it's the Fourth of July, for heaven's sake," she shouted into the phone to E.Z.'s manager. "Leave the poor guy alone."

E.Z. moaned and stepped toward the phone, holding out a hand to take it. Grimly, Jo surrendered it.

"Guy comes from Australia and automatically thinks none of the American holidays matter," she mumbled, taking Carmen from E.Z. and holding her tightly as E.Z. spoke quietly into the receiver.

Tess watched Jo's face fall even farther in sheer disappointment as E.Z. hung up the phone, his eyebrows cocked apologetically. "I'm sorry, babe," he said. "There's a problem with the song I cut last week. I have to go back and remix it."

"E.Z.," Jo said, and if E.Z.'s mind could have been changed, Tess was certain the pouty lilt to Jo's voice and the way she tugged at his shirt could have changed it. "We just got here."

Tess couldn't help smiling as E.Z. pulled his wife into his arms and dropped a kiss on her lips. "I'll fly back, and you and Carmen can stay as long as you want and come on back when you're ready."

Jo didn't like it, but in the end, she surrendered her husband gracefully. Tess wondered what it was like to share the man she loved with so many others. Idly, she told herself that it wouldn't matter to her as long as he loved her.

As she stood pensively at the window watching Jo say goodbye to E.Z., Eden stepped up behind her. "It's a shame to waste all that food, with E.Z. leaving and everything," she said. "We made way too much."

"We always do," Tess said with a smile. "That's what makes it so special." She sighed. "Too bad we don't have more men around here."

"Yeah," Eden said wistfully. "Too bad."

SETH WAS IN the process of putting two TV dinners in the oven, hoping to coax Jason out of his room with the promise of sustenance, when the telephone rang.

"Hello," he said without much interest.

"Seth?"

He recognized Eden's voice immediately. "Yeah, Eden. How ya doin'?"

"Fine," Eden said, her voice low, as if she didn't want to be heard. "Listen, Mariah told me that she'd invited you to our Fourth of July picnic, but that you and your son were going fishing. I thought I'd try again, anyway. We have all this food, and—"

"I don't think so," Seth cut in, glancing toward Jason's bedroom. "Jason's not too happy about being here. The fishing trip didn't exactly come off, and I think he's better off if I just leave him alone for a while."

"Maybe he just needs to be around people," Eden ventured. "Might help break the ice between you, if there's any that needs breaking. It'd be our chance to welcome him to Calloway Corners."

"I don't know," he said.

He heard her pause a moment before she showed her ace. "Tess would love to see you, too," she said. "She's been really lonely lately. I think she could use a friend."

Something in Seth's heart twisted, and he looked at his watch. It was still early, and there was plenty of time yet to salvage the day. Maybe it was what he and Jason needed, he thought. Neutral territory, surrounded by people who knew how real families were supposed to act.

And Tess.

"Well, maybe we could stop by just for a while."

"Great," Eden said. "I'll see you as soon as you can get here."

Seth hung up the phone and started toward Jason's room, feeling a sudden burst of excitement in his heart that things were looking up already.

As THE DAY wore on, Tess felt a renewed sense of spirit and gloried in the familiar antics and camaraderie with her sisters.

With the four of them in the kitchen, it was almost like old times again. Mariah, Tess noticed, still took great delight in pestering Jo by choosing the opposite side of any and every debatable conversational issue, simply for the pleasure of watching Jo steam.

And, as usual, when Jo and Mariah were in the same house—let alone the same room—Eden was forced to act occasionally as referee between the duo. In spite of this pattern, which had been going on for as long as Tess could remember, she sensed a change in the two women—a subtle difference in their relationship. Though they both still joked and poked and generally sought to antagonize each other, like children forced to sit on opposite ends of the same divan, Tess perceived a kind of mellowing in each of them. Where once their teasing might have led to an outburst of real anger or crushed feelings, each now seemed more tolerant, and almost seemed to appreciate the extreme personality traits that had formerly served to create so much friction between them. Both Jo and Mariah seemed more satisfied with themselves now. And Tess couldn't help wondering if their new attitudes were owed, at least in part, to each having discovered and married the respective love of her life. Strange, she thought. Of the four of them, the two sisters who had seemed the least likely to settle down were now happily married, while the remaining two, who had seemed the most likely to get married and to stay that way, were single.

The scent of ribs barbecuing on the grill, along with the scent of charbroiled fat Eden-burgers, wafted over the yard and into the house, signaling to the family that it was almost time to eat. Out back, Tess saw Ford and Mariah playing ball with Carmen, and Jo hovered over the grills with a plate and a barbecue brush, waiting to apply the finishing touches.

The doorbell rang, and Tess looked at Eden. "Were you expecting someone else?" she asked.

If Eden had ever shown the slightest guilt in her life, Tess saw it now. Almost wincing, she blurted out, "Don't be mad at me, okay?"

Tess frowned. "Eden, what did you do?"

"Nothing," she said, looking as troubled as if she were about to be caught at a major crime. "Just answer the door."

A sense of foreboding rose inside Tess as she started for the door, wondering what surprise was going to jump out at her. But the surprise didn't jump when she opened the door. Instead, he flashed that unself-conscious grin that had always cut straight to her heart.

"Hi, Tess," Seth said. "Sorry we're late."

Tess caught her breath and threw a condemning look over her shoulder at Eden, who stood in the doorway, far enough out of reach not to be pounced on. Pulling herself together, she returned her gaze to Seth. "That's okay," she forced herself to say. "We haven't even taken the ribs off the grill yet."

He stepped in, followed by a tall, blond youth who looked about as comfortable as a caged falcon. Though his eyes were a rich brown, unlike Seth's, his hair and the structure of his face closely resembled those of the man beside him. Tess knew even before Seth touched her arm in light preamble to his introduction who the boy was.

"Tess and Eden Calloway, I'd like you to meet my son, Jason. Jase, this is . . ."

"Langford," Tess corrected him, without really knowing why. "My name is Tess Langford now." Did she imagine it? Or did the pressure of Seth's hand on her arm tighten a fraction just before he pulled it away?

With a reluctant effort, Jason nodded, and Tess thought she sensed an odd undercurrent of tension between them. She didn't question it, however, but almost welcomed it as a diversion from her own unsettled state.

She reached out a hand to him in formal greeting. "How do you do, Jason? I've heard a lot about you, and I'm glad to finally meet you."

Jason made a point of glancing down at Tess's extended hand. And then, with a belligerent lift of his chin, he shoved both his hands into the rear pockets of his jeans. His young face was hard-set and cold as the dark eyes that glared at her. "You married?" he asked, and his question was as disconcerting as his expression and the sneering tone of his voice.

Tess caught Eden's eye, and mentally lashed her sister for creating such an awkward situation. Flushing deeply, Tess withdrew her hand as inconspicuously as possible and tried to maintain her smile. "I was," she managed to answer evenly. "But I'm divorced now."

For some reason, her answer seemed to be exactly what he expected, and the boy gave a kind of self-satisfied snort, his dark eyes shifting to his father's blue ones. Tess saw the way Jason cocked his head to the side, as if to balance the chip he was obviously carrying on his shoulder. And it seemed to her that he was testing his father somehow, silently challenging him to react to his insolent display.

They stared at each other, and the moment seemed to go on forever, while Tess, not knowing what to expect from either of them, felt helplessly trapped in an emotionally charged situation that had nothing to do with her.

He's a hard one to reach. Suddenly, she remembered what Mariah's husband had said concerning Seth's son. And when she looked at his hard, defiant face, she could certainly understand Ford's reasoning.

Just then, Eden stepped up and patted Seth on the shoulder. "Come on in, guys. We have enough food to feed a stadium full of people. Maybe you two can help put a dent in it."

"Just a minute, Eden," Seth said, settling his penetrating gaze on his son. Though his voice was soft, Tess sensed its edge of suppressed fury, and wondered if Jason recognized it, too.

"Apologize," Seth commanded softly.

Jason's mouth dropped open, and he blinked, dumbfounded, staring at his father as if his plan, whatever it had been, had suddenly gone awry. "W—what? I mean . . . sir?"

Tess saw how quickly the boy's attitude changed once the controls had clearly changed hands.

Without altering his bland expression or his commanding tone of voice, Seth repeated, "Apologize to the lady, Jason. She offered you her hand in friendship. And since I'm sure you wouldn't have been so rude as to deliberately ignore it, you must have failed to notice it. Now, I think you should apologize for your oversight and for making her feel uncomfortable."

Eden flashed an alarmed glance at Tess, who tried to smile. "It's okay, Seth. Really—"

"No," Seth said calmly, looking at his son. "Jason?"

Tess glanced at Seth. She didn't know how she would have handled this situation had Jason been her son, but she couldn't help admiring the man's control or the way in which he was able to exert his authority smoothly, and yet without brow-beating or berating the boy in front of them.

Jason, too, seemed somewhat startled and unnerved by his father's reaction. "I, uh...I'm sorry, Ms..." He glanced uncertainly at his father, who nodded for him to continue. "Mrs. Langford."

Jason seemed relieved that he had managed to retain her name, and with one more uncomfortable glance at Seth, he withdrew his right hand from his pocket and extended it to Tess. She accepted it with a smile. "As I said, I'm very pleased to meet you, Jason. I'm glad you both came."

Suppressing a smile of his own that was part satisfaction and part pride in his son, Seth turned back to Tess and Eden. "Well, lead us to the food. I'm starved."

Tess hung back as Eden led the Taylors to the back door. They joined the others, then Eden went back inside. She winced as she turned to her sister. "Go ahead. Chew me out."

Tess was in no mood to make light of things. Shaking her head, she asked, "Eden, why didn't you tell me you invited them?"

Eden sighed helplessly. "It was kind of a last minute thing when E.Z. left. And I knew that if I told you, you'd find some excuse not to be here. And after all, I only invited him because of you."

"Me?" she cried. "Why?"

Eden turned and looked out on the lawn, where Jason stood alone beside a tree while his father talked to Ford and Mariah. "I don't know, Tess. I guess I thought maybe that old spark might still be there."

"Old spark?" Tess asked. "What old spark?"

"Right," Eden said with a smile that said she wouldn't play along. "What old spark? Certainly not the one that made you read Thomas Wolfe for hours, then sit out on the front porch waiting for the sound of Seth's car coming down the road. And by all means, not the old spark that had you not speaking to anybody for weeks after Seth and Celia got married."

Tess caught her breath and held it, kicking herself for having been so obvious. "He was just a friend I was helping with his term paper," she said weakly.

"Well, even if that *was* the case," Eden pointed out, "it wouldn't hurt for the two of you to be friends again." She stepped across the kitchen and cupped Tess's chin. "So perk up and get out there, and help me get the food on the picnic table."

Tess leaned against the doorjamb for a moment after Eden had left the kitchen and watched out the window as Seth bent and spoke to Carmen. She saw the smile of pure enjoyment on his face, then watched as he glanced toward the house as if wondering when she'd come out.

It's going to be a long day, she told herself grimly. *You might as well enjoy it.*

Finally, she got the stack of paper cups and the bag of ice, and joined the others in the yard.

As if the tension already pulsating between Tess and Seth was not enough, Eden seated them next to each other. The sun beat down with unmerciful diligence, but a gentle breeze through the trees shading the table kept it cool enough for comfort.

But Tess wasn't comfortable. The table was too small for eight people, so they sat too close together. Each time Seth's hand brushed hers, he muttered, "Excuse me."

Each time her thigh brushed his, she jerked it back.

"Could someone pass the salt?" he asked once, and when Jo handed it across the table, his shoulder gently grazed Tess's cheek.

She couldn't help noticing his scent as he sat beside her...the same scent she had dreamed about years ago, the unpretentious, natural scent of wind and soap and man. Something in her heart fluttered unevenly.

"I meant to ask about your car," he asked quietly when they were each on second helpings, and the conversations around them provided a low, muffled roar to buffer theirs. "Is it running okay?"

"Well, yes, I guess so," Tess said.

"Good. I've been meaning to call and check, but—"

"Oh, that's all right," she cut in. "I understand."

Understand what? Why had she interrupted him so abruptly? It wasn't like her. *Get control!* she told herself, and she did her best. "I was...uh, thinking of calling you, in fact."

His brows raised curiously, and he looked at her. His face was much too close, and she smelled the faint scent of barbecue sauce and cold beer on his breath.

"To thank you," she hastened to explain. "And to see how much I owed you. You must think me terrible that I would let you take the expense—"

This time it was Seth who interrupted. "I thought we agreed this was to be a favor. Something I wanted to do for you—not for money."

"But, Seth, the parts," she persisted. "Surely you understand that even if you refuse to let me compensate you for your time and trouble, I can't let you pay for the parts, too."

"It was nothing, Tess." His voice dropped to a flat level, and she sensed his irritation. "A hose and a clamp. I think I might have spent five whole dollars. Maybe I can handle that."

Tess saw the sudden stubborn set of his jaw, and realized that she had touched him somewhere near his pride. It reminded her of the time, all those years ago, when she had bought the books he needed—the ones that hadn't been in the library—and had, at first, refused to let him pay her back.

I'm not destitute yet, he'd said, his pride sharpening his voice. *I think I can afford a stupid book.*

Now she decided to back off the subject of money. A slight smile touched her lips. "Well, then, all I can say is thank you," she offered sincerely, her voice quiet against the rumble of voices around them. "For rescuing me and for saving my car. In between building a house for my sister. It seems you really are a jack of all trades."

She did smile then, but he did not, and she watched as his gaze lowered, trailing languidly, intently, down the straight of her nose to the small brown mole at the corner of her mouth, and then to her lips.

"And master of none," he murmured.

He didn't touch her, but his eyes were like flames, burning down into the soft flesh of her lips, until they seemed to grow heavy and swollen with the throbbing concentration of heat.

Suddenly, she realized that she wanted him to kiss her. The realization came with a dizzying rush of blood to her brain. It didn't matter that they were sitting at a table full of people; for a moment, she didn't care. In that instant, she had no thoughts of caution or propriety, only a driving need to assuage the surging ache of desire that rose like a hunger inside her.

It hasn't gone away, she thought. *I want him. After all these years.* And suddenly she felt overwhelmed with confusion and shock at her own thoughts. Her hands trembled as she reached for her iced tea, but he didn't take his eyes from her.

She looked around, wondering if anyone else had seen the desire on her face, but everyone was chattering as if nothing drastic had changed in the atmosphere…as if no cataclysmic event had taken place. Everyone except Jason.

Her eyes met the boy's across the table, and she saw the censure in his expression, as if he'd read her every thought concerning his father.

Suddenly, the heat was too much to bear, and the closeness of those around her stole her breath away. "I . . . I'll get the dessert," she said, her words issued on a raspy breath. She slid off the bench and came to her feet.

No one seemed to notice the clumsy way she took the empty plates, but as she went inside, Tess looked over her shoulder. Seth was watching her with the solemn expression of someone who divined her exact thoughts. And Tess wondered how she would get through the rest of the day.

IT WAS ALMOST THREE O'CLOCK when Eden rose from the table. "Who needs more iced tea?" She was about to head to the house for the pitcher, but Ford stopped her.

"Eden, I wish you'd wait a minute before you go inside. Mariah and I have a little announcement we'd like to make first."

"Oh?" Eden's expression was puzzled and a little concerned as she regarded Ford, then turned her gaze to Mariah.

Ford cleared his throat. "Well, you see, with this family growing the way it is, Mariah and I didn't think you'd mind if we contributed our share."

"What are you talking about?" Eden still appeared confused, but Tess felt a sudden prickling of excitement even before Mariah laughed.

"Oh, Eden," she declared. "I'm pregnant! Ford and I are going to have a baby."

Tess gasped with delight, Eden slumped down in her chair, and Jo made sure everyone knew that she had already been let in on the secret.

"I can't believe it," Eden murmured.

"When is it due?" Tess asked.

Eden sat up then, rigid with curiosity. "How long have you known?"

"It's due in February," Mariah said. "And I've known a few weeks." She looked at Ford meaningfully, then at Jo. "We would have announced it sooner, but I really wasn't feeling very well, and we didn't want anyone to worry."

Eden laughed out loud, and clapped her hands over her mouth. "Well, I guess that mean's you're better now," she said. "I can't believe it. A baby!"

Seth pretended to be hearing the news for the first time, and shook Ford's hand with a wink while the sisters hovered around Mariah. Tess stood back, waiting quietly until the excitement had reached its peak. Only then did she step forward with a loving hug for her sister. "Congratulations," she whispered. "I know you'll make a wonderful mother."

Mariah glanced up and saw a faint shimmer of tears in Tess's eyes. "And so will you," she said softly. "Someday you'll have a family, too."

No, Tess thought. *I don't think so.* Still, she couldn't help being happy for Mariah. Smiling, she turned to Ford and gave him a hug, too.

She walked away from the group, surrendering Mariah to Eden, who had a million questions for her. Absently, Tess noticed that Jason had strayed from the table and was strolling near the arbor, kicking a rock at his feet. He was uncomfortable being in this family moment, she thought. They hadn't yet made him feel welcome.

Deciding not to wallow in the fact that Mariah was the first to become pregnant instead of her, she picked up the little Nerf football that Carmen had been playing with and went over to the boy. "Hey, Jason," she said casually. "You like to play touch football? It's sort of a tradition around here. We eat enough to gain ten pounds, and then we work it off by running around acting like fools."

Jason shrugged. "I guess."

Tess turned to the others and got Ford and Seth started dividing teams.

Tess was Ford's second pick, after Mariah, and Seth chose Jason, Eden and Jo. Carmen became Ford's final pick as the token two-year-old mascot, chosen to keep things interesting. Jason didn't put his heart into the game, Tess noticed, and more than once he missed a pass that was thrown right into his hands. His father didn't get upset, however, at the lack of enthusiasm on Jason's part. He merely kept on trying to get him more involved.

Once, when Jason finally caught the ball and ran for a touchdown, he tripped over a tree root protruding from the ground and fumbled the ball. Tess recovered it, thinking it was all in good fun, and high-tailed it for the opposite imaginary goal line they had designated. Seth was fast on her heels, determined not to let her make that touchdown.

Just as she had almost reached the goal line, Seth grabbed her around the waist and lifted her feet off the ground. "I got her!" he shouted victoriously. "The ball's ours now."

Eden and Jo did a high-five and shouted as if they had just won the Super Bowl. Eden dashed to Jason, holding up a hand for another high-five, but Jason didn't seem to see. Instead, he watched his father sullenly as he kept his arms around Tess's waist.

"It's touch football," Tess said, breathing rapidly from her jaunt across the lawn. "Not tackle."

"I didn't tackle you," he whispered in her ear. His breath tickled her neck just below her earlobe. "If I had, I might not have ever let you up."

Her heart stumbled in triple time, but it had nothing to do with the adrenaline pulsing through her. Seth dropped his hands from her waist, and she turned to face him. His eyes smoldered, and the hint of amusement made them even more compelling.

The rest of the game lacked the competitiveness that the first part had, because Tess's mind was more on the way Seth's arms had felt around her waist, the way his mouth had felt so near her ear, the way his eyes had looked when he'd teased her.

She didn't even notice when Carmen made the final touchdown for her team, or what the score turned out to be.

DUSK WAS INVADING the sky when the dishes had been done and Ford announced that it was time for the fireworks. Seth watched the kitchen for Tess to come into the living room, where he and Ford and Jason were watching a baseball game. She was avoiding him, he thought. Maybe he shouldn't have tried to tackle her. Maybe that was too much too soon.

She stepped into the doorway, and he swallowed at the rush of hormones that pulsed through him with every sight of her. It had been a long time since he'd seen her in shorts, he thought. Her legs incited fantasies that he had no business entertaining. At least not here, with his son in the room, and her family all around them.

They assembled outside, Jo holding Carmen as if protecting her from shell fire in a war, and for the first time Jason began to take an interest in what was going on. Seth had little interest in the firecrackers and bottle rockets, however, for he had his own fireworks taking place in his head. He saw Tess sit on the top of the picnic table, folding her arms across her bare knees. He wondered how soft the skin there felt. He wondered if he'd ever have the chance to find out.

A rocket shot into the sky, exploding into a thousand particles of bright pink light, and everyone oohed and ahed. Seth ambled over to the picnic table, leaning against it. "Mind if I sit here, too?" he asked.

He noticed the slightest hesitation before Tess smiled and nodded. "Sure."

He sat down next to her, his shoulder brushing hers. The sky lit up with another bright light, illuminating her face for a moment. "You look pretty today," he said. "Have I told you that?"

He couldn't tell for sure in the approaching darkness, but he could have sworn she blushed. "Thanks," Tess whispered. "Do you think Jason's enjoyed himself?"

She was changing the subject, he realized. But that was okay. "I'm sure he has. He's not much of a joiner, but I'm glad I brought him."

"He's a handsome kid," Tess said, focusing her eyes on the boy, who was intent on lighting the rockets. "He looks just like you."

She caught herself then, and glanced at him almost apologetically. He smiled.

"I mean, you can tell—"

"I know what you mean," he whispered. "Thank you."

Their eyes locked for a stretch of time that seemed oddly timeless. For a moment, Seth forgot that others were nearby, or that all those years had passed between them. For a moment, all he saw was Tess, the girl who had made him believe in himself, the girl who had made his mouth go dry with desire.

He wondered what she would do if he leaned over, just a few inches, and kissed her. Would she pull away, once and for all? Or worse, would she push him away? The risk was too great, so he only let his gaze fall to those full, moist lips, let himself imagine the way they would feel right now, the way her mouth would taste . . .

"You want to do any, Seth?" Jo shouted, shaking him out of his fantasy. "Tess?"

Tess cleared her throat and came to her feet, making a clean exit from the daydream that had temporarily bound her. "No, I..." She turned to Seth. "You go ahead, though."

Seth's heart sank with frustration, and he nodded benignly. "Yeah," he shouted to Jo. "Save a couple for me."

Tess felt a withering sense of relief when Seth joined the others, releasing her from the tension that had plagued her all afternoon. She had to get away, she thought, had to be alone long enough to calm her heart.

Without telling anyone, she wandered off as darkness began to close in. Her intention had been to walk down beside the small, shallow creek that ran on the east side of the house, close to the woods. But oddly, her steps didn't carry her in that direction. Before she knew it, she had crossed the backyard and was climbing the steps to the garage apartment, which had been closed up now for years. The apartment where she and Seth had spent so many evenings together, before he'd married Celia.

She had just put her hand on the knob when she heard her name called. She glanced up to see Jo coming toward her.

"Hey, whatcha doing?"

Tess shrugged. "I just thought I'd see what it looked like. I haven't been in here in so long, I thought maybe the termites had carried it off."

Jo laughed and bounded up the stairs, arriving breathlessly beside Tess. "Come on, then," she said, smiling. "We'll check out the damage together."

The building was old. The foundation had settled, and it took both of them to wrench open the door. But surprisingly, as they stepped inside, Tess noticed the three small rooms were neither as hot nor musty-smelling as she had expected.

"I wonder if Eden's been airing this place out," Jo mused aloud, as if she had shared Tess's thought. "Where's the light switch?"

"Over there... by the door, I think."

Jo located the switch and Tess heard it click, but nothing happened. "I guess the bulb's blown out," she said.

"Probably." Tess wasn't surprised.

They stood in the shadows for a moment, glancing around at what little they could see of the furnishings. The sofa bed and a chair were covered with sheets. Finally, when there hardly seemed any valid reason to linger any longer, Tess met Jo's gaze from across the room. "Everything seems to be here." She smiled wanly. "Not much to see, though, especially with no lights."

"Well, to tell you the truth..." Jo took a step toward her. "I didn't really come up here for the view."

Tess frowned slightly. "Is there something the matter?"

"That's just what I was going to ask you."

Uncomfortable suddenly with the concern she heard in her sister's voice, Tess wrapped her arms around herself and walked to the window. She stared at the night through the dusty pane. "What makes you think something is the matter?"

"Oh, Tess." Jo's tone was commiserating as she came to stand beside her. "I saw your face when Mariah and Ford were talking about the baby. And I know it can't be easy for you to be around all of us. We're all so happy now, and you're just coming out of a painful divorce. I only wished there was something I could do."

Tess had to smile. Jo wasn't normally perceptive, and she was deeply moved. "Thank you," she murmured.

"You probably won't believe it, but just knowing you care means more to me than you can imagine."

"Well, of course, I care. You're my sister." Jo reached out to squeeze Tess's hand in a rare show of affection and moral support. "But I wouldn't be me if I didn't go on to tell you that I think you've been wallowing around in a lot of self-pity these last few months. And that isn't like you. You've always been so strong and . . ."

"No, I haven't," Tess interrupted. "Don't you see that's all been an act? I've never been strong—"

"Oh, please." Jo rolled her eyes. "You see what I mean? You've got yourself all tangled up in this. Vance didn't die, for heaven's sake. He gave you a divorce. And by now, you should be getting back into the world of the living. Even having some fun with being single again."

"And how would you suggest I go about it?" Tess asked dryly.

Jo met her gaze. "Maybe you should have an affair."

Tess stared at her sister. "You know, you're beginning to sound just like Mariah."

"Perish the thought," Jo murmured, before she continued, "I'm really serious. I think you need to start dating again."

"I'll take that advice under consideration."

"Good." Jo grinned.

And, though Tess had no real intention of acting on Jo's suggestion, she found her thoughts willfully drifting to Seth Taylor.

CHAPTER SEVEN

BY NINE O'CLOCK on Tuesday, July fifth, Mariah Dunning was already busy answering the phone and silently threatening the rusty keys of the old manual Underwood typewriter that blemished her desktop at the Calloway Lumber Mill.

At just before ten, Mariah's husband, Ford, was pulling into the paved lot of the Family Counseling Center in Bossier City, where he worked two days a week.

A short twenty minutes later, Jo and Carmen Ellis were in their Astro bound for New Orleans and a reunion with E.Z.

Everyone seemed to have a purpose or a cause. Or at least, Tess thought dismally, almost everyone.

It was just after noon, and she was standing at the refrigerator, holding a pitcher of grape drink and feeling about as useful as a wooden Indian as she watched Eden doling out bowls of chicken noodle soup and Saltine crackers to the five youngsters who sat at the table.

"Eden? Are you sure there's not something else I can help you do?" Tess asked, knowing already, from having posed the same question a half dozen times, what her sister's answer would be. Since the children had arrived, two at six o'clock that morning and three more at seven forty-five, Eden had thrown herself into her role as an in-home day-care manager. She seemed to have established the systematic routine of a trained professional, requiring little assistance from her younger sister.

"No," Eden replied, exactly as Tess had predicted. "Just pour the drinks into those glasses on the sink ledge, there. The rest I've about narrowed down to a one-woman job."

"So I see," Tess murmured, turning to fill the plastic tumblers with "purple punch," as the children called it.

She told herself it was silly, and that she was probably experiencing no more than a touch of the post-holiday blues. But the fact remained that from the moment Tess had opened her eyes that morning, she had felt restless and despondent. It was almost as if she'd left something unfinished, something important. And then her mind provided the answer she hadn't really sought.

Seth Taylor.

She shouldn't have avoided him last night after he'd sat next to her on the picnic table, she told herself. She shouldn't have hidden behind the convenient cover her family provided, like a little girl afraid of her first kiss. Seth probably hadn't wanted to kiss her at all. It had probably been her imagination, another cruel trick her heart was playing on her. It had just been wishful thinking.

She passed the cups to the children, absently remembering how, when Seth and Jason had left last night, his eyes had kept straying to her. She had smiled and told Jason that it had been a pleasure getting to know him, but he hadn't really responded. Seth had thanked Eden again for inviting them, and just before getting into his car, he had turned back.

"See you later, Tess," he'd said, and she could have sworn there was a hopeful lilt to his voice.

"Bye," she had said simply, fighting the urge to name a place and time, preferably a location where they could be alone, to see each other again. But something inside had held her back, making her want to play it safe and isolate herself against the risk he represented.

With the passing of the Fourth, summer was already half over. She was home, and yet she was beginning to realize that she hardly seemed to fit in any longer. Every one of her sisters, including Eden, had a life and responsibilities of her own. Still, Tess couldn't bring herself to even think about going back to Dallas. Not now, anyway. Not until school was ready to start.

There was a lot to be said for keeping busy, Tess thought, and her teaching certainly helped her to do that. In the meantime, however, Tess realized she couldn't go on all summer pouring drinks for Eden's kids. Somehow, she was just going to have to find something more productive to do.

"I'M SORRY, MR. TAYLOR," Mr. D'Arberville, principal of the local junior high, said quietly. "But you see, we only offer one session of summer school here, and we're already into our last week. There just simply isn't time to apply for Jason's transcripts from his last school and get him into the proper class. And even if there were, you understand, of course, every school is a little different. No two teachers or classrooms are alike. And there is also the problem of our not being in the same parish, and therefore we don't use the same textbooks as Jason's other school."

"Then what you're saying is that Jason can't pick up where he left off. That he can't reenter summer school here and finish the session?"

"I'm afraid that's exactly right." The man removed his glasses and leaned forward in his chair. "I do hope you understand, though, if it were up to me, I'd be glad to have Jason in school here." He smiled briefly at the boy before his gaze returned to Seth. "But it wouldn't help him, Mr. Taylor. When a student changes schools there are always adjustments to be made, and in this case there simply isn't time. I'm sorry, Jason." Mr. D'Arberville turned his attention to the boy. "I know you were probably looking forward to attending high school in the fall. But as I'm sure you know, it isn't within my power to promote you unless you've passed your courses. I'm sorry," he apologized again.

Jason said nothing. For the last half-hour, he had been sitting rigidly beside his father, staring down at his hands, speaking only when he was forced to reply to a direct question.

Seth glanced briefly at his son, then back at the school principal. "But isn't there some way?" he asked. "Even if he can't continue his studies in summer school, what about a private tutor?"

Mr. D'Arberville nodded his head thoughtfully. "I suppose that might be an option. In which case, Jason could be given a competency test just before the beginning of the term to determine if he's mastered the material required for high-school promotion."

"All right, then." Seth felt they were finally getting somewhere. "Who would you recommend?"

Mr. D'Arberville sighed. "Unfortunately, that, too, poses a problem," he admitted. "This late in the season, I know of no qualified teacher who doesn't already have a load of students. As I've said, Mr. Taylor, you've managed to hit us at a very bad time."

"So I see." This time it was Seth's turn to sigh. But as he rose to his feet, the man offered one last thread of hope.

"You might try checking with the parish school board. Perhaps they know of someone. Meanwhile, I'll be glad to request Jason's transcripts from his old school."

"Yes, I'd appreciate that," Seth said. Then, thanking the man for his time and his trouble, he and Jason left the office and crossed the parking lot to Seth's truck.

"Well, what do you think?" Seth asked his son minutes later as they were headed away from the school and toward his job site off Oliver Road.

Jason shrugged. "About what?"

"About school, Jason." Seth sighed and glanced at his son in exasperation. "What else have we been discussing all afternoon?"

The boy gave another careless lift of his shoulder, indicating that, like most adolescents, school wasn't his favorite topic, and the subject of private tutoring was equally unappealing.

Shaking his head, Seth turned his attention to the road. He was of a good mind just to let the issue go without further ado. How much harm could it do to let Jason repeat a grade? It wasn't going to kill him, and he certainly didn't seem too torn up at the present.

Furthermore, Seth thought, trying to locate a tutor wasn't going to be easy. In fact, it would be time-consuming and bothersome. And no doubt costly. Not that the expense mattered. When it came to his son, Seth wasn't concerned with either the trouble or the money. But the tempting truth was that he'd probably come nearer earning favor in Jason's eyes if he were to simply drop the issue of summer school altogether. That, of course, would be the most convenient solution. But would it be the best one?

Surreptitiously, Seth let his gaze slide back to his son. No, he silently answered his own question. As deeply as he longed for Jason's affection, Seth didn't want to win it through a permissive attitude that would leave Jason the loser in the long run.

Somehow, he'd come up with something. He just didn't know what yet.

AT JUST AFTER ONE O'CLOCK, Eden put the children down for a nap, as was her routine in the heat of the day. The older ones, she explained, usually didn't fall asleep, but the rest put them in a better mood, and gave Eden a minute or two to catch her breath.

At the moment, she was relaxing by taking inventory of the pantry. "I'm running short of a few things," she said to Tess, handing her a can of pork and beans and a jar of pickled tomatoes to hold for a minute while she shifted things around.

"I guess I'll have to run to the store. Let's see…peanut butter, cornflakes… Would you mind watching over the kids for a little while?"

Tess shook her head. "No, but if you'd rather, I'd be glad to take your list and shop for you."

"Would you?" Eden turned with a relieved smile, raking a wisp of hair off her forehead. "Oh, I would appreciate that. If you went, I might even have time to pick that squash I've been meaning to bring in from the garden before it gets so tough we won't be able to eat it."

"Then you better wear something cool," Tess warned her. "It's got to be a hundred degrees out there."

Correction, Tess thought moments later, as she slid into the suffocating interior of her car. *One hundred and ten is more like it.* Her car had been sitting in the sun all day, and now the steering wheel was so hot she couldn't touch it. She rolled down the windows and then reached over, yanking a couple of tissues from the box beside her. These she used like thin towels, draped on the wheel, to protect her hands until the air conditioner began to do its job.

In spite of the heat, Tess was glad for a reason to get out of the house for a while. She hadn't realized until she'd pulled out of the drive and was headed up the dirt road toward the Calloway Corner Store that something as small as a change of scenery, however hot, could go a long way toward reviving her sagging spirits.

As she passed the mill, she glanced at its rough exterior and considered stopping in to say hello to Mariah. But she changed her mind, reasoning that her sister was probably busy, and Eden would be wondering what happened to her if she were detained.

The drive was a short one and her air conditioner had only just begun to cool when Tess braked to a halt in the graveled drive outside the store.

Inside, the little structure was dark and cool compared to the blaze of sunlight outdoors.

"Hi, Dan." Tess smiled as she addressed the slightly balding, middle-aged man behind the counter.

"Well, hello there, stranger!" Dan Morgan exclaimed, tossing down his newspaper and grinning from ear to ear. "Good to see you."

"Thanks, Dan. How have you been?" Tess had known Dan Morgan almost all her life. The store his family leased was part of the Calloway property, and it had originally been built to serve the employees of the Calloway mill, across the street.

"Oh, fine, fine," Dan replied, as good-naturedly as usual. "Business could be better, but other than that, I really can't complain."

Tess frowned slightly. "Things are pretty slow, huh?"

It was no secret to those concerned that since Ben Calloway's death, the mill business had been rapidly deteriorating. A number of workers had already been laid off, and if distributors continued to cancel orders, according to Eden, there was a possibility more would eventually lose their jobs.

"Well, you know how it is." Dan tried to shrug the matter off. "Money's tight all over. But I'm sure you didn't come in here to talk about my problems. So tell me...what can we do for you, today?"

When Tess explained that she needed to pick up a few things for Eden, Dan's interest peaked. Since his wife had died, over five years ago, he'd made no secret of his hopeful intentions toward the eldest Calloway sister. "Oh? And how is Eden? I missed her in church Sunday. She's seldom absent, you know. I hope she wasn't sick."

"Oh, no, she's fine," Tess insisted. "Just trying to keep up with her gardening and her baby-sitting. All growing faster than she can keep up with, she says."

"I'll bet they are." Dan chuckled. "Well, uh..." He flushed with vague embarrassment. "Give her my love, would you? And let me know if you have trouble finding anything?"

Tess committed herself to honor both requests. Turning, she picked up a small wire basket from the stack beside the door. She slipped the handle over her arm and started down the narrow aisle, picking up an item or two as she worked her way toward the cooler in the back of the store.

She was just reaching inside the refrigerated compartment for a half gallon of milk when the front door swung
open, jingling the tin bell above it. Tess didn't look up,
but instinctively turned her eyes away from the sudden
flash of blinding sunlight that lit the store for an instant.

"Howdy." She heard Dan greet the newcomers cheerfully as the door closed.

"How ya doin?" Seth Taylor murmured, and Tess
jumped at the unexpected sound of his voice, banging her
knuckles against the cooler doors and nearly dropping
the slippery milk carton in the process.

Disgusted with herself and her silly reaction, she
shifted the milk container to the other hand and pressed
her throbbing knuckles to her lips. All the while, she was
convinced that her clumsiness had created enough com-
motion to draw every eye in the place.

In fact, Tess thought she could almost feel Seth's pale
gaze boring down the back of her neck. Closing her eyes,
she drew a deep breath and silently commanded her heart
to cease its ridiculous pounding, even as she schooled her
features into an expression she hoped would bear some
reasonable resemblance to calm.

Later, Tess wondered how Seth had managed to come
up behind her so soundlessly. The building was raised on
piers, and the floor—constructed of hard oak planks—
should have easily given away the strike of his boot heels
as he'd made his way down the narrow aisle toward her.
But it wasn't until she'd opened her eyes, prepared to turn
around and act as if she were confronting an old friend
she felt comfortable with, that Tess saw his face reflected in the glass doors in front of her.

"Need help with that?" he asked.

Drawing a breath for courage, Tess turned with a polite smile. Her gaze gravitated to the almost staggering

blue of Seth Taylor's eyes. Her heart skipped three short beats. And she damned herself for the color she felt seeping into her cheeks.

"How are you, Seth?" she managed to ask, as if last night had never happened. "It's nice to see you."

A strange shadow passed over Seth's eyes, and Tess watched his expression change, hardening almost imperceptibly as he seemed to draw himself up, rigid and formal, the earlier casualness of his stance transformed.

As he straightened, she couldn't help noticing the way he was dressed, as usual, in faded jeans that molded to his upper thighs as sleek and tight as buckskin leather. A black T-shirt was stretched tautly across the broad expanse of his chest, serving to cover but not to conceal the powerful mounds of muscled flesh and the leaner contours of sinew and bone underneath.

A quiver of feminine longing, which she was at a loss to prevent, darted through Tess's stomach and shook her legs. How was it, she wondered, that after thirteen years and numerous visits to her hometown, without so much as a passing glimpse of this man, she now couldn't seem to avoid running into him?

"I saw your car outside," he said, "and thought I'd stop in and tell you how much Jason and I enjoyed last night. I could tell Eden probably invited us without telling you—"

"No," she said quickly. "I was glad to see you. Both of you. Really."

Behind Seth, she saw Jason standing in the aisle with a soda and a bag of potato chips in his hand. She waved. "Hi, Jason," she said.

Jason mumbled something that she interpreted as hi and ambled to the cash register.

"Looks like you've got a handful there," Seth observed, his pale eyes flickering briefly over her grocery basket and the milk carton she still held. "Why don't you let me take it to the car for you when you're finished?"

"N—no, I can manage," Tess insisted. "It's not much, really. But I appreciate it."

"You sure?"

"Yes." She nodded and started to the front of the store. "And I do hate to rush, but if I don't get this stuff paid for and get out of here, Eden will be wondering if I've had car trouble again."

He grinned. "Well, we wouldn't want her to think that, would we? It wouldn't reflect well on my image."

Jack of all trades, he didn't bother to add, but Tess knew that he was thinking of her remark last night, just as she was thinking of his modest reply, which seemed to have volumes of other meaning behind it. Still, as she paid for her purchases and made her way out the door, her private conjecture was that, in one area at least, she'd be willing to bet Seth Taylor was a master of the art.

"I'D LIKE TO KNOW what all that was about back there." Seth glanced at his son ten minutes later, as they were headed down the highway toward Seth's construction site.

Jason took a swig of his soda, then continued to stare out the windshield in silence.

Seth hissed a breath through his teeth, struggling for patience. "Jason, she was only trying to be nice to you. Tess Langford is an old friend of mine. And even if she weren't, I won't have you behaving disrespectfully to your elders. Especially when the elder in question is a lady."

Jason glared at his father sullenly. "What is she? Your girlfriend or something?"

"Would it matter to you if she were?"

"Would you care?" the boy fired back.

Turning his attention away from the road for a moment, Seth regarded his son steadily. "Yes, Jase. As a matter of fact, I would care very much."

Uncertainty lit the boy's dark eyes for a brief second before distrust blotted it out. "Mom never cared whether I liked her boyfriends or not," he muttered bitterly.

Seth wheeled the truck into the drive and killed the engine. "I'm not your mother, Jason. Don't compare me to her."

"Afternoon, boss," Jim Spier called out with a wave, and started toward them as he spotted Seth and Jason climbing out of the pickup.

"Jim, you know my son, Jason?"

"Why, sure 'nuff." The older man gave Jason a playful sock to the shoulder. "How ya doin', boy?" He didn't wait for an answer, but addressed his next comments to Seth. "Things got a little hairy around my house this morning, and I had to bring Tony to work with me. Thought I'd let him earn a little dough working as a carpenter's helper. Hope it's okay?"

Jim Spier's son was fourteen, a year older than Jason. But the two boys were acquainted with each other and seemed to get along fairly well. Maybe, Seth thought, it would be good for Jase to have someone his own age to pal around with. His eyes flickered briefly over Jim and then back to his son.

"Fine," he said with a half-smile. "Now Jason will have somebody besides me to provoke."

Jason looked at his father, and for the first time in days, Seth thought he saw the boy's lips twitch with a grudging smile.

"I don't know, though." Jim stroked his chin in a mocking gesture of consideration. "Reckon we can trust those two together?"

"Well, I 'spose that'll depend on what we're trusting them to do."

Jim threw back his head and laughed. "Yeah, that's it, all right. Trust 'em to trouble, and they'll be dependable enough." He turned to Jason, still grinning. "Tony's around back, boy. Go see if you can roust him."

Jason tossed his father a questioning glance. "Go on if you want to," Seth said. And in a matter of seconds, Jason Taylor was out of sight.

"Hey, what's the story?" Jim asked curiously, once the two of them were alone. "I thought you only got your boy on Sundays and holidays?"

Blue eyes narrowed in the direction Jason had taken. "Not anymore, Jim. I've got him for good, now. And I'm not giving him up again."

CHAPTER EIGHT

"SO, HOW DO YOU THINK you're gonna like living with your father?" Tony Spier asked Jason over the telephone Wednesday night.

Jason sighed and leaned back against the headboard, reaching around to adjust the pillows behind his head. "I don't know, man. So far, I guess it's not as bad as I thought it would be. I still miss my friends and all. But at least I get to play my music and talk on the phone when I want to."

"Didn't your mom let you do all that stuff? It's always my *dad* that's hasslin' me."

"Well, it wasn't my mother so much as her boyfriends. She lets them move in, and all of a sudden they think they own you."

"Oh, yeah? What'd they do?"

"Man, you wouldn't believe some of the jerks I've had to act respectful to. Like every time there's a new guy? Well, he's got a new set of rules you're supposed to abide by. And they're just waiting for you to screw up. 'Cause all they wanta do is get rid of you. Puts a cramp in their style when their ol' lady's got a kid."

Tony drew a deep breath. "Yeah, I can see where that could get to be a pretty crummy deal. But listen, Jase, you don't know how lucky you are that your parents are divorced. What if you had folks like mine? They fight all the time. They can't stand to be in the same room together without starting up. Sometimes I wished they'd just get it over with. Split the sheet, man, and hang it up!''

Jason laughed. ''Aw, you don't mean that. Listen, I'll tell you what scares me. When they get married again—that's when the real trouble starts. Because *everybody* hates stepkids. I think it's a law.''

This time it was Tony who laughed, but his amusement was cut short. ''Look,'' he murmured urgently. ''I gotta go. I just heard the TV click off, and my dad'll be poking his head in here any minute.''

''All right,'' Jason said. ''I'll see ya later, then. At church on Sunday if not before.''

The line went dead, and Jason rolled over to hang up the phone on the small table beside him. Then he reached over and flicked on his stereo before leaning back on the bed, his arms folded behind his head. For long moments, he stared at the ceiling and thought about what Tony had said about wishing his parents would get a divorce. Sighing, he rolled his head to the side and stared at the phone. He didn't really want to talk to her, Jason assured himself. But it wouldn't hurt his mother to call.

FOR TESS, THE NEXT FEW DAYS might well have been carbon copies of one another, with one exception: she didn't see Seth Taylor again. Not that she expected to—or even wanted to. But on Sunday morning when she realized that he and Jason would very likely be in church, just as she was planning to be, Tess found herself taking care with her hair and her dress.

She told herself it was because she had looked so terrible when she had encountered the two Taylor men in the store earlier in the week. But then, when she asked herself why it mattered—why should she care what Jason

Taylor thought of her?—Tess had decided she really didn't want to know the answer. And so she tried to put such questions out of her mind.

It had been a long while since Tess had attended services at the small church where her brother-in-law was pastor. But she had always loved the little white building for its simplicity and for the sense of peace and serenity it evoked.

The sanctuary was almost full by the time she and Eden arrived, but Dan Morgan had saved them a seat in a pew near the back of the church. As he stood in the aisle, affording them room to slide in, Tess caught sight of a dark blond head and a pair of ruggedly masculine shoulders. Her heart began to thud as she recognized Seth and, beside him, Jason.

Seating herself, Tess watched as Seth bent his head to say something to his son. To his right, the sunlight shone through the stained-glass windows and glanced off the pale streaks of his hair, creating an illusion of silver spun with gold and shimmering under a red sun.

The organist sounded the chord for the first hymn, and as everyone stood, Tess dragged her gaze from Seth and forced herself to concentrate on the service. Ford spoke—appropriately enough, Tess thought—on loving one another. Each time his eyes met Mariah's, if only for a moment, during the delivery of his sermon, pride and love seemed to emanate from him.

So obvious to Tess was the depth of emotion openly shared between her sister and her husband, she felt certain that everyone in the congregation could see it as clearly as she did. But as her eyes filled with tears and she scanned the serene faces of people surrounding her, Tess was surprised to note that no one else seemed to be moved. No one else seemed ready to cry because the kind of love Ford and Mariah shared didn't come to all who willed it.

Or was it possible, Tess thought suddenly, that the opportunity for that forever kind of love was there for everyone and some simply failed to see it? The notion was disconcerting, and she wondered, painfully, if she had already missed her one chance for happiness. Closing her eyes, she sighed dejectedly. When she opened her eyes again, her hazel gaze collided with the fire-lit blue of Seth Taylor's. Stunned, Tess realized he had turned completely around and was staring at her as if they were the only two people in the room.

When church was over, Tess was one of the first people out the door. She didn't know why every time she came within fifty yards of Seth Taylor her mind seemed intent on reverting to some adolescent stage of development. And she wasn't about to act like a lovesick teenager today.

Maybe Jo had been right, she thought. Maybe she had let herself wallow in the self-pity of this whole divorce until she wasn't even behaving like herself anymore. In fact, she wasn't even *thinking* like herself anymore! She was—

"Tess?"

At the sound of the familiar drawling voice calling her, Tess's runaway thoughts screeched to an abrupt halt. She turned and saw Seth coming toward her.

His eyes crinkled and he regarded her with lazy bemusement. "You look great," he said.

"Thanks." She couldn't help noticing that he didn't look half bad, either, dressed in a light blue sports coat with his white collar open, revealing a sprinkle of hair at the base of his throat. She looked around, struggling for something else to think about. She caught sight of Ford

shaking hands at the door of the church, and recalled the
way Seth had looked at her during the service. "The sermon was good, wasn't it?" she asked for lack of anything better to say.

Seth nodded and followed the direction of her gaze.
"Yeah. Ford always knows how to get to the heart of
things."

Tess brought her eyes back to Seth, and saw that his
words carried some deeper meaning. She had thought
that only she had been touched by Ford's sermon about
love, but now she saw that Seth's heart had been moved,
as well.

A warm breeze wafted through her hair, pushing a
stray wisp against her moist lips. Seth reached up and
gently stroked it back into place. "Let me buy you
lunch," he said softly.

Tess's heart lurched, but a faint sense of warning
chilled her, despite the heat. "I . . . I don't think so."

"Why not?" he asked.

Tess looked at the people heading toward their cars,
searching for some excuse to get away from his disturbing presence. "I have a car here, and Eden—"

"Can't Eden drive?"

"Well, yes, of course. But . . ."

"Then I don't see the problem." His conclusion was
delivered in a no-nonsense rumble that made Tess feel
powerless to reject him again. "Eden can drive your car
home. Jason is going home with the Spiers, and I really
do need to talk to you."

Tess noted how quickly his mood had altered from
amusement to curt impatience. She licked her lips and
swallowed. "What do you want to talk about?"

His eyes pinned hers, glaring straight into her pupils
with a hard, searching look that almost dared her to

glance away. "I've got a proposition for you." He grinned when her mouth came open to protest. "No, not that kind. It concerns Jason. He's had some trouble in school this past year," Seth explained. "And now that I'm trying to get him set up for the fall term here, I find the boy's in a mess. He can barely read, and Ford said that you might be willing to help out."

Tess's eyes narrowed. "What do you mean help out? You mean teach him?"

"Well, yeah," Seth said. "You are a teacher, and a good one, from all I remember."

Tess drew a lengthy breath and released it as a sigh. "I don't know, Seth. I don't think I'm the right person to do this." She thought of Jason's reaction to her both times she had met him, and the uncomfortable feeling she had experienced being caught up in the tension between father and son. A conflict like that was the last thing she needed in her already unsettled life. It simply wouldn't work. "Maybe you should try someone else."

"There isn't anyone else," Seth contended, and vaguely Tess became aware of all the vehicles pulling out of the church parking lot. In a minute, she thought, there wouldn't be anyone else around. Just Seth and her standing alone in the dust and the sun, with Eden waiting at the car. "Is it because he's my son?" Seth demanded, dragging her attention back to him.

She looked up at him, saw that his eyes had suddenly lost their luster and were opaque with defensiveness. It was the look he carried from another time, a time when he was a teenager and considered an outcast, a "bad boy," a no-account who would end up in jail or dead or lying in a gutter somewhere. Because he was a Taylor. Because he was his father's son.

Strange, Tess thought. If Jason's eyes were not brown, but blue like his father's, she could almost swear she was looking into the same hard young face that had glared at her just days ago.

"Seth..." She looked in his eyes and answered honestly. "You know I'm not like that. I'd never turn away from Jason because he's your son." If anything, she could have added, it would only make her care for the boy more. Which could end up hurting them all in the long run. No. Her answer still stood.

Tess saw the reflection of memory and the dawning admiration of truth lighten Seth's turquoise eyes like sunlight shining on a mountain stream. He released her slowly, unfurling his fingers from her upper arms and gently smoothing the wide, pink flounce of her off-the-shoulder sundress.

"I'm sorry," he said, raking his hand through the wave of hair that had fallen down on his forehead. "I'm just a little desperate, I guess. That boy means everything to me."

At that moment, Eden Calloway abandoned Dan Morgan, who was just climbing into his car to leave. There were only a handful of worshipers still lingering. Eden strolled over to join Seth and Tess. "Is this a private conversation?" she teased. "Or have the fireworks fizzled out by now?"

Tess blushed hotly, and even Seth looked a little uneasy, shifting his weight and jamming his hands in his pockets. Tess wondered how much of their conversation her sister had figured out.

"No. Come on, join us," Seth invited, inclining his head. How quickly he had recovered his control! "I was just trying to talk some sense into your little sister here," Seth told Eden. "She won't go out with me, so I thought

I'd drive her home from church. Would you mind driving her car? It's the only way I can tempt her into that blue truck."

Tess wheeled around, glaring at him, her mouth opened to protest. But Eden was quicker. "Why, I think that is a very good idea. I might even stop by the Grovers' and see how the twins are doing. It's been quite a while since I've looked in on them." She turned to Tess. "You don't mind if I use your car?"

She was trapped. There was absolutely no gracious way she could refuse Seth now. But at least it would be no more than a ten-minute drive, which she supposed was less restricting than a two-hour lunch date. Especially when she wasn't even dating him.

Seconds later, she was sitting beside him on the seat of the truck. Neither Tess nor Seth was aware of Jason Taylor's watchful eyes on them as they pulled out of the gravel parking lot.

"Who's that? Your dad's girlfriend?" Tony Spier asked idly as he drew back and threw another rock at the cement culvert across the road.

Jason's eyes narrowed. "No," he snapped. "I told you before. He doesn't have a girlfriend."

"Hmm..." Tony seemed to ponder the matter with heavy consideration. "Which seems to me all the more reason for him to be getting one," he finally said.

"Well, he's not going to. And if he was, it wouldn't be her. He's already told me. They're just friends."

Tony grinned slyly. "Friends, huh? Well, they looked pretty cozy to me. And she's sure not hard to look at. Your ol' man would be a fool to pass that up."

Gritting his teeth, Jason turned cold eyes on his friend. "Anybody ever tell you, Spier, you got a big damn mouth?"

THE FIRST FIVE MINUTES of the drive down Camp Zion
Road was endured in silence. Tess took care to sit as far
over on her side of the truck as possible, her hands
pressed together in her lap.

"I like your dress," Seth finally offered, because it was
true, and because he couldn't think of anything more
debonair to say.

"Thank you," Tess replied simply. Why was she so
nervous?

Four more minutes lapsed into wordless oblivion, and
then Seth slowed the pickup, turning into the Calloway
drive.

"Would you . . . like some coffee or something?" Tess
asked, noticing that he'd cut the engine and apparently
had intentions of walking her to the door.

"No, thanks." Seth slid out from behind the wheel.
Skirting the hood of his truck, he went around to help
Tess out on the passenger side. "I haven't given up yet,"
he said cryptically, as he took her hand, and she glanced
up at him in question. "I still want you to tutor my son."

Tess watched her footing as she stepped on the running board and then to the ground. "Seth, the boy
doesn't even like me. You saw that for yourself."

"He doesn't know you," Seth persisted. "And the
truth is, Jason doesn't like anyone too much, right now."

Steady on her feet, Tess started to pull her hand from
Seth's, but he caught her fingers and squeezed them
gently.

"Don't go in now," he implored. "I want to talk to
you. It's been a long time since you and I have really
talked. Remember all those nights . . . ?" He smiled a little and his eyes grew soft, like evening shadows, gentle
with memory.

A warmth spread through her, filling her heart with the poignant wine of remembrance, and later, Tess thought, it must have gone to her head as well. Seth took her hand and she let him lead her to the small stream that ran beside the house. Years ago, her father had built the narrow, arching bridge that still served as its only crossing.

Now, as she followed Seth to its highest point, she let her free hand caress the curving rails. Constructed of wood and surrounded by Japanese tulip trees, fan-leaf fern and weeping willows, the little red bridge had always reminded Tess of a private Oriental garden.

It hadn't changed. It was still beautiful, she thought as she rested her forearms on the railing and leaned over to see if she could spot any of the numerous goldfish that had been set free here over the years.

"A penny for your thoughts?" Seth murmured, reaching out to brush the tumble of shiny hair off her shoulder.

"I was just thinking," she said honestly, "how we've all grown up. Eden, Jo, Mariah and me. Somehow it doesn't seem possible. Sometimes I look at myself in the mirror and think, here you are, all grown up in a woman's body. But inside, you know, you're still just a little girl."

Seth leaned beside her, his arm brushing hers. "I guess we all feel that way sometimes," he said quietly. "Like it isn't real. Like we've got the whole world fooled into believing we're adults and in control, managing our lives with the greatest of ease. But deep down, we know ourselves, and we know there's a coward in there somewhere. Inside, I'm the same little boy who used to be afraid his dad would get drunk and give him a couple of black eyes to wear to school the next day."

He turned to look at her, a vague smile crooking his lips. "Or maybe there's still that little girl in you who never liked to make decisions and was always afraid of taking risks."

Tess's heart felt suddenly as if someone had squeezed it. "You remember that?" she whispered disbelievingly. "You remember I said that once to you?"

His gaze dropped to the tip of her nose, and he lifted his hand, tracing the curve gently with one long tanned finger. "I remember a lot of things you probably thought I had forgotten."

"Such as?" Her voice was only a wisp of air.

He slid his hand to her temple, his fingers combing through her hair. "*'O Lost.'*" He recited the words softly. "*'O Lost, and by the wind grieved, ghost, come back again.'*"

Tess had to fight to keep the tears from filling her eyes. The poignant line he had recited from Thomas Wolfe's *Look Homeward, Angel* was her favorite, and it never failed to move her. That he would remember something so small, and yet of such enormous importance for all these years, flooded her with emotion.

"Thank you," she choked out. "Thank you for remembering those beautiful words."

Seth smiled. "Thank you for teaching them to me."

They looked at each other, seeking, remembering all the sweet embracing places they had discovered, long ago, in each other's eyes. Slowly, Seth began to lean toward her, drawn as if by the slow pull of a hidden magnet, the magnet of a beating heart.

But Tess turned away. "No," she whispered. "I'm not ready, Seth. Please understand."

He sighed and pulled himself up straight. "I want to," he said. "I want to understand. But first you have to tell me.'' Reaching around her shoulder, he took her hand and drew her gently around to face him. ''What is it, Tess?'' he coaxed, and then as if he'd read her mind: ''Was there someone else? Was that why your marriage went wrong?''

He watched as her eyes strayed past him, their expression vague and distant. And he saw, too, the shadow of pain that clouded their hazel depths like smoke. Was she still in love with her ex-husband? Seth wondered. Was that the reason the eyes he had remembered for so long as being only soft and vulnerable and so full of dreams were shaded now with a kind of bewildered despair? He waited, and watched, as she turned back to him.

''Yes,'' she said simply. ''There was someone else.''

She tried to smile, but the effort came off badly, and for one desperate moment, as Seth stared at the same ashen twist of her beautiful mouth and the bright flame of anguish that lit her shadowed eyes, he could hardly stop himself from reaching for her. She looked so lost, so fragile. He wanted to draw her into his arms and hold her close until all her pain went away. How he wished he had the power to take it from her, to protect her from anything that might ever hurt her again.

But as much as he longed to, Seth knew he couldn't take away Tess's hurt. He could only ache for himself at seeing her grief. For the harshest pain, which was the pain of private disillusionment, was a burden that couldn't be shared.

''Do you still love him?'' Seth asked, needing to learn and yet not certain he wanted to know.

His question surprised her. Strange, Tess realized suddenly that no one, not even any of her sisters, had asked her that question before. Not that her family hadn't been supportive through her divorce. But they hadn't asked for

details, and she hadn't offered them. She told them only
that Vance had left her, and that there had been another
woman involved. But she had told no one about the baby.
How did a woman admit that her husband had gotten
another woman pregnant, while he was still married to
her?

Do I still love him? Tess's heart twisted, and she answered, shaking her head slowly. "No. I did once. But
not anymore."

Seth slid his hand to the nape of her neck and forced
her head up with his thumb at her jaw. "Your husband
was a fool, Tess." The flame of his gaze blazed, scorch-
ing hers with bright intensity. "No man in his right mind
would let a woman like you get away from him."

Tess almost laughed, realizing he had no idea of the
irony she found in his words. Instead, she murmured, her
mouth twisting, "I don't know. I've counted two men
who have so far."

Seth stared at her. Did she mean him? Was she including him as one of the two? Or did he think so only because he wanted to believe he had been that important to
her once?

Swallowing suddenly, vaguely disconcerted, Seth bus-
ied himself by plucking a leaf off a nearby tree. Tess
watched as he bent to rest his arms on the bridge rail once
more. Below him, the creek shimmered in the afternoon
sun. Idly, he drew the willow blade between his forefin-
ger and thumb.

"I came to your graduation." It was a soft, pained
admission, and he spoke almost absently.

Tess frowned in confusion. "M—my graduation?"

Seth didn't look at her. His eyes were fastened to the
slender emerald leaf, which he continued to slide like a
satin ribbon through his hands. "I know. It was a stu-

pid, crazy thing to do. There you were, looking so young and shining in your little white cap and gown, making your plans to go off to college. And there I was, a married man with a baby, caught up in a divorce suit and a battle for custody. I told myself I shouldn't even be thinking about you. Much less sitting there watching you. But...I was there." He shrugged and glanced at her with a strange, sad smile. "Valedictorian. I was really proud of you."

Tess's chest constricted. A welter of confused emotions rose as a lump formed in her throat. She felt like crying. Why had he done that? Why would he have even cared to see her graduate from high school? Memories flashed through her mind: her fellow students; their caps and gowns; the commencement ceremony; and the speech she had worked on for weeks, only to have it flee her mind in an instant. It all seemed so hokey and insignificant now.

But she *had* gone to college. And she *had* met Vance. And if her marriage had been the success she'd tried to make of it, Tess realized, she wouldn't be having this conversation now. She would never have known that Seth Taylor had thought enough of her, then, to go out of his way to attend her high-school graduation ceremony.

She didn't quite know what to say, and so she asked, "Why are you telling me this now?"

Seth laughed, but it was an odd, rasping kind of sound. "I don't know." He dropped the willow leaf to the water and stared after it. "It's something I've been carrying for a long time. I guess I just wanted you to know."

The sound of gravel crunching beneath car tires drew Tess's attention to the sight of Eden pulling into the driveway. As Eden glimpsed the two of them on the bridge, she gave a brief wave and Tess returned it. Then she turned to Seth with a sigh. "I suppose I really should be getting back now."

He nodded and shoved away from the bridge's railing, drawing himself upright. "Sure. I'll walk you over."

This time, however, he didn't offer to hold her hand. Gliding his hands into the back pockets of the starched indigo jeans he'd worn to church with a plaid dress shirt, he followed her down the sloping walk. When they'd crossed the yard and reached the porch, he stood gazing up at her as she paused for a moment on the steps.

"Thank you for bringing me home," she said.

"Thank you for letting me."

Blue eyes clung to hers, quietly probing, compelling her to repeat a truth she had already implied. "I'm not ready to start dating again."

Seth's eyes didn't waver. "I understand that."

Drawing a breath, Tess pulled her shoulders up stiffly. "If I were to tutor your son, it would have to be strictly that and nothing more. Nothing personal." *Between us,* she didn't add.

His face remained expressively blank, impassive as a stone. "Nothing personal," he agreed. "My son is my concern."

Sighing, Tess shoved a trembling hand through her hair. "All right, then," she finally agreed. "I'll, uh... I'll call you tomorrow and set up something." *I must be crazy,* she thought.

His eyes held hers for a moment longer, but his features gave none of his feelings away. Perhaps, Tess thought later, that was the reason his reply surprised her.

"I won't forget this," he promised, still without smiling. Then he turned and walked to his truck.

CHAPTER NINE

IT WAS RIDICULOUS; Tess knew it, and yet she realized the moment Seth opened the door she hadn't been prepared for the sight of him. She had fixed a smile on her face, and was about to say something—some polite but casual greeting, until she found herself staring into those stunning blue eyes of his, and for a brief second Tess thought she forgot even to breathe.

"I'm glad you came," he said as if there had been some question that she might not. There seemed something almost intimate about his statement. But it wasn't so much his words as the caressing drawl of his voice that reached her, seeping deep into her consciousness and drawing her out of a mist as though she had stood on his doorstep, dreaming.

"I'm, uh... I'm not too early, am I?" Tess managed to ask haltingly, as she shifted her small attaché case containing the supplies and teaching aids she had purchased the day before, and glanced down at her watch. She knew that she was right on time and her question was purely diversionary, meant to draw attention away from the fiery rush of heat to her cheeks.

This wasn't going to work, she realized instantly. How could it, when she wasn't even inside the house yet, and already her nerves felt like crackling hot wires under her skin? If she had any sense at all, Tess told herself, she would turn around now, get back in her car and drive away as fast as she could.

But obviously, she had no sense. Otherwise, Tess concluded, she wouldn't be here, staring at him through the screen, clutching her books to her breast with the trembling hands of a smitten schoolgirl.

"Come on in," Seth invited, smiling captivatingly as he shoved the door open. Spring hinges moaned, and he moved to straddle the threshold, stretching one long, muscled arm around to brace the screen against the outer wall.

The doorway was narrow, and Tess realized that there was no way she could pass through it without touching him, the way his body was angled towards hers. At the thought of physical contact, her pulse rate surged, but she told herself she was just being silly. He was holding the door, for heaven's sake! And she could hardly justify loitering around outside on the hot porch for fear that part of her body might inadvertently brush his.

"Well?" Seth lowered his head. Amusement danced in the fire-bright eyes that squinted at her as if he were trying to view her through an imaginary pair of new bifocals. "You wanna come in now? Or should I go in and catch a couple of movies on the VCR while you take a minute to decide?"

He was making fun of her, and yet Tess found she had to bite her lip to keep from laughing with him, and at herself. It was one of her flaws: grave expectations. That she tended to take herself and life a little too seriously and occasionally needed someone to remind her to "loosen up," as Mariah would say, was no news to Tess. She knew well that she was a pessimist at heart. And especially since her divorce she seemed to have fallen into the habit of preparing herself for the worst in every situation. That way, if the worst happened, she wouldn't be completely devastated; and if it didn't, she would be pleasantly surprised.

At the moment, she was pleasantly surprised. Crouched down and peering at her the way he was, Seth suddenly didn't seem as imposing or intimidating. Her heart rate calmed and she permitted herself the smile his teasing had coaxed to her lips. "I think I'll come in now," she answered finally, "if you don't mind."

She was still smiling as she made the step up from the porch and brushed past Seth, moving into the wide expanse of his den. *Now,* she thought, *that wasn't so bad, was it?* Her shoulder grazed his chest. There were no sparks, no jolting currents of electricity shooting up her arms or tingling to make her hair stand on end. He didn't grab her and crush her in a harsh embrace. And she came nowhere near suffering a cardiac arrest. *Aren't you relieved?* an inner voice questioned. Tess felt her smile waver slightly as she realized that relief had never felt more like disappointment.

"Can I get you something cold to drink?" Seth's voice intruded upon Tess's thoughts, and she sighed, grateful for the interruption.

"Yes," she said, and smiled. "That would be nice."

"What would you like? Cola? Iced tea? A beer?" He glanced over his shoulder as she followed him into the kitchen.

"Cola would be great. Eden can't keep it," she explained. "The kids she baby-sits drink it up too fast. And I don't mind telling you, I've started to develop a near phobia to even the smell of grape juice."

Seth laughed. "That bad, huh?" Reaching into the refrigerator, he came up with a canned soft drink for her and a beer for himself.

"Well, maybe not that bad," Tess hedged, watching as he dropped ice cubes into a glass and poured the cola on top. The drink was still fizzing when he handed it to her. "You didn't have to go to this trouble, you know," she said, taking a sip. "It wouldn't have killed me to drink it from the can."

He twisted the cap off his beer and crossed his arms, leaning his hip against the kitchen counter. "First-time guests always get first-rate treatment." He gave her a half-cocked grin. "Next time you get the can."

Tess laughed and took another drink, wondering how plain cola could possibly make her feel so warm and light-headed. Or was it just this man's company? At the thought, the glass wobbled suddenly in her grasp. She set it on the counter and ran her hands down her thighs.

"Your, uh... your house is great," she said nervously, seeking some safe topic of conversation. But it was true. The single-story gray framehouse, with its gabled roof and mock turret, was attractive from the outside, and roomy and comfortable on the inside. "Did you build it yourself?" Tess asked idly, running her hand over the ceramic-tile countertop.

Seth had just taken a drink of his beer. "No. Actually, I had it moved here."

He swallowed, then touched the corner of his mouth with the back of his hand. The same long, tanned masculine hand, holding the beer bottle loosely by the neck. The gesture was casual, and yet so absolutely male, that Tess found herself staring, wishing he would do it again. Oddly, she wondered if this was the very reason Seth Taylor had always fascinated her. That he was almost hypnotically male.

"They were widening a highway south of Shreveport," Seth continued, forcing Tess's wandering thoughts back to the conversation. "This was one of the houses that had to go. So I bought it for a fraction of nothing, then paid a near fortune to have it moved. And spent more money and time than anyone in their right mind would ever consider, remodeling and fixing it up the way I wanted it."

"Oh?" Raising her brows, Tess feigned stark innocence. "Does that mean you'd actually admit you're not in your right mind?"

Seth's eyes met hers, and the blue flames in his grew suddenly dark and cryptic. "It comes and goes," he murmured. "And if you knew what I was considering right now, you'd probably think I'd lost it for good."

She watched his gaze lower to her lips, and her heart thudded out a pounding rhythm that echoed in her ears. Her mouth felt dry and she tried to swallow. Then, finding that she couldn't, she tore her gaze away from his in near panic.

"Well, I . . . I like what you've done with the place."

Seth couldn't help smiling as he watched her retrieve her glass of cola, tipping it up and drinking as if she were dying of thirst. He had rattled her. He hadn't intended to, but now he was almost glad. Despite their bargain—that there would be nothing personal between them while she was working with Jason—Seth had to admit he wanted to have an effect on her. Because she certainly had one on him.

What was it about her? he wondered. And how could any woman who had been through both marriage and divorce still manage to exude such a beguiling sense of innocence? And yet, she was all woman.

Memory served Seth suddenly with a recollection of their conversation on Sunday afternoon, when they had stood together on the little bridge beside her house. He knew how much it must have cost her to confess, essentially, that there were times when she still felt as helpless and frightened as a little girl.

Her admission had stirred every protective male instinct inside him. And even now, as she turned to meet his eyes, her expression composed, emotions clearly under control again, Seth experienced that same compulsive rush of protectiveness for the fragile girl he wanted to shelter, the beautiful woman he wanted to possess.

"I'm sorry," she said and gave her head a little shake, her lips crooked with a wry smile. "I seem to have forgotten what we were talking about."

Seth's eyes flickered with a gentle warmth. "Don't worry about it." He smiled. "I don't think it was anything too earth-shattering."

Reluctantly, he pulled his gaze away from Tess, and reached for the file he had picked up at the school from Mr. D'Arberville. His smile vanished and his warm expression changed radically as he placed the documents on the kitchen table in front of Tess. "I thought you might like to have a look at these. So I had the school make copies."

Tess's brows raised. "Jason's transcripts?" Seth drew out a chair from the table, remaining behind it until she was seated.

"Yes," he confirmed with a curt nod and took the chair across from her. "And, while I admit most of that 'mean' and 'level' jargon is Greek to me, I have an idea from what I *was* able to grasp, and from the way Mr. D'Arberville talked, that Jason's in a lot more trouble scholastically than I ever thought."

"Oh?" Responding to the gravity in Seth's tone, Tess frowned almost automatically as she glanced down and opened the folder. But as she began her slow perusal of the documents contained inside—basic skills tests, level mastery scores, patterns of grades and percentile ranks on intelligence capacity and aptitude scales—Tess's frown deepened.

"Well? What do you think?" Seth asked quietly, although he wasn't sure he wanted the answer. For long moments he had sat in tense silence, carefully scrutinizing every nuance of Tess's expression, while she carefully looked over each sheet in Jason's file.

After a few minutes, she sighed and leaned back in her chair. But she was still frowning as her eyes met Seth's. "Where is Jason now?" she asked intently. "Is he here?"

Seth frowned, too. "Well, yeah, of course. He's in his room. I told him you were coming. Why? Is something wrong?"

Tess drew a deep breath and leaned forward, resting her elbows on the transcript folder, her hands clasped, her eyes bright with concern. "Seth, when was the first time you realized Jason was having trouble in school?"

He shrugged and tried to remember. "I don't know. He hasn't been with me—I mean, you know, he's been living with his mother, and the news I get is usually selective." His tone was bitter. "He was retained in the eighth grade last year, as I told you, and as you can see for yourself, Jason has never been a real strong student. I knew he was struggling, but I suppose it's only been in the last couple of years that I realized—or was given the opportunity to realize—that he was actually failing."

Tess nodded as if she wasn't surprised. "What about sports? Has Jason ever gone out for any type of athletics?"

Seth shook his head, failing to see the question's relevance but willing to go along. "No. He's never shown much interest in sports. Ford tried to get him involved in the youth basketball team last spring at church. But Jason refused.''

"But have you ever seen him play? I mean even when he was small—basketball, baseball, hopscotch?" She saw Seth's frown of consternation. "What I'm trying to find out is if you've ever noticed Jason's being, say—" Tess searched for the right way to phrase her question so that Seth wouldn't be offended "—a little clumsy?" She tried to put it as gently as possible. "Maybe not quite as co-ordinated as other boys his age?"

"I don't see what all this has to do with Jason's schoolwork." His voice took on a note of impatience, but he answered her honestly. "As far as I can see, Jason is as normal and coordinated as any other gangly-legged adolescent. He has been known to trip over his own feet, if that's what you mean. But I don't think it's affected his ability to hold a pencil. So, what are you leading up to, here?"

Blazing blue eyes bored into hers with a fierce pater-nal protectiveness Tess couldn't help but admire. If she had had any reservations about Seth's relationship with his son, she could see now, without a doubt, just how deeply he cared for the boy.

"Jason has an above-average IQ, yet he's barely read-ing at a sixth-grade level. He does average work in math-ematics, industrial arts and any subject that deals with numbers. But when it comes to science, social studies, language arts or other areas where the ability to read, comprehend and retain material is essential to the learn-ing process, Jason falls far short of the mark.''

"But his IQ . . ."

"Is 119, well above the average. But people have a lot of misconceptions about IQ tests. They are, in fact, only a projected measurement of his learning potential.''

"Which translated means...?"

"That some people never reach their estimated potential, while others exceed theirs."

"So what good are they? IQ tests, I mean."

"Well, in Jason's case at least, the results indicate that he's basically a very bright boy, and not by any means mentally retarded. In other words, he has the capacity to learn, if the material is presented in a way that he can understand."

"I don't think I understand."

Tess laughed. "It is kind of confusing, isn't it? But actually I'd rather not go into any detailed explanations until I'm certain of the problem. I'd like to spend a few days putting Jason through some tests."

"Whatever it takes. But I'm not sure he'll be too thrilled. He thinks he's allergic to tests."

"Don't worry. These aren't your ordinary multiple-choice variety. They shouldn't tax his brain, and he might even find himself having fun with some of them."

"Oh, yeah?" Seth's expression conveyed his reservations. "I'll have to see it to believe it, but I still don't understand what basketball and coordination have to do with scholastic ability."

"Well, I do. And you will, too, if my assumption proves correct. I'll explain everything, I promise."

"Everything? You promise?" His voice lowered to a seductive rumble, and though he smiled teasingly, Tess thought that his eyes held a curious glimmer of challenge.

Was he making certain she hadn't changed her mind about any personal involvement? Or was it her own attraction to him that had her reading more into his expression than was there?

Forcing herself to answer as calmly as possible, despite the leaping pulse in her throat, she countered, "Within reason."

Seth grinned impishly. "I should have known there'd be a catch somewhere." Then, surprising her, he dropped his teasing facade and rose from the table, coming around to help her from her chair. "Come on," he said. "I'll show you to Jason's room."

As they headed down the dim, narrow hall, Tess was extremely aware of Seth's imposing presence behind her. His muscular shoulders seemed to barely clear the walls on either side, and she wondered why she hadn't remembered to notice how tall he was. Or had she?

When they paused at the door to Jason's room, Tess turned and tilted her head slightly to look at Seth.

"I have to warn you." He spoke softly, but she sensed the strain in his voice. "Jason wasn't real crazy about the idea of a tutor, and you may have trouble getting him to cooperate at first."

"Don't worry," she said, smiling. "I won't let him scare me away."

"Is that a promise?" His eyes darkened and searched hers for a moment. But before she could recover from the unexpected intensity of his gaze to respond with a reasonable comeback, he turned and rapped quickly on Jason's door.

"Jason?" The door wasn't locked. He eased it open as he announced, "Ms Langford is here."

Whoopee do, Tess imagined she could almost read the boy's first thought as the door swung open, and he rolled his eyes, his lips taut and compressed.

He was standing before a gleaming wall of expensive stereo equipment, his stance careless and slouching in profile. A huge black headset was strung haphazardly around his lean neck. And when he turned, stiffly, Tess caught the hardened sheen of resentment in his eyes.

He's a hard one to reach. Ford Dunning's words flashed like a caution light through her mind, and for the second time in less than two hours, Tess couldn't help wondering if she had made a mistake in coming here.

It was Seth's voice she heard behind her. "Ms Langford is here to help you, Jason," he reminded his son, and though he sounded calm, Tess sensed the steeliness of authority in his tone. "She's a guest in our home and you will treat her with cooperation and respect. Just as you would expect me to treat any friend of yours who was doing a favor for you."

Jason gave a bitter snort. "I don't have any friends, and I don't need no favors," he said sullenly.

Tess felt Seth tense, and realized that as long as she was here she might as well try to make the best of it. She had dealt with hostile youths before, and if her assumptions, based on Jason's school records, were accurate, she knew there was a psychological if not justifiable motive behind his behavior. Moving quickly to intercede before there could be any further exchange between father and son, Tess approached Jason with an easy smile and a sympathetic eye.

"No friends? I can't believe that. Maybe you're just too selective." Tess paused for a moment, and realized that professional observations weren't what Jason needed now. She was going to have to dig down in her heart and come up with a genuine way to relate to the boy. But that was easy, she thought, because when it came to loneliness, she understood more than most. "That's my problem sometimes, you know. I don't open up very well, and I hold everything inside. And sometimes I just feel like I don't belong. Maybe we could help each other. Maybe we could be friends.''

Jason looked at her, and his dark eyes narrowed suspiciously. But after a few moments, he seemed to vacillate, not too convinced and yet not totally unconvinced of her sincerity. Tess watched as he shifted his gaze and glanced over her shoulder to Seth, who was still standing close behind her, with a look that seemed to ask, is she for real?

Tess couldn't see Seth's expression, and she had no idea what kind of wordless assurance he might have offered his son, if any. But in a matter of seconds, Jason lowered his eyes and leveled them, once again, on hers, his expression wary but considering.

It was a start, she thought. "Great." Her smile broadened into a full grin as she hastily accepted what she interpreted as a small concession on his part as a positive step in the right direction. "Now, the first thing I want us to do is start getting acquainted. We're not going to study today, just talk. And to tell you the truth, hardly anybody calls me Ms Langford." Only her students, she might have added, but thought it best not to. They weren't in a classroom. This arrangement was more personal. More so, maybe, than she cared to admit. Still smiling, despite the subtly upsetting implications that thought brought to mind, Tess shrugged and slid her hands into her slash pockets. "How 'bout if you just call me Tess? For short."

Jason's face remained impassive, but Tess thought his eyes betrayed a fleeting glimmer of emotion that seemed to hover somewhere along the spectrum between mild curiosity and cautious amusement.

This kid was no dummy, Tess thought. And she was no psychic, but it didn't take a mind reader to guess at Jason's thoughts. *Okay, teacher lady, you rolled in here on a line of bull. Now let's see which one of us slips on it first.*

They had taken each other's measure and, while Tess harbored no illusions concerning Jason's attitude toward her, she hadn't expected that he would withdraw again completely and so soon—almost the instant Seth excused himself and closed the door, leaving the two of them alone to talk.

"You really have a nice room here," she began in an effort to strike up a conversation. If they were to work together successfully, Tess needed to learn more about Jason. Some of her questions would be personal, while others might make him uncomfortable simply because of their vague nature.

But much like a psychologist or a professional counselor, she knew her first step was to find some common ground on which to begin the process of building trust and the necessary rapport. Somehow she had to find a way to get Jason to relax and open up to her.

But how? Tess wondered as she watched Jason slowly slide his back down the wall, taking a seat flat on the floor. Flanked by the bed on one side and a huge stereo speaker on the other, he sat as far away from her as possible, with his knees drawn up, his arms folded and clenched defensively across his chest. His stereo headset, with earphones so large they nearly obscured his narrow shoulders, still hung, suspended like weights from the curve of his neck, and a long black wire connected him to the system as if it he depended upon it for life support.

It occurred to her suddenly that Jason had yet to address a single word to her. He had spoken to his father, but even then it was only briefly, to inform him that he had no friends, and furthermore didn't want any. Tess doubted that was the case. Everyone needed someone, and teenagers, especially, required the close companionship and the nurturing social support of their peers.

And yet, as she looked at Jason, his cold, dark eyes—so like his mother's, Tess realized suddenly—staring at her with bitter distrust and insolence, she couldn't help thinking that if the boy's intention was indeed to discourage friends, he was certainly on the right track, so far.

"You like music, I see," she remarked, glancing around his room at the myriad rock-band posters, album covers and other related memorabilia covering his walls with scarcely a spot left vacant.

Jason only looked at her, his expression conveying something close to disgust. It didn't take a genius to figure out that one. Maybe *he* should be tutoring *her.*

Tess drew a long-suffering breath. *Okay, Jason,* she thought, becoming a little irritated with the situation herself. *They say music is the universal language, and if that's true, then it stands to reason that somewhere in this room, there's bound to be a tune we can hum together.*

With her hands clasped behind her, Tess strolled the length of the room to where Jason sat. Standing before him, she faced the wall and leaned forward slightly. Her eyes narrowed as she pretended to study, with the critical interest of a fine-art connoisseur, the motley array of posters and pictures taped above his head.

"Hmm." She raised one eyebrow and pursed her lips. But besides this deliberately ambiguous cluster of gestures, she offered no comment as she drew back, politely stepped over the boy's feet and moved on to inspect the next collage.

Jason said nothing, maintaining his tight, surly-faced vigil. But Tess could feel the heat of his eyes upon her, and the defensiveness building inside him was like a pressure force. He was waiting, Tess knew, in seething readiness, for her to make some comment, some typically censuring adult remark against the art of rock music and the derelict appearance of some of its creators. And that was what she was counting on. That, and . . .

This.

It had been behind her all along, Tess realized, barely able to conceal her smile as she halted before Jason's closet door. The larger-than-life-size poster bearing the image of a tall, dark-haired, bare-chested man, provocatively posed in skin-tight jeans and fringed suede boots. Around his neck was draped a white silk scarf that trailed to the floor in lazy abandon.

The rock star's autograph was neatly stenciled in the lower right-hand corner. But Tess had no need to read the signature. The face, the clothes...she'd grown used to it all by now, until it almost seemed commonplace. Little did the star know that he had suddenly become her ace in the hole.

With her back to Jason, Tess bit her lip and struggled to make her tone sound heavy with disdain. "E.Z. Ellis, huh? Well, I guess we won't be hearing much out of him, anymore. He's given up touring, you know. And since stage appeal and a certain teenie-bopper charm were about all the talent he ever had anyway, I doubt anyone will continue buying records he has no intention of promoting in live concerts."

"Are you crazy?" In a matter of seconds, Jason had wrenched off his headset, tossed it on the bed and scrambled angrily to his feet. "E.Z. rules, man. He's the best! And if you knew anything about music, you'd know the man is a legend. He doesn't need to go on the road to sell records. His last album went platinum the same day it hit the stands!''

A devoted fan! Thank goodness. Tess fought to keep herself from laughing in sheer satisfaction. She'd gotten exactly the response she had hoped for. No longer closed-faced and silent, Jason was animated and more than ready to talk, his dark eyes snapping with emotion.

"Well, then—" she shrugged nonchalantly "—I suppose you wouldn't mind meeting him in person sometime?"

Jason frowned at her as if he wondered what would make her ask something so stupid and obviously out of the realm of possibility. But after a few moments, he sighed and raised his eyes to the man in the poster.

When he answered, his voice was almost wistful. "Well, yeah, I'd like to meet him. Who wouldn't want to meet E.Z.? But like you said, he's not doing any more live concerts. And since he's probably out globe-trotting, while I'm stuck in Hicksville, U.S.A., I'm not gonna hold my breath for the big meet."

"Maybe I could arrange it for you," Tess offered casually, and watched as Jason turned his head to stare at her.

His mouth opened slightly and he blinked, then cocked his head at her, baffled. "Sure, great. You do that, and while you're at it, I'll see if I can get you a lunch date with the president."

"Well, I appreciate the thought, but actually I'm not interested in meeting the president. But I'll tell you what. If you promise me that you'll work hard and make my work easier over the next few weeks, I'll not only arrange for you to meet good ol' E.Z., I'll ask him to let you sit in on a recording session."

"What do you think? That just because I flunked out a grade I'm some kind of a moron? You can't just call up somebody like E.Z. Ellis."

"I don't see why not. His wife calls me."

Jason's eyes widened.

Tess smiled. "E.Z. Ellis is my brother-in-law, Jason. He's married to my sister, Jo."

CHAPTER TEN

IN THE SUSPENDED STILLNESS of those next few seconds, Tess hadn't known what to expect as Jason stared at her, dumbstruck, his expression wavering between disbelief and euphoric delirium.

"You're kidding."

"Nope. D'you remember a few months ago, when the music industry was all up in arms over a group in Washington that was trying to get the government to pass a law that would ban and control the lyrics in rock music?"

Jason nodded.

"Well, at that time, my sister was—what you might call—the spokeswoman for that group. And E.Z. was . . . uh, he was pretty outspoken, too. But to make a long story short, when the law failed to pass, they both decided that the only way to shut the other one up was to marry him—or her, depending on your point of view. And so they did—get married, that is. But they haven't shut up."

"Then all that stuff you said about E.Z. not having any talent . . ."

"That's an inside joke. Something my sister said about him once, when she was mad at him. But of course, it isn't true—and, if you value your life, you'll never tell either of them I even dared to repeat it!"

Jason was coming out of his daze, and excitement went through him like a current, snapping him to sudden life.

"You mean it? You really aren't joking? E.Z. Ellis! Oh, man! I can't believe it! This is—it's just... Oh, man, too much! When can I meet him? Will he come here? No, his recording studio. I'll meet him there, right? Where is it? When—"

"Wait. Slow down." Tess laughed, then went on to explain that E.Z. and Jo were working on a special project now and wouldn't be back until the end of the summer. But maybe she would get E.Z. to call him, to set things up in advance.

"But remember, Jason," she reminded him. "This isn't something I'm doing out of the goodness of my heart. If you agree to this, we're going to consider it sort of like a business arrangement, a trade-off, so to speak. You promise me no more sulking, no more closing yourself up and swallowing the key. We're going to work together, and we're going to get you ready for high school, without a lot of griping and complaining. And then, if you keep your end of the bargain, I'll keep mine."

"A bargain, you say?" Tess nodded and Jason grinned. "Don't you mean a bribe?"

One brow lifted in devilish teasing. And in that moment, Tess thought, it was amazing how much he looked like his father.

Strangely, her heart gave a little twist. *This boy could have been my son,* she thought. Strong. Handsome. Witty. Like his father. No—that's foolish thinking. Jason could never have been her son. Despite Seth's teasing comments and his single invitation to lunch, Tess was convinced he had probably never thought of her as anything other than an old friend.

And, in spite of thoughts of his father, Tess found she was taken in by Jason's grin. She even had to bite the inside of her cheek to suppress the grin that tugged at her own lips. "I said bargain. Not bribe. And you better not quibble. I've got your number, Jason Taylor and don't forget it!"

"No, ma'am." Jason grinned. "And please don't forget it when you talk to E.Z."

EVEN UNDER THE BEST of circumstances, Seth readily admitted, he was not the greatest of cooks. One might assume that for someone who had lived alone for as many years as he had, a working knowledge of basic culinary skills would not only have come naturally, but would have, in all probability, been impossible to avoid. After all, a man had to survive, and to survive he had to eat. But Seth had long since concluded that should his survival depend on his own cooking, he'd rather be dead.

Only he had Jason to think of now. Nutrition and all that. He couldn't expect, nor did he wish, his son to fall into the same habit he had of living on cornflakes, bologna sandwiches, colas and ready-wrapped hamburgers, grabbed and eaten on the run.

And so here he was, slaving over a hot skillet of hamburger dinner mix, wondering if those little white disk things really tasted anything like scalloped potatoes, and if Tess had any idea how much he had longed to lead her down the hall, past his son's room and into his own bedroom—and not with any altruistic motive in mind—instead of leaving her with Jason, fifty agonizingly long minutes ago.

Fifty-one, he corrected himself, glancing at the clock over the stove. It was nearly eight o'clock. Supper was ready, and he had heard the stereo come on in Jason's room a little while ago. It was a signal, indicating to Seth that Tess and Jason were either finished with the serious side of their conversation, or that Jason was tuning her out, no longer willing to listen. Maybe he should go and check.

Sighing, Seth dragged his hand through a thick wave of sweat-damp hair that had fallen across his forehead. The music became progressively louder as he crossed the living room and turned down the narrow hall. Seth frowned. If only he could understand what was going on in Jason's mind, then maybe he could reach him, reassure him—prove to him that he would always be safe here. No one would leave him or kick him out. That he would always be loved. That, unlike Celia, Seth would never allow anyone to jeopardize their relationship. If only he could get Jason to trust and open up....

Reaching his son's door, Seth rapped once before he turned the knob and stuck his head inside. "Supper's ready, Jase. You better go wa—"

Seth thought he felt his lips move to form the words "wash up" but he couldn't be sure, since the sound of his voice never reached his ears. Or anyone else's. Which was no mystery, considering the volume of the "music" blaring out from the stereo and the fairly screaming conversation taking place. Seth thought he might as well have been whistling Dixie into the eye of a hurricane. Not even his presence was noted, amid the pandemonium of noise. After a few seconds, he decided that was a distinct advantage.

"What'dya think, man? Is that killer or what?" Jason shouted above the wall-quaking vibrations of some hard-metal rock band's screechingly amplified improvisation of dueling guitars.

Heavy on the bass. Light on the treble. Hell on the central nervous system, Seth mused. His eyes moved to Tess.

"Killer? Is that anything like 'far out'?" she asked Jason, lifting her head lightly and glancing toward him as he leaned over to adjust a knob on his stereo system.

She was sitting on the floor cross-legged, her right shoulder blocking her view of Seth, although because he was standing, he could see her clearly. She had taken her shoes off, and records and album covers lay strewn all around her. Her hair was all mussed as if she had been running her hands through it, and when she lowered her head the brown tresses tumbled like a curtain of silk, dark and gleaming against her tawny gold skin with its faint blush of coral that added tint to her cheeks.

"Far out where?" Jason answered her question with a question. And Seth quickly shifted his gaze to his son, searching, looking for any sign of his earlier insolence, his sullen resentment of Tess. What he saw was his son drop down on the floor beside her, with an indulgent grin and a casual, almost affectionate brush against her shoulder.

Head to head, they leaned over the album cover she was holding as if it were a treasure and they'd been friends for years. What had she done? How could anyone have gotten Jason to turn around so suddenly? It seemed impossible, and yet he was seeing it with his own eyes.

"Far out? Is that what you said?"

"Never mind. I think we've stumbled upon a minor generation gap. Or do they even use that expression anymore? Anyway, the sound is . . . very powerful. What did you say was the name of this group?"

"Rank'n Foul. But don't let the name throw you. It's just a gimmick. They're really some pretty cool dudes. The lead singer's big into RAD."

"Rad?" Tess asked, realizing that she was totally out of her element. "Is that some kind of a sport?"

Jason laughed. "Naw, man. RAD. Rock Against Drugs. You know, sorta like MADD."

"Oh, yes." Tess nodded. Mothers Against Drunk Drivers. Tess was aware of that organization, at least. "RAD," she muttered, again repeating the word to herself. "Sounds like a very good cause. My sister must have thought it up." With a smile Tess thought of Jo, the tireless crusader, one of her never-ending struggles to save the world from itself.

Maybe you should have an affair. Find someone to be crazy with. Jo's words boomeranged through her mind, and Tess tossed back her head with a jolt, impatiently shoving at her hair, its heaviness suddenly a smothering irritant on her face and neck. And it was then that she spotted a pair of scuffed leather boots and the long, denim-sheathed legs that went with them.

"Seth!" His name burst past the pumping constriction in her throat, but was swept away in the pounding surge of a drum solo.

But then he smiled at her, his eyes soft and lazy, and for a moment, words and even the music were forgotten. When he looked at her, thoughts evaporated, and her spirit seemed to quiet in fragile anticipation. Yet, strangely, she felt as if her body was floating, drawn up in the cloud of his eyes, caressed and consumed in a swirl of blue.

"Dad!" It was the sound of Jason's voice that penetrated the haze. When he noticed his father standing at the door, he sprang to his feet and rushed to lower the volume on the stereo. Glad for the diversion, Tess glanced away quickly, feeling suddenly both ridiculous and exposed.

"Dad, why didn't you tell me!" Jason charged, his voice excited and loud despite the fact that the room was quiet now. "She's related! Can you believe it? Actually related to E.Z. Ellis!"

Seth passed Tess a baffled look. "Who?"

She smiled and explained. "Jo's husband. You've met him, haven't you?" She pointed at the poster on Jason's door. "In real life he wears glasses and his clothes are..." She couldn't help smiling. "Well, let's just say he wears more of them. He likes to keep a lower profile when he's not on stage. But it is true. He's a star." She shrugged.

"A star?" Jason echoed. "The man's a legend, I tell you. And I'm gonna meet him. Wait till I tell Tony. He won't believe it. If I'm dreaming, please don't wake me up."

"Then you better start sleepwalking into the bathroom and get washed up for supper."

"But Dad..." Jason started to protest when Tess interjected. "Don't worry, Jason. We'll tap three times if any limos pull up out front."

Jason gave her an exasperated look, but in the end he complied with his father's command almost cheerfully. "E.Z. Ellis." His voice trailed out the door and down the hall. "I can't believe it. Man, oh, man. I just can't—"

The bathroom door slammed shut. Seth and Tess looked at each other. "Believe it," they finished in unison and laughed.

Their voices mingled well together, Tess noted. His so deep and rumbling in his chest, hers lighter and more hesitant. She wished that they could laugh together more often. And then, realizing that she was staring at him again, she ducked her head and reached for her shoes. One of them was half hidden under the bed.

"I'm having a little trouble believing it myself," Seth said softly, as Tess, feeling more comfortable now that she was fully dressed, gathered up the stack of records and stood.

"About E.Z.?" She turned and slid Jason's albums in the rack under the turntable and closed the glass doors that protected them.

"No," Seth answered. "I mean about Jason." He watched as Tess straightened away from the stereo and ran her palms down the legs of her jumpsuit.

"I don't understand." Her eyes had the wide-open innocence of a child, and Seth found himself wanting to drown in them. He dragged his attention back to his son with an effort.

"Jason. Are you sure that's the same kid I left in here an hour ago? I've heard of miracle make-overs, but I had no idea you carried a magic wand up your sleeve. How did you do it?"

Her features softened, and she glanced toward the door Jason had just exited through. "He does seem to be in a better mood, doesn't he? But I'm afraid I can't take the credit for it." With a tilt of her head, Tess indicated the poster of Jason's idol. "It helps to know persons in high places." She grinned. "Connections. You'd be surprised at their value."

"Do I, by any chance, sense the crime of bribery in the works?"

Tess's eyes narrowed in mock reproof. "Bargain," she corrected. "The word is bargain. Did anyone ever tell you you Taylors seem to share the joint workings of a criminal mind?"

Seth's face suddenly blanched and Tess realized in a flash what she'd just said and could have died from embarrassment. "Oh, Seth. I'm sorry." Her face burned and she stumbled over her words, trying to find the right ones to say, a verbal stitch to reseal the wound accidentally opened through her insensitive words. "You know I didn't mean—"

But Seth dismissed her verbal slip. "Forget it. It was a long time ago, the old man's dead now, and even when he was alive, his prison record was certainly no secret in this town." His voice sounded bitter, and Tess realized the old pain—the stigma—was still there, regardless of what he said.

How could you be such a clod? she admonished herself. And then, because she couldn't bear the guilt of knowing she had hurt him, she reached out and touched him, putting her hand on his arm. "I'm sorry. Please forgive me. You know that I never cared about where you came from, or what your father did when we were growing up. And it surely doesn't matter now."

Seth stared at her, aware of the feel of her small, warm hand on his forearm. Hadn't she already assured him, numerous times in the past, and once only lately, that the old slights against the Taylor name had no effect on her? Nor did they matter to him any longer; he had risen above all that social nonsense, years ago. Then why was he getting so sensitive all of sudden?

Sensitive. Maybe, Seth thought, it was because he seemed almost uncannily sensitive to everything about this woman.

I don't care where you came from. Her soft-spoken declaration taunted his mind with the flip side of the same issue.

"And what do you care about, Tess?" Seth heard himself ask, although his voice sounded strange, detached, as if the question had not come from him at all.

Tess felt the subtle shift in his mood, too. That almost frightening sense of being connected somehow, in a way that defied and transcended the powers of language. Her instinct was to pull away, but she found she could not. Entranced, she answered softly, "I care about you."

Was this a dream? Was she fantasizing again? Or had she tripped over some hidden dimensional barrier, called back in time to say the words she should have said thirteen years ago, had things been different, had their date been kept, had he not married. And had a son.

Jason.

It was the very tangible reality of Jason and the recollection of his presence just down the hall that brought Tess back to her wits. With jerky motions, she withdrew her hand from Seth's arm and took a step back, her joints as stiff as if they had rusted while she stood.

"I, uh...I care about you, of course—and Jason," she added, hoping to make it appear that she had meant to include him all along. "You...you and Jason caught me at a time in my life when I really need to feel needed." Now why did she tell him that? "And I really want to help Jason with his scholastic problems, if I can, and maybe I'll see the two of you grow closer." She smiled faintly, but her gaze was steady and dark.

Seth had been watching her intently, and the changing emotions on her face were fleeting and impossible to read as they always had been, for him at least. One moment she was trembling, vulnerable as a tiny wildflower caught in the rage of a battering storm, and the next she was secretive, restless, dark as the rain itself. A flower in a storm. Wasn't that how he'd always seen her? A contradiction within a contradiction. Flower child; rainy-day woman. Seth smiled to himself. Bob Dylan would've loved it.

Once in the kitchen, Tess went straight to the table and picked up her attaché case, along with Jason's transcripts. "I'd like to take these home with me if you don't mind." She turned to Seth. "I want to check them over again, just to make sure I didn't miss anything."

Seth shrugged. "Sure. We're here to please." He smiled. "Does that mean you'll be back, same time, tomorrow night?"

"Well, yes. I mean, that is, if you still want me. It was our agreement, unless you've changed your mind?"

His eyes dropped to her lips, and her breath caught. "No, Tess. I haven't changed my mind, and I don't think I ever will. I still want you... more than you know."

Something went wrong with Tess's heart; it stopped. And for one interminable second, the only sense of life that pulsed through her otherwise numb body was a renewed and undeniable desire for the first man she had ever physically wanted. But she would be a fool! an inner voice shouted. A fool to let herself become involved with a man who had already rejected her once.

"Hey, Dad!" Jason's voice suddenly ricocheted through the room. "Can Tess stay for supper?" the boy asked. Oblivious to the tension in the room, he flopped down at his place at the table and closed his hand around a tall glass of milk.

Seth lifted a quizzical brow, implying with his look that she'd be welcome to stay if she were so inclined.

But Tess shook her head. "No, thank you both. I appreciate it. But I have some things to do, and I really need to get home early tonight. Maybe some other time."

"Tomorrow?" Jason persisted. "We'll fix something special, like steaks or spaghetti."

Tess bit her lip and deftly avoided Seth's gaze. "We'll see," she said. Then, picking up her purse, she adjusted the shoulder strap and bid Jason good-night.

"You sure you won't stay?" Seth asked seconds later as he walked her across the narrow strip of lawn that stretched between his front porch step and the driveway where her car was parked.

"I'm sure. But thanks anyway. You and Jason have been more than kind already."

It wasn't quite nine yet, but the moon was high, and the stars were bright and shining, illuminating their path.

As they arrived at her car, Tess automatically reached for the door handle. Her hand was already touching the lever when she felt the warmth and the strength of Seth's long fingers close over hers. "Tess?" His voice was deep, warm and flowing like a lazy river in the sun. And she was drawn to it with the fascination of a child, wandering the banks.

Very slowly, she turned her head to look at him, and his face was so close, she could define, even in the moonlight, every line and plane of it, the clean, square jaw, the faint white scar that was crescent-shaped and looked almost a like dimple, off center and to the left, near the blade of his chin.

His hair seemed darker in the silver light, maple-blond with streaks of gold and burnished copper that shimmered on iridescent silk. A cluster of waves tumbled down over his forehead, and beneath the dark wings of his brows his eyes blazed. Bright fires that seemed to glow from the tan of his face as if they were independent entities, alive and apart.

Again, Tess found herself caught up in the brilliant spell of his eyes. What would she do, she wondered, if he leaned forward and kissed her at that very moment when she felt incapable of resistance? Or was it that she didn't want to resist?

"Here," he murmured, his muscled chest momentarily pressed against the curve of her shoulder as he brushed her hand aside and opened the car door for her. He then stepped back and slid his hands into the back pockets of his jeans. "You've been in the city too long. Around here ladies never open a door for themselves when there's someone else to do it for them."

There was something in his eyes, something that said he was saying one thing and thinking another. Had he been about to kiss her? And if so, she wondered, what had changed his mind?

Later, Tess had no recollection of climbing behind the wheel of her car. She didn't remember slipping the key into the ignition or turning it over, sparking the engine to life. What she recalled was Seth easing the door shut and bending down to view her through the open window.

"Drive careful, and watch those bumps on the way out," he said and then, taking her totally by surprise, he reached out to tuck a strand of hair behind her ear. His fingertips lingering on her jaw, he traced her lips with the pad of his thumb. "You've grown into a beautiful woman, Tess. But then, you were a beautiful girl, especially in the moonlight." His eyes met hers, and something in their depths left no question that he was remembering, just as she was, their last night together as teenagers. The night he'd kissed her on the porch under the moonlight, then left her with a broken promise...

"Tomorrow," he whispered huskily. "I'll see you tomorrow."

She drove away with her knees shaking, her mind a blur and her body aching for more than the promise of a touch.

Seth stood with his hands resting lamely on his hips, watching the taillights of Tess's car disappear into the night. He had wanted to kiss her. What had come over him? Why hadn't he drawn her into his arms and taken her when he'd had the chance?

Nothing personal. Tess's terms of agreement flashed through Seth's mind. That was why he hadn't kissed her. Because he'd made her a promise, and he knew he had to keep it. For Jason's sake.

Inside the house, the phone rang and Jason answered it in the living room.

"So how did it go?" Tony Spier asked. It had been over a week now since Jason had come to town, and his nightly phone calls to and from Tony were becoming a habit.

"Okay, I guess," Jason answered his friend, abstracted. Holding the curtain back from the window, he had watched his father walk Tess Langford to her car. He had seen them hover there beside the door for a moment, and every muscle in his body had gone rigid as he waited to see if Seth was going to kiss her. He knew what that meant. One kiss and the next thing you knew they were moving in, and you were being shoved out.

When Jason saw there was no kiss exchanged, his body relaxed. Seconds later, as his father turned and started to the house, Jason quickly let the curtain fall into place and flung himself down on the couch. He didn't want his father to know he'd been watching.

By the time Seth came through the door, Jason was telling Tony the news about E.Z. Ellis. Even so, he didn't miss the odd slump of his father's shoulders. And for some reason he couldn't clearly define, a tremor of dread ran through him.

"What's the matter?" Tony heard the muffled sound of the phone being shifted around.

"Nothing," Jason muttered. Then, suddenly remembering the old saying, he added, "Just a rabbit running over my grave."

FOR THE REST OF THE WEEK and into the next, Tess devoted nearly every waking hour to avoiding thoughts of Seth and concentrating instead on his son. Though she was more than convinced that Jason's academic deficiency was directly related to poor reading performance, she knew it was impossible to help him until she was able to isolate the specific problem and determine the degree of his learning dysfunction.

By day, mostly in the early mornings when the sun was not so unbearably hot, they worked outside, going through a battery of exercises that were more like games. She coaxed him into playing hopscotch, a game that he considered "wimpy" and generally beneath his dignity. When he had trouble hopping on one foot, however, several of her questions about his problem were answered. She continued with tests for his perceptual motor control, making him balance seesaw style on a board supported by a soccer ball, and found that he couldn't stay there for any degree of time. And then there was the old tried-and-true experiment in which he was told to pat his head with one hand while rubbing his stomach in a circle with the other. Just as she'd expected, he'd been unable to do them both simultaneously, once again indicating that both sides of his brain weren't working together, the way they should.

At night they worked inside. Tess would show Jason a simple picture, such as a square with a diagonal series of dots, or a crude drawing of a man. His job, then, was to try reproducing, as accurately as he could, the simple picture as he perceived it. Nearly always, he reproduced the diagonal backward, and the picture of the man came out distorted, with one part of the body too large or too small.

While they worked, she would often look up to see Seth lingering in Jason's bedroom doorway, listening with a puzzled frown as she asked him important questions. How old was he when he'd learned to walk? Did he daydream? Were there times when he'd have to stop and think before he could remember which hand was right and which was left? Had he ever had his eyes checked? Did he get mixed up or confused sometimes about what day it was? Or forget for a moment what something was called, the word symbol for an object, for instance, like "lamp" or "dog"?

"What? Do you think I'm stupid?" Jason asked, insulted, when she posed that particular question. "It don't take an Einstein to tell a light bulb from a German shepherd."

Tess had laughed then, letting him know the question was neither an accusation or a judgment. "That's not what I mean, Jason. I'm talking about the word. Not how quickly the picture comes to mind, but whether or not you forget the word."

"Pardon me for a second, okay?" he said. "I think I'll turn off this overhead dog and go put a plate of something out for the light."

She had pursed her lips, trying to appear serious. "Very funny."

"So are these questions," he'd said with an unmistakable Seth smile. "Arf, arf."

It was Wednesday night. Tess had a headache, and Jason was in one of his moods. Though he seldom shut her out anymore, there were times when he lapsed into his typical pattern of aggressive-resistance behavior, making a joke out of everything she said. And it was those times that she found most difficult to evaluate him objectively.

His mood swings were to be expected, Tess knew, first because, at thirteen, Jason still straddled the fence between adolescence and manhood. It was no wonder, then, that at one moment, she could communicate with him as naturally as if he were an adult. Then, five seconds later, he would be swollen up like a pouting three-year-old who didn't want to play this silly game anymore.

But Tess had been trained to recognize a cluster of both physical and behavioral symptoms relating to learning disabilities. Poor concentration, avoidance reactions and the defensiveness Jason often displayed were classic indications of a learning disorder.

Knowing this didn't always make it automatically easier to deal with the volatile thirteen-year-old, however. She was, after all, only human—an astute revelation that had never seemed more apparent, or less escapable, than twenty minutes later, when Jason was dismissed to the bathroom to wash for supper, and Tess found herself in the kitchen alone with Seth.

"What's the matter?" he asked the moment he saw her face. He'd thought that she had looked unusually pale and tired when she had arrived that evening. Now, he thought, she looked as if she hadn't slept in weeks.

Tess smiled wanly but was careful to keep her gaze averted from Seth's. "Oh, it's nothing, really. Just a slight headache," she said, touching her fingertips to her temple.

But the truth was it was more than a headache. The truth was she hadn't slept in days. And how could she admit that, since the night Seth had walked her out to her car and she had stood with him in the moonlight, thinking he was about to kiss her, she'd grown obsessed with him? What a fool he'd believe her to be, if he knew that night after night, when she'd finished making notes and mental evaluations of Jason's tests for that day, she'd turn out the light and lie awake for restless hours praying for sleep.

But sleep wouldn't come. Instead, her mind tormented her with thoughts and images of Seth, replaying each nuance of his expression, his voice, his stance. Taking scenes out of context, rearranging and changing his words, so that in her mind, when he whispered, "I still want you," as he had that first evening, it was always just before he drew her into his arms and kissed her, hard and fiercely and passionately. And then sometimes, when she did finally manage to fall asleep, her dreams would draw her even deeper into what had become her preoccupation with such erotic fantasies. She would wake up flushed and breathless, yearning for release, and miserable that propriety stood between her and what she dreamed of.

Logically, she tried to convince herself that her feelings were normal. She'd been a married woman, and without a man now for over a year. But logic had little to do with feelings. She had never been with any man but Vance. And Vance had left her. For another woman. Just like Seth had done so long ago.

Because of this thought, and her secret humiliation at the infatuation she should have outgrown in her teens, Tess found it difficult to look Seth in the eye when he put two aspirin and a glass of water in her hand.

"Here, take these," he said. "They might not help, but they sure won't hurt...unless they get stuck in your throat."

Tess smiled wryly and swallowed the pills.

Jason barreled in and plopped down in his chair. "Hey, you gonna stay for dinner tonight?"

Tess was opening her mouth to refuse when Seth spoke.

"Yes, she is," he answered firmly and emphatically for her. "She's complaining of a headache this time." He directed his conversation to Jason, but Tess saw the conspiring glint of humor in his eyes that was undeniably meant for her.

"But to tell you the truth," he continued in a teasing tone, "I think the only reason she's turned down our generous dinner invitations so far is that she's on to the house rule: if you eat, you have to help clean up. And Jason—" he looked at his son before turning to Tess with a grave shake of his head "—I don't know about you, but I never would have figured her for the lazy type."

"I know what you mean, Dad," Jason said solemnly, getting in on the gag. "But she just doesn't want to do those dishes, does she?"

When they both turned to her, their faces long in mirrored expression of mock despair, it occurred to Tess this was the first time she had seen father and son joined together in the pursuit of pure fun.

It didn't bother her that she had become the object of their teasing. In fact, her spirits lifted, and she couldn't help laughing at their ridiculous expressions. An odd feeling of warmth permeated her body. And she wondered if perhaps she might have acted in part as a catalyst for their newfound alliance. The notion filled her with such a feeling of worth and belonging, she couldn't bring herself to refuse them.

"All right! All right, I'll stay!" But only, she insisted, to clear her name.

CHAPTER ELEVEN

THE MEAT LOAF WASN'T quite done. The mashed potatoes were a little lumpy, and the rolls were too white on top and too black on the bottom. But it was endearing, somehow, to see the honest attempt to create a home life where there hadn't been much of one before, and Tess ate as if a French chef had prepared the dinner.

"Dad's not much of a cook," Jason told her with amused apology, watching with admiration as Tess ate every morsel.

"The trick," Seth admitted, "is to make sure everyone's starving to death before I put the food on the table. You don't get many complaints that way."

Jason set down his fork and leaned toward Tess, animated with a memory. "One time when I was little and my dad had me for the weekend, he only had a pack of hot dogs in the refrigerator. We ate those for six meals in a row."

Tess shot Seth a disbelieving look, but already he was laughing and shaking his head in denial. "Now, wait a minute, Jason. You're gonna have Tess reporting me to the child welfare office. You forgot to mention that your mother dropped you off with a whopping case of chicken pox, and you were so sick with fever and nausea that I couldn't take you out to go to the grocery store."

"Oh, yeah," Jason said with a chuckle. "I did forget to mention that, didn't I?"

They laughed then, the first time Tess remembered seeing them do so together, and when the laughter died down, she could see more memories, better ones, reflected in both father's and son's eyes. The poignant expressions on their faces seemed almost surprised, as if the struggles they'd encountered with each other lately had clouded any happiness they might have shared.

"There were a couple of years there when Jason refused to eat anything but hamburgers and potato chips when he came to stay with me. I tried everything to get him to eat balanced meals. The doctor finally told me to quit worrying about it and just feed him what he would eat. So I started sneaking tomatoes and lettuce and cheese on the burgers, hoping at least those would provide a little nutrition."

Jason looked at his father, his brown eyes containing a look of tentative amazement. "You went to the doctor about what I ate?"

"Yeah," Seth said, chuckling. "I felt a little silly, going in there without a kid for him to examine. But you weren't with me at the time, so . . ."

Tess noted the way Jason lowered his eyes to his food, trying to imagine the scene. It was as if the new picture he saw of his father was completely foreign to him, completely opposite from the one his mother had drawn all his life. Tess took a sip of her iced tea and tried to keep the conversation going. She couldn't help suspecting that their openness wasn't an everyday event. "Well, you don't look any worse for all those hamburgers. Your mother must have kept you on a balanced diet."

Jason lifted his shoulder thoughtfully, then let it fall. "Not really. Mom never has been too good in the kitchen. I pretty much fended for myself." He glanced at Seth, awkward at the admission he was about to make.

"Truth is, I only wanted hamburgers at Dad's because he made them so good."

Seth laughed at that and turned apologetic eyes on Tess. "Well, I guess I blew it. I should have made hamburgers tonight. But you know what I always say about taking risks..."

The reference to his old philosophy, the one that he'd spent weeks making her believe only to show her that it led to heartbreak, sobered her a little. But before she could acknowledge what he'd said, Jason piped up again.

"You got any kids?" he asked.

Tess felt her spirits sink even lower. "No, I'm afraid I don't."

Jason took a mouthful of potatoes, but spoke anyway. "Do you want some?"

Tess felt Seth's eyes boring into her, waiting for that vulnerability that she was certain was her trademark. She tried not to let it share her expression. Smiling and keeping her tone as light as she could, she said, "There was a time in my life when I wanted some very much. But now I think I'm better suited to helping children in the classroom instead of raising my own. I get a lot of satisfaction out of the kids I work with."

Seth wasn't going to let the subject drop that easily. "I remember when you said your main goal in life was to raise a family," he said. "When you were tutoring me, and I told you what a good teacher you'd make. Remember?"

The reminder sent a cold draft of anger blowing through her. Why was he bringing that up now? Was he trying to make a point that she'd failed at that, too, now that it was too late to change things?

Jason missed the tension between the two adults. "Tutoring you?" he asked his father. "Tess tutored you, too?"

Tess looked down at her food, forced herself to take another bite.

Seth nodded, not taking his eyes from Tess. "Yeah. I was flunking English. Without her, I never would have graduated."

"But wasn't she younger than you?" Jason asked.

"Yeah," Seth said, his eyes smiling as he looked at his son. "But a hell of a lot smarter."

Jason forgot his food and moved his eyes to Tess, then back to his father, as if seeing him, really seeing him, for the first time. "I never knew you had trouble in school," he said. "I always thought you were smart."

"Your father *is* smart," Tess interjected. "By the time he finished, he knew more about Thomas Wolfe than I did. I think I learned more from our tutoring sessions than he did."

Seth's eyes flashed back to hers, held them captive, and she instantly realized that what she'd said held more truth than she'd intended. Heaven help her, she had learned so much and too little. Seth's eyes told her that he had learned lessons, too, lessons that had nothing to do with Thomas Wolfe. What Tess had learned had led her down a path all those years ago to make painful mistakes. And she wasn't sure she could survive that kind of heartbreak again.

Jason snorted with derision, shaking her and Seth out of their solemn reverie. "Guess it runs in the family."

Seth tore his eyes from Tess and focused his attention on his son again. "What does?"

"Bad grades. Getting behind. Flunking."

"You can't inherit bad grades, son," he said. "But there's no crime in getting behind. And if anybody understands what it's like to flunk, I do."

Jason lifted a hopeful eyebrow and offered a cocky grin. "Then what's the big deal? Why don't we just let it ride?"

"Understanding it and accepting it are two different things," Seth said, messing up Jason's hair with an affectionate tenderness Tess didn't miss. "When Tess gets through with you, you'll probably be spouting Shakespeare."

Jason grimaced as if the thought was appalling. "I'd rather eat your meat loaf," he said.

Again, laughter came as easily as the warm feeling enveloping Tess's heart.

Dinner was almost over when the telephone rang. "That's for me. I'll get it!" Jason said, and leaped from his chair, nearly tipping it over as he raced to answer the extension in his room.

Tess turned astonished eyes on Seth. "What was that all about?"

"Tony Spier." Seth chuckled. "He and Jason have become pretty tight over the last little while. And they're both at the age where a fascination with the telephone seems to be part of the growth process."

"Oh, yes," Tess said, standing up and automatically stacking the plates. "I remember those days. I guess Jason can't wait to tell his friend about the grueling battery of tests I've put him through today."

Seth came to his feet, took the plates out of Tess's hand and finished stacking the dishes himself. "You were great with him. I don't think you can fully appreciate what a breakthrough you've made."

Tess smiled. "I think I have an idea. He's a great kid, though, Seth. We're going to get him back on the right track."

She began gathering the silverware, but Seth reached out and stopped her. A spark ignited in her heart at his touch, and she looked up and met his eyes. "I never doubted you for a minute. You worked wonders with me, after all."

That old hurt swelled inside her, reminding her that this feeling led to eventual devastation. "Yes, well, this is a little less risky, I guess. At least Jason can't run off and get married just as I get attached to him."

Seth broke his hold on her hand and gaped at her, but she wrenched her eyes away and went back to the silverware. *You idiot,* she berated herself. *Now why'd you go and say that?*

Seth cupped her chin with a callused hand and drew her to him, forcing her to meet his eyes again. "I didn't know you'd gotten attached to me," he said.

Tess laughed, though there was no joy in the sound. "Come on, Seth. That last night we were together, I would have followed you to the moon. You couldn't have been that blind."

She saw his throat convulse, and his eyes bored deeply into her, years of regret and worthless wishes glimmering there. "I guess I was too caught up in my own misery," he said. "When I found out Celia was pregnant, I saw my relationship with you as just one more thing in my life that I had screwed up. I wanted to call, but I knew the gossip had already gotten out, and I couldn't stand to see your disgust."

Tess dropped the silverware on the stack of plates, then picked the plates up. "It wasn't gossip, Seth. It was true."

Seth took the plates once and for all and set them in the sink. "Stop with the dishes," he told her. "Just look at me, okay?"

Tess told herself not to cry, not to lash out at him like she'd wanted to do when she wasn't fantasizing about that night when he'd held her and kissed her... She was a woman now, not a little girl, and she'd gotten over the pain, hadn't she? "It's okay," she said, forcing herself to sound light. "Really. I never should have brought it up."

He was much too close to her in the tiny kitchen, and she could smell the scent of iced tea on his breath. His hands came up to rest on her waist, as if they belonged there. "But you did. And I'm glad, because I've wondered. Sometimes I wondered what would have happened if things had worked out differently, and we had gone on..."

Tess turned on the water to run over the plates in the sink. But Seth shut the water off.

"Look at me, Tess," he whispered. "Look at me."

Knowing what would happen if she did, that her heart would pay a dear price, Tess brought her eyes to Seth. He touched her bottom lip with his thumb.

"When I was seventeen years old I was standing at the locker on the first day of school. All the guys—the hoods, the misfits—we were standing in a cluster checking out the new blood, the freshmen girls coming in. I had my eyes on a hot little blond in a black leather skirt and a tight sweater that looked like it might split down the middle if she took a deep breath...and then you walked by." He caught his breath and framed her face with his hand.

"I didn't even see you at first. I only...I caught the fragrance of your skin. When I wheeled around, you were halfway down the hall. But I saw you stop and turn to say something to someone, and when you smiled . . ." He sighed as if the moment were happening now. "I couldn't stop thinking about you. It took me the rest of the year and most of the next year to figure out an excuse to see you."

Tess swallowed as his eyes dropped to her mouth, and when she wet her lips, he ran his thumb across the moisture there. "I must have been quite a disappointment," she whispered. "You kissed me one night, and the next day you were getting married."

Seth shook his head, intent on making her understand. "It wasn't like that, Tess. That night when I went home, that was the night Celia called to tell me . . . she was pregnant. It happened before I started seeing you."

A look of despair distorted his features, and he threw a glance to the ceiling, as if trying to figure out the past. "It was kind of a private joke I had going with myself, the way Celia and her rich friends came to me. I used to laugh and think, they're no better than me. They wouldn't speak to me in the hall—it might tarnish their lily-white images. But after hours, when there was nobody to impress, they didn't mind slumming with ol' Seth Taylor, the bad boy who could give them a quick thrill. I gave them what they wanted, because it was one way I had of convincing myself that I was just as good as them. Even Celia wouldn't be seen with me in public. But she sure as hell didn't mind me seeing her . . . in private."

The explanation didn't make the past any easier to bear, and Tess felt her old anger hardening her against him again. "I wasn't like that, Seth," she pointed out.

He smiled then, a soft, pensive smile packed with years of regret. "No, you weren't like that. You weren't embarrassed to be seen with me. And you made me feel good in real ways, not in secret ways that I had to hide. That's why I fell for you."

She caught her breath at the unintentionally ironic statement. "Come on, Seth," she said. "You married Celia."

"She was carrying my son," he said. "I wasn't going to turn my back on her." He rubbed his face and breathed out a ragged sigh. "The marriage was an act of defiance on her part as much as anything. She wanted to get her father's attention, and she got it, all right. But even then, heaven help me, I tried as hard as I could to make that marriage work. But she wasn't . . . she wasn't you. And I was still Seth Taylor."

Tears welled up in Tess's eyes, and she reached up to touch his face, rough with the day's stubble. Despite herself, she forgave him, for all the pain, the heartache and the wasted years that came after. He'd had it worse than she had, after all. "Seth Taylor was always good enough for me," she whispered.

She swallowed as his face began descending to hers, and let her eyes close in sweet relief coupled with gentle anguish. Why couldn't she have avoided him tonight, she asked herself. Why couldn't she have refused dinner? Why couldn't she have forgotten him?

And as the kiss deepened, pulling her back into the vortex of memory, old questions reemerged. Why hadn't he known his own worth, and avoided the rich girls who preyed on him for their private thrills? Why couldn't he have approached her sooner, and stayed with her longer? Why had life worked out the way it had? She felt tears forming at the back of her throat, felt her breath forming a sob. Her hands came up to push him away, but she clutched the front of his shirt in her fists, and realized she was clinging instead of breaking free.

The kiss ended, but Seth didn't release her. He set his elbows on her shoulders, and nested his hands around her head, burying his face in her hair. "I'm sorry," he whispered. "So sorry."

Tess loosened her hold on his shirt, and allowed herself to lay her head against his chest. "For what?" she breathed.

"For blowing it with you. But it's not too late to make it right."

Tess looked up at him, and felt her heart melting. It wouldn't work, she told herself. It was too soon after her divorce, and she didn't want to depend on anyone again, the way she felt herself doing already. She wanted to get her life back on the right track, wanted to show herself that she could do it without a man. There were too many memories, too many obstacles...

"I don't know," she whispered, pulling out of his arms. "I just don't know."

"I do," Seth said. "I've never been more sure of anything."

"And I've never been more confused," Tess said. "I...I really should go."

"Don't," he said.

Tess turned away, then, and forced herself to go and get her purse from the living-room couch. "I have to, Seth. I have to...to think."

Reluctantly, he followed her to the door. "As long as you're thinking about me," he whispered.

Tess wished she had a choice in the matter, but as she started out the door, she realized that that choice had been taken from her long ago. Seth Taylor had become a vital part of her soul, and she wasn't sure she was strong enough to erase his presence there, now.

"HE TOLD ME HIMSELF," Jason told Tony, propping the telephone on his shoulder as he held the E.Z. Ellis album cover in his hands. "She used to tutor my dad. He had trouble in school, too."

"Yeah, well, who doesn't?" Tony asked. "So how was the tutoring? Did she bore you to death?"

"Not really. We didn't do much. Just played some more games, and she asked a lot of questions and stuff. Then she stayed for dinner."

"Dinner!" Tony uttered the word as if it were the closest thing to torture he could imagine. "Why?"

"My dad and her are old friends. He asked her to stay."

"Uh-oh," Tony said. "That explains it."

"Explains what?"

"Her interest in you," Tony said. "She's trying to get to your dad through you. Old friends, huh? Jeez."

Jason dropped the album cover and switched the phone to his other ear. "It's not like that, Tony. My dad isn't interested in her. He just hired her to—"

Jason heard a car door slam, and lifted the blind to peer out. Tess was in her car, and his father was leaning down with his hands propped on the door, talking quietly to her. A cold gust of apprehension made him shiver. He wouldn't be so lucky this time as he'd been the last time he'd watched them at her car. This time he was sure his father would kiss her.

"Jase? You still there?" Tony asked.

"Yeah, I'm here," he said quietly, not taking his eyes off his father and Tess. "She just got in her car. Guess she's leaving."

"Did your dad walk her to the car?"

"Yeah," Jason said in a what-do-you-wanna-make-of-it tone.

"Uh-oh. I'm tellin' you, man. You can't ignore the signs."

Jason watched, holding his breath as his father stepped back from the car. *He isn't going to kiss her,* he thought joyously. *She's just going to drive away.*

He saw her start the car and watched her pull out of the driveway. Seth stood there for a moment, watching her disappear from sight. Something about the way he stood, shoulders slumped, head cocked pensively, brought Jason's worry back. He was losing him, he thought. Little by little, he was losing him.

"They didn't do nothin'," he said. "She's gone now."

SHE'S GONE NOW. The realization came like a jolt that shook him out of his thoughts, and Seth told himself to quit standing there in the driveway like a fool and go on inside.

He went to the kitchen and began mechanically washing the dishes he'd stacked in the sink. *You couldn't have been that blind.*

His mind raced back to that night when he'd kissed her at her garage apartment, when he'd held her against him and wondered why he'd ever seen anything in any other girl. He'd wanted her so badly...he had come so close to crossing that threshold between necking and making love. But she wasn't like the other girls he saw, the ones who sneaked around, looking for the thrill that came from being with the town's bad boy. She didn't see him as a bad boy. Instead, Tess had made him feel like someone who measured up, someone who could hold his own, someone worthy.

And so he had kept control that night, and had made himself go home and take a cold shower, telling himself there would be other nights, that he had plenty of time with her. There was no rush, because she wasn't going to flit back to some jock or class president who looked better in the yearbook. Tess wanted him.

Seth bent over the sink and dropped his head down, agonizing over what had never been. The phone call had come that night from Celia, and his private hell had begun. And from that moment on, he'd been so busy nursing his own heartaches over losing Tess that he hadn't given that much consideration to the fact that she had suffered, too.

It's not too late, he told himself as he had told her. It was time he made things right. It was time he made her love him again.

EARLY MORNING SUNLIGHT sifted through the thin curtains in Tess's room, and she rubbed her eyes and looked up from the test results that lay spread across her bed. She'd been working on them since four that morning, when she had finally given up on the effort to sleep.

She'd given it a good try, she told herself. She had taken a hot bath, gotten into her gown, had even crawled into bed. But thoughts of Seth and the things he'd said last night had plagued her mercilessly. And that kiss... It hadn't begun to fulfill the longing inside her, but it had done a lot to stir the hunger she had carried for so long. She wanted more, she told herself. So much more. But she didn't want to want him.

Finally, she had given up and gotten out of bed, intent on doing something—anything—to get her mind off Seth. And so she had turned her attention to Jason and the tests she had put him through.

Now that she was finished, her eyes drifted to the phone beside her bed. She wondered if Seth was awake yet. If he had slept well. If he had wrestled with the same feelings that kiss evoked.

She climbed onto the bed, pulled her feet up under her and picked up the phone. She would call him about the results of the tests, she told herself. She had to do that, anyway. She wasn't calling him just to hear his voice, or to bask in the sound of his affection...

She dialed his number, waited as it rang.

"Hello?" Seth's voice was gravelly with early morning sleepiness.

"Seth?" she asked softly. "I hope I didn't wake you."

She could sense his smile. "Wake me? Who says I got any sleep last night?"

Tess decided not to tell him that she'd had the same problem. "I got up early this morning and finished evaluating Jason's tests," she said. "I need to talk to you about them."

She heard the sheets rustle, and imagined Seth sitting up. "Go ahead. I'm listening."

"Not on the phone," she said. "It's too complicated. If I came over, do you think we could talk about it privately?"

Seth considered the idea for a moment. "Not really," he said. "Tony's coming over today, and the boys will be in and out. Listen, I promised Ford and Mariah I'd drive out to the trailer sometime this afternoon. I've got to drop off some carpet and wallpaper samples. Why don't you ride with me? We'll be alone on the way, and we can talk."

Alone. The prospect made her heartbeat accelerate. She thought of being alone in the cabin of that truck again, close to Seth. What if he kissed her again? What if he didn't?

"I guess that's fine," she said. "I have some errands to run first. Why don't I just come pick you up, and we can take my car? Is three o'clock okay?"

"Oh." Seth's disappointment was obvious in the single word. "I have to wait that long to see you?"

Tess felt a warm heat scoring her cheeks, and she smiled. "Seth, this is business. About Jason."

"I know," he said. "But I can dream, can't I?"

And he did dream. Seth dreamed of sweeping her off her feet and making up for lost time in one afternoon. He dreamed of having a second chance to finish what he'd started over thirteen years ago. He dreamed of having her want him the way he wanted her. They were adults now, and her father wasn't lurking in the house waiting for her to come in. They had more freedom now, and yet he didn't feel free at all.

Tess pulled into the driveway at four minutes before three and saw Seth sitting on his front porch waiting for her. He came to his feet when she stopped her car, and stepped onto the lawn, allowing the sun to favor him with a golden crown. The wind swept through his hair, giving him the wild look he'd had in high school, the look that said he played by his own rules. His shirt was a crisp white that made his tan look deeper and his eyes bluer, and when he smiled, she felt all her resolve to keep him at arm's length melting away.

"Are you ready?" she asked him, getting out of the car.

She noted the way he watched the wind swirl her skirt around her legs, and fleetingly, she wished she'd worn a slip. "I've been ready all day," he said.

She swallowed. "Should we tell Jason you're leaving?"

Seth shook his head. "I told him already. He and Tony are busy building a go-cart in my shop out back."

As he stepped closer, carrying the book of carpet samples under one arm and three wallpaper books under another, Tess caught the masculine scent of soap and wind, and her hands began to tremble. She wasn't strong enough for this, she told herself, not after thinking of him all night, wishing things could work out...

She tossed him the keys, and he caught them. "You drive," she said. "I'll need to refer to the test results."

He helped her into the car, then took his seat behind the wheel. His mood was tense, too thoughtful, and she could feel that the tests weren't the main thing on his mind.

"Aren't you worried about Jason riding a go-cart?" she asked to lighten things. "It's dangerous, isn't it?"

"Not if they know the rules and only ride it in a pasture or out at the sand pits." He looked at her as he backed the car out of his driveway. "You know, a lot of things are dangerous. The trick is knowing what you're getting into and being willing to pay the price if you wind up falling on your face."

Tess looked out the window, away from Seth's probing gaze. "I seem to be falling on my face a lot these days."

"So do I," he said. "But sometimes it's worth it."

She knew he wasn't talking about go-carts, and neither was she. Neither of them spoke for a stretch of time, and finally Seth sighed. "So...you said we needed to talk about Jase. What's all the mystery? Is it bad?"

Tess felt Seth's tension lifting, and thankfully she took up the subject of the boy. "No, of course not. It's just that I wanted you alone, so that Jason wouldn't hear what I have to say and overreact. Sometimes, when a child sees his parent's initial reaction to finding out he has a learning disability, he feels ashamed and embarrassed. I didn't want that to happen."

"A learning disability!" Seth looked at Tess, his astonished eyes revealing just the reaction she had feared.

"Yes," she said, hoping a calm tone would influence him into not panicking. "Have you ever heard the term 'dyslexic?'"

"Yeah, I've heard of it. That's when a child turns his letters around. Writes b for d, and that kind of thing."

"That's one symptom," Tess said. "But the problem is a lot more complicated than that."

Seth's frown cut deep into his forehead as he drove. "Are you saying Jason is dyslexic?"

"I don't like labels," she said. "The fact is, there are a number of specific learning disabilities. Some of them are so slight that the person learns to compensate, so no one ever detects the problem. But sometimes a problem can be so severe that a child never even learns to read."

"And in Jason's case?"

Tess decided to confront the subject with as much honesty as she could. "His problem is mild compared to a lot of children I've worked with. With proper teaching, he can be taught to cope."

Seth slapped the heel of his hand on the steering wheel and shook his head in frustration. "To cope? Tess, you make it sound like he's suffering from some...some disease."

"Not a disease, Seth," she said. "A learning dysfunction. It has to do with how the brain interprets what the eyes see, and how the body responds to the stimulus." She shifted in her seat to face him, to better illustrate her point. He kept his eyes on the road, but she knew his mind was on his son. "You see, when Jason is asked to look at a picture and copy it, he isn't able to...at least not in the right way. He sees the same picture you or I see, but his brain distorts it. And then things are complicated even more when he tries to draw it . . . or in the case of a written word, when he tries to *read* it."

Some imperceptible thought swept across Seth's face, and revealed itself in a sober frown. "How did he get this? What caused it?"

Tess shuffled the papers in her lap. "No one knows. Sometimes it's inherited," she said.

"That's what I thought." The words were delivered in a pensive monotone, and Tess looked at him again.

"What do you mean?" she asked.

Seth didn't answer for a moment, but on his face she saw the struggle of fragments of bitter memories coming together. "My mother couldn't read at all," he whispered. "And I was always a bad reader. I could memorize and understand the most convoluted concepts, but when I tried to read them..." He swallowed and glanced at Tess, as if assessing her for a reaction. "I still have trouble reading blueprints. Jim Spier handles a lot of that for me."

He came to an intersection and brought the car to a temporary halt, then threw another look at Tess, as if waiting for her to express disgust.

But there was neither shock nor judgment in her expression, instead, she smiled. "And you see how well you turned out?" she asked softly. "I guess that's the best evidence I can show you that Jason can be taught to cope."

The smile that was becoming imprinted on her heart returned to Seth's face. "You're right," he agreed softly. "I haven't done so bad, have I?"

"Not bad at all," Tess said.

The light changed, and Seth drove on. A new peace seemed to settle on his features as he considered Jason's problem. "Then Jason isn't having trouble just because he isn't trying," he said, more to himself than to Tess. "Any more than I was."

He breathed and gave a half laugh. "Of course, that still doesn't explain his behavior problems."

"Yes, it does." Tess flipped through Jason's transcript, confirming, as she'd done a number of times already, that it all fell into place. "Sometimes students like Jason get labeled 'dumb' and 'lazy.' And the child feels frustrated most of the time. So he does things to compensate."

"Compensate?" Seth asked. "How do you mean?"

"Delinquency, aggression, destructiveness."

Seth took a deep breath and leaned his head on the headrest. "And vandalism," he finished. "Oh, man."

Tess closed the file and focused on Seth's face, on the thoughts obviously wheeling through his mind.

"Slashing the tires and the seats of that guy's car...they were signs. Symptoms. If I'd been any kind of parent I'd have figured that out."

Tess reached across the seat and set her hand on his arm. "How? You weren't trained to recognize these problems. Not many people are. You couldn't even see it in yourself. How could you have known?"

Seth released a heavy breath. "I don't know. Maybe I could have been around more. Maybe forced Celia to let me have more of a part in his life. Maybe I could have seen it."

"Parents who live with their kids don't always notice a problem, Seth. You're doing something about it now. That's a start."

He tossed her a hopeful look as he turned down the dirt road leading to Ford and Mariah's trailer. "Then it isn't too late? Something can still be done?"

"Of course," Tess said. "And we should start with repairing his self-image. Making him feel good about himself and letting him know that he has a problem that can be dealt with."

Seth cut off the engine and turned to face her, his body swiveled at the waist, one arm draped over the steering wheel. "What if we hadn't figured this out? What if we'd just gone on letting Jase think he was dumb?"

"We didn't," she said softly.

Seth's mouth slowly curved in a gentle smile, and he reached over and pushed a wisp of hair off of her cheek. "Thanks to you," he said. "What would I have done without you?"

Tess swallowed and willed her heart to slow down. "You'd have found someone else to do the same things," she said.

Seth took a handful of her hair, wadded it in his hand. His fingers gently massaged her neck just below her earlobe. "No, I don't think so. You see, I tried to find someone else. It just didn't work out."

The double meaning in his words made her lips go dry, made her heart plummet, made her breath quicken. "I'm glad I was here to help," she whispered, knowing that he sensed her meaning, as well.

"Are you?" he asked, leaning closer to her while drawing her face nearer to him. "Glad, I mean?"

She nodded, knowing the admission was much too honest for her own good, but helpless to deny it.

"Last night you weren't so sure," he whispered. "You were—" his gaze dropped to her lips as her tongue swept across them "—confused."

Mesmerized, she watched his lips coming closer to hers. "Things . . . are a little . . . clearer today," she whispered.

His lips found hers in the space of a heartbeat, and no more words had to be exchanged. He wouldn't make her confess that she'd thought about him all night, that she'd ached with wanting him, that this kiss was the first peace she'd had since he'd kissed her last night. All those truths spilled out in their kiss and hammered home in their hearts.

His touch was bolder now, even more unsettling, and his tongue made a daring mating dance against her own, drawing out years of loneliness and emptiness and filling those voids with the smell and feel and taste of Seth.

She felt her hands riding up his ribs, over the chest hardened from years of heavy labor. His heart tripped against her hand, and she felt his breath growing as ragged as hers. A deep ache lodged in the pit of her stomach, coupled with a yearning to take this moment to completion, unlike the last time, to feel his skin beneath her hand, his body crushing hers, his passion swirling through her . . .

But they weren't really alone, and their privacy was as fleeting as the moment itself.

"Mariah," she whispered against his lips.

The word seemed to remind him, unwelcomely, that this was no place to unleash the passion he'd contained for so long. "Oh, hell," he mumbled. "Mariah."

He kissed her again, one last, lingering kiss, then pulled back enough to brush her lip with his thumb, wiping the dampness away. "You sure your sister wouldn't understand if I lost my head right here in your car?" he breathed.

"Mariah probably would," Tess whispered with a wry grin. "But Ford might not be too thrilled."

Seth opened the car door and pulled her out with him. He took a deep, cleansing breath, straightened his clothes and took Tess's hand. "All right. I think I can show some semblance of professionalism now. What do you think?"

Tess grinned and straightened her hair. Reluctantly, with her heart still pounding, she followed him to the door. A big Harley-Davidson stood near the front entrance to the trailer, and Seth expelled a low whistle. "Whose is that?"

"I don't know," Tess said. "Ford doesn't ride a motorcycle, does he?"

Seth knocked on the door, and Mariah opened it. Her eyebrows lifted in sheer delight when she saw Tess with Seth. "Hi, you two."

"Hi, yourself," Tess said, giving her sister a look that said, "Not now, don't tease us now." "I rode with Seth so we could talk about Jason."

"Jason," Mariah said, unconvinced. "Uh-huh."

Tess felt her lips curling up in a grudging smile. It wasn't the first time she'd wanted to kill her sister. "I'm tutoring him, you know."

"Yeah. I know." Mariah bit her lip to keep her smile from being quite so obvious and turned to Seth. "Did you bring the samples, Seth? We've been dying to see them."

"They're in the car," he said. "I'll get them, if you're ready."

"Not yet," Mariah cut in. "Come in, first. I want you both to meet my life-long buddy."

Seth and Tess stepped inside, and Tess didn't miss the wink that Mariah gave to Ford. Tess looked at the handsome stranger standing in the kitchen with a long-necked beer bottle hanging from his hand. His smile was charismatic, charming, not at all the smile she'd expected to see on someone who rode a Harley.

"This is Nick Logan," Mariah announced proudly.

Tess had heard that name many times before. She extended her hand to shake his, then turned to Seth as he shook hands. "Mariah and Nick used to jump out of airplanes together," she said, then turned back to the dark, handsome hunk. Mariah claimed he'd never been more than a friend, despite his obvious appeal to any woman worthy of her sex. "I've wondered when I was going to finally meet you."

"I had to come by and check on Mariah," Nick said, reaching out to pat Mariah's stomach. Mariah slapped his hand away from her belly. "Wanted to make sure this marriage and pregnancy bit wasn't some sort of con."

"No con," Ford said, laughing as he pulled Mariah against him. "Nick had trouble believing Mariah could settle down with a preacher."

"No offense, man," Nick said. "Just had to see it to believe it."

Seth leaned against the counter in the kitchen. "Have they shown you the house yet, Nick?"

"Yeah," he said. "We rode out there earlier today. It's lookin' good."

Tess noted the unmistakable pride on Seth's face. "Thanks. It's coming along." He turned to Ford and slapped his thigh. "Well, if you're ready, you can help me bring the samples in."

The men followed Seth out the door, leaving Mariah and Tess alone. Mariah turned to Tess, waiting for what she had always called "the scoop."

"It's nothing, Mariah. I'm tutoring his son. That's all."

"Uh-huh," Mariah said again. "Just like that's all it was when you were tutoring *him*?"

"That was a long time ago," Tess said. "A lot's changed since then."

"And a lot hasn't," Mariah pointed out. She went to the refrigerator and got out a can of soda, popped the top and handed it to Tess.

Tess took a sip, wishing to heaven for a change of subject. Mariah's swelling stomach provided one. "Speaking of changes," she said, "how's the pregnancy coming along? Have you been feeling all right?"

"Oh, yeah," Mariah said, touching her stomach affectionately. "A little morning sickness still, but the doctor says it'll pass. My hormones must be working overtime, though. I'm an emotional basket case lately."

"I know the feeling," Tess said, her smile fading by degrees. She caught herself, then took a deep breath. "So, I haven't had a chance to ask you yet. What do you want? A boy or a girl?"

Mariah filled the teakettle with water and set it on the stove. "Oh, I don't know. Sometimes I think I'd love to have a little boy who looks just like Ford. And then other times I say, 'What, and break a family tradition?' Do you realize there hasn't been a boy born to this family for over fifty years?"

Tess ran her finger around the rim of her soft drink can. "I hadn't really thought about it. I guess Dad was the last Calloway male."

Mariah leaned against the counter, looking pensively at her sister. "It seems a little strange, sometimes, when I think of the four of us having different last names now. Do you realize that if Eden ever marries, the Calloway family name will disappear?"

Tess offered a self-deprecating smirk. "Maybe not. If it ever comes to that, maybe I'll just assume my maiden name again."

Mariah was quiet for a moment, as if she heard volumes more in Tess's words than what she was saying. "Or maybe you'll get married again."

Tess almost laughed, but the sound contained no mirth. "No, I don't think so. Once was enough for me." Her eyes strayed out the kitchen window to her car, where Seth and the others were talking.

Mariah peered over her shoulder. "Stranger things have happened. Take you and Seth, for instance."

Tess felt her cheeks reddening. She had never been one to open up to her sisters, but they never stopped prying, anyway. She turned, trying to look as if the thought had never crossed her mind. "What do you mean? There's nothing between Seth and me except his son."

"My point exactly," Mariah said, like a lawyer resting her case. "You know, I've always believed in fate, myself. Like some people were meant to be together, but sometimes something gets in the way." The teakettle began to boil over, and Mariah went to the stove to turn it off.

"What are you getting at, Mariah?" Tess asked.

Mariah got two cups from the overhead cabinet and dropped a tea bag in each. "I'm just saying, if it's meant to be, it's meant to be, right? And if those people are destined to get together, they will ... eventually. Maybe just a few years later than fate originally intended."

Tess had never believed in fate. She had always imagined that people created their own destinies. Since her separation from Vance, though, she'd come to realize that some things couldn't be controlled simply through action or will. Still, she didn't like the way the conversation was turning. "I didn't know pregnancy affected the mind."

Mariah gave her a withering look. "Oh, come off it, Tess. Did you think we were all blind back then, when Seth used to come over twice a week? Did you think we couldn't see how crazy you were about him?" She poured water into the cups and went on. "But you never talked to any of us about him, and so we pretended not to notice."

Tess wilted and covered her face. "Everyone knew about it?" she asked quietly. "And I thought my feelings were so well hidden."

"Well, it wasn't that you were obvious," Mariah said, as if the thought struck her as absurd. "Nothing about you has ever been obvious, Tess. Sometimes I can still sense you shutting me out, shutting everyone out. You never confided in us. We always told you all the gory details of our love lives, but you never returned the favor. I had to get all my information through either spying on you or listening to you talk in your sleep!"

Tess jerked her head up and saw that Mariah didn't mean a word of it. She was laughing, waiting for Tess's reaction. "If I never confided in you," she said, "it's because I never had anything interesting to tell."

Mariah stepped closer and dropped her voice to a conspiratorial level. "Well, you do now. So, tell me, ex-roomie. What do you think the odds are against two people who might have fallen in love years ago if it hadn't been for a child, finding themselves together again as the result of that same child?"

Tess slipped off the countertop and turned her back on Mariah, too caught up in her sister's words to reveal her feelings. She looked out the window again, saw Seth laughing and describing something with sweeping gestures of his hands, making Nick and Ford laugh with him. What were the odds of her falling in love with Seth again? she asked herself.

Slowly, she turned to Mariah. Maybe it was time she started opening up a little, after all. "Like you said," she told her sister. "Stranger things have happened."

CHAPTER TWELVE

THE DRIVE FROM Mariah's trailer was charged with anticipation, for neither of them had forgotten what had happened earlier. But beneath the passion they contained like volcanic lava smoldering underground was an undercurrent of emotional tension, as well. Seth's face was almost sad as he set his hand on her thigh. Without allowing her judgment to censor her instincts, Tess covered his hand with her own.

"So..." Seth began quietly. "Where do we go from here?"

His question made her mouth go dry. Mutely she looked at him.

"With Jason, I mean?" he clarified quickly, as though he feared any other reference might frighten her away. "You said his problem wasn't curable but he could be taught to cope. I was just wondering how long something like that takes."

Tess drew in a breath. "In Jason's case, I'd say a year, maybe two at the most. He'll need remedial training, outside of his regular schoolwork."

Slowly Seth turned his gaze back to the road, but not before Tess caught the fleeting shadow of emotion that darkened his eyes for an instant. "Are you going to stay that long?" he asked, his voice low. She saw him swallow, a muscle leaping in his jaw.

Looking away, she answered softly, "That's a long time. I . . . I don't know."

They drove on in silence, and when Seth made no further comment Tess stole a furtive glance at him through lowered lashes. His face was hard-set, harder than she had ever seen it, and she couldn't help wondering what was going on in his mind.

She couldn't stay. Not a whole year in Calloway Corners, she reasoned silently. She had a job to go back to in Dallas. And what did she have here?

Unfinished business, she told herself curtly.

Leaning her head against the seat, she closed her eyes in the scarlet rays of the reluctantly sinking sun and let her thoughts drift with the wind wafting in through the car's open windows.

Would it end like this? she wondered. Would she walk out of Seth Taylor's life, just as he had walked out of hers years ago? When summer was over, only a few weeks from now, would they simply say goodbye like old friends who had shared a few kisses, some memories, but nothing more?

A dull, aching chill crept over her heart at the prospect, and she rolled her head to one side, opening her eyes. Behind the wheel, Seth stared straight ahead, but the lines furrowing his brow suggested that he was deep in thought.

She wanted to touch more than just his hand. She wanted to ease the brooding lines from his forehead and trace the smooth, hard ridge of his mouth with her fingers. She wanted him to kiss her again as he had earlier that afternoon, when he'd almost made her lose control. It had been so long . . . so long since she had been with a man. And this was the man she'd wanted since she'd been fifteen years old. What would it be like to become his lover this time, instead of just his friend?

They had been driving for thirty minutes. Tess had been so caught up in her own thoughts and fantasies that she had failed to notice when Seth had turned off the main highway. When she finally looked up and saw that they were traveling down a narrow dirt road that she didn't recognize, she sat up straight.

"Where are we going?"

Taunting blue eyes flickered to hers, and the smug hint of a smile twitched at his lips. "Just sit tight. We'll be there in a minute or two."

His cryptic reply in no way answered her question. But Tess was relieved by the sudden change in his mood. Her own spirits seemed to lighten with his, and she raised a brow in mock skepticism. "Why do I have the feeling I'm not going to like this?"

"Oh, I don't know about that," he countered. "You might just surprise yourself. And me."

She started to ask him what he meant, but just then he halted the car in a small clearing where the road ended abruptly. A thick stand of pine surrounded them.

"Seth...?" Tess began, uncertainty threading her voice in earnest now. Seth ignored her.

"Come on," he said. Shouldering open the driver's door, he stepped to the ground and turned back, offering her the support of his upturned hand. "We have to walk from here. But it's not very far."

Tess hesitated. "If I had known we were going hiking, I'd have worn boots. I can't possibly forge through these woods in a skirt and sandals."

"Sure you can." Seth wasn't listening to her arguments. Reaching into the Audi, he laid gentle claim on the hand she refused to surrender willingly. Still, it required less than a tug to urge her from the seat. "There's a nice clean path right through there," he explained. "Hardly anyone uses it. Only the deer and the snakes."

"Snakes?" Tess's feet had no sooner touched the ground than something cold and alien slithered up the back of her leg. She jumped a clear foot, then swung around, slapping furiously at her lower right calf. "Look. I think you better start telling me what this is about."

"Can't," he said, touching his nose to hide his grin. He had seen her jump, and he turned his head now to keep from laughing. Never had he known anyone to move so fast. "This is a secret place," he managed to relate in a reasonably sober tone. Then, striding forward to the spot where she had stood just seconds ago, he bent to pluck the yellow bud from a blooming weed. "And don't worry," he said, handing her the flower as he straightened beside the car. "Dandelions are seldom deadly; even when they bite."

Tess shot him a withering look, but he only chuckled and reached into the back seat, lifting a brown paper bag he had set there with the samples.

Curiosity got the best of her. "Seth, what are you up to?" she demanded, though her voice trembled with a cautious excitement that undermined her stern words.

Seth caught her hand and gave her a wink. "Shh. It's a secret. Remember? Now come on. We're going to be late."

"*Late?* Late for what?"

He didn't answer, not that she really expected him to. And after a few moments of finding herself dragged, half stumbling, along an overgrown, briar-thicketed patch of winding ground that Seth had loosely referred to as a path, Tess forgot she'd even asked the question.

Inside the forest was a cool, dark enclosure, silent except for the rustling of their footsteps treading dry leaves and ground. Through the lush green canopy of spreading oaks and tall, aromatic pine the wind moved listlessly, occasionally turning over a leaf or a branch so that the sunlight glittered like gold dust fallen from the sky.

Seth was right, Tess mused, her fingers curling tighter around his hand. This *was* a secret place. Its beautifully natural seclusion evoked a sacredness that filled her with awe.

"It's not far now." His voice was a reverent whisper, appropriate for the exquisite peace of these surroundings. So complete was the orchestration of the forest, she thought, that even the birds stilled their songs to listen.

As they grew closer to what Tess perceived as a small clearing up ahead, the pine and hardwoods began to thin, giving way to palmetto bushes and wildflowers. The farther they walked, the lighter the air became, and the scent of water, wet earth and thriving vegetation teased her senses.

Seth stopped and released her hand, slipping his arm around her waist instead. "All right, this is it," he announced, propelling her around to stand in front of him. His hands rested on either side of her waist, and he held the paper bag tucked under his arm. "Now close your eyes," he whispered, "and I'm going to show you something in a minute that I know you're going to love."

She felt ridiculous, but she didn't argue. "What if I fall down?" she asked, closing her eyes and smiling as he guided her forward toward the clearing.

"Then I'll catch you," he murmured. The words were a soft, seductive promise against her ear. Her heart pounded, filling her senses with the warmth of his nearness.

Tess was almost sorry when he sidestepped around her and lead her out past the shaded edge of the forest, until she could feel the brightness of sunlight against her closed eyelids. But then, while her eyes were still closed, he moved up behind her once more, and this time his arms went around her, drawing her close against the muscled contour of his chest.

"Now," he sighed, and she felt his chest at her back, the heat of his breath in her hair. "Now you can look."

Very slowly Tess opened her eyes, and for one breath-taking moment she couldn't speak. Her gaze absorbed the sight of the setting sun reflecting off the mirrored surface of a clear blue-gray pond.

"Seth, it's...it's lovely," she said at last, her eyes taking in the gnarled cypress and willow trees shading the banks. Along the ground, emerald-colored moss, wild grass and dark woodland fern created the illusion of a leprechaun's garden. Every shade of green in the world seemed represented here. "What is this place?" she asked, so mesmerized that she couldn't pull her gaze away.

Seth smiled down at her, then rested his chin on the crown of her head. "I call it Shadow Lake," he murmured, taking pleasure not only in the beauty of the sights around him but in the warmth of the woman in his arms. "I found it a couple of years ago," he explained quietly. "I think it was probably part of Lake Bistineau once. But through the years the woods grew to enclose it. And now it's landlocked. Sort of like a little cove."

Tess inclined her head to look up at him. "Who does it belong to?"

The sun caught his eyes, and a glittering spark leaped like firelight in his gaze. Tess held her breath as she turned in his arms, her heart pounding against her ribs.

"And what do we do when we have a lake all to ourselves?" Her voice shook, despite her attempt to conceal her sudden breathlessness.

Blue eyes darkened with the spell of a dream. "First we celebrate," he whispered huskily, his eyes drifting to her lips. "And then we see what happens next."

He wanted her, Seth thought. The force of his need had been building inside him since he had seen her on the roadside that first day, her face heat-flushed and her clothes damp and molded to her soft curves, much as they were now.

He didn't lower his eyes from her face, but Seth knew the shape of her small, firm breasts. The cotton of her coral camisole top outlined them exquisitely, revealing even the beadlike thrust of tiny nipples. Desire coiled inside him, and he had to clench his fists and turn away to keep from reaching for her now, as he longed to do.

But, Seth told himself, he wasn't going to rush. If he made love to Tess, now or ever, it would be because he was certain she wanted him, too. He'd waited years. Years to touch her, to woo her, to feel the tawny satin of her body, warm and bare, against his. A few more minutes wouldn't matter. And he already knew she was worth the wait.

"Come on over here," he said. Linking his hand with hers, he drew her along with him to the base of a giant cypress. He set the mysterious bag he'd lugged all the way from the car upright beside the tree. Then, reaching for the hem of his black T-shirt, he peeled it over his shoulders and head. Straightening the folds, he spread it out on the ground for her to sit on.

Tingling with exhilaration, and the kind of fear that sent adrenaline pulsing through her, she slipped off her sandals and sat down as he had urged her.

Slowly Seth eased his weight down beside her, and Tess's pulse thundered in her ears. She had never seen him without his shirt, and though she'd recognized his muscular build, even through his clothing, nothing—no single thread of clinging garment, even coupled with imagination—could have prepared her for the truly masculine beauty of his lean, powerful body.

His skin was golden tan and sleek as suede leather. Not a flaw, not even a hair, marred the smoothness of his broad, muscled chest. His jeans hugged his hips, low-slung and revealing the hard flatness of his belly. And when he turned at the waist, reaching for the paper bag beside him, Tess caught her breath in sensual reckoning with the sight of muscles cording and stirring between the welts of his ribs.

Sensation washed over her. Need. Desire. And hunger. A hunger like none she had ever known before. It was frightening and yet amazing the way her head seemed suddenly light as a vapor while her body felt heavy, as if her blood had thickened to a viscous syrup in her veins.

"I hope you like wine," Seth said, the seductive sound of his voice enhancing the moment.

"Yes . . . yes, I do," she whispered.

With the bottle of wine still sheathed in the paper bag, he filled two plastic stemmed glasses with bubbling pink liquid. "I hope you like this stuff," he said. "I don't know exactly what kind of wine it is, actually. But it was on the top shelf, and the man in the liquor store assured me it was pretty good."

Tess laughed and took the glass he offered her. "This is crazy. I can't believe I'm sitting in the woods, watching the sun set over a pond and drinking rosé." She took a sip of her wine and thought that the man in the liquor store had been right. But then, plain water would have tasted like champagne today.

Relaxation and sensual abandon seeped into her body and mind as she finished two glasses, watching until the sun sank low behind the trees in an explosive final burst of color. Seth closed his eyes and leaned his head against the trunk of the tree, and Tess let her eyes roam over that chest, down to his hard, flat stomach, which was subtly rising and falling with his rhythmic breaths. Her lips ached to touch that supple flesh, to mold to the shape of his ribs, to taste the dark male nipples teasing her with their bareness. Trying to hold herself in check for fear that it would sweep her into a whirlwind of desire she couldn't control, Tess got to her feet and wandered to the water's edge, searching for relief from her feelings.

Glancing over her shoulder, she saw that Seth's eyes were still closed. For several long moments she just stood, watching his face in repose. How she wished she had the nerve to walk over and slide her hands over him . . . to kneel down beside him and press her lips to his until he opened his eyes and took her into his arms.

But fear of failure, of disappointing him, stopped her. She turned back to the water, wishing that, just once, she could borrow Mariah's free-spirited daringness, or Jo's straightforward aggressiveness, or Eden's honest openness. But those traits belonged to her sisters—not to her. Tess kept things inside, sometimes until it was too late.

Seth opened his eyes and watched Tess carefully. He couldn't see her face, but he knew by her lowered head and the dejected slant of her shoulders that something was bothering her. Was it him? Was he pushing her too far, too fast, by bringing her to a place so secluded? Or was he just getting paranoid because she wouldn't commit herself today, when he had asked about her plans for the future?

Damn, he couldn't help it! He needed to know, didn't he, if she was going to walk out of his life right about the time he surrendered his heart completely? Hadn't he given her the space and time she'd wanted to make up her mind about him?

But space was just an illusion, and time was fact, Seth thought. Autumn was creeping up on them, and he couldn't bear the thought of Tess going back to Dallas to start a new life without him. When summer was over he didn't want her to remember him as she always had...just an acquaintance from her past. This time there had to be more.

Raking a hand through his hair, Seth rose and went toward her.

"A penny for your thoughts," he said softly as he approached.

At the sound of his voice, Tess smiled, remembering that he had said the same thing to her only a few weeks ago, on the bridge. She turned to view him over her shoulder. Her heart tripped over again at the sight of him, bare chested and so recklessly handsome. A tremor of yearning shot through her. She tried not to let it show. "Only a penny?" she responded lightly. "I'd have thought the price would've gone up by now. Maybe you're suggesting my thoughts are cheap."

She had meant it as a joke, but something in his eyes told her he wasn't taking it that way. There was pain in his face, and uncertainty, and when he spoke his voice held a strange, ragged note. "No, Tess. Nothing about you has ever been cheap. From the first time I ever saw you I knew you were like a rare jewel that wasn't for sale. And that I'd do anything I could...to get close to you."

Blue eyes looked straight into hers with an expression so intense they seemed to burn, liquid and bright as fire on water. "I want you, Tess," he confessed gravely. "I've always wanted you. Ever since we were in high school and you were so unaware of what you did to me..." He swallowed, and his body trembled. "Your innocence and your age always stopped me. But there's nothing to stop us now, Tess. Nothing to keep us from what we want."

He took a step closer, his eyes searching, pleading, and she could see the emotion-racked heaving of his chest. The thundering of his heart was almost audible, and the sound seemed to vibrate through her, singing through her bloodstream like the tingling hum of a tuning fork. Her own heart raced with a fierceness that made her search for breath. And Tess knew he was right. There was nothing to stop them now. And nothing was going to...

With trembling hands she reached down to the waist of her skirt. Her eyes clung to his as she slowly began to unfasten the buttons.

Seth watched her slow, deliberate movements and prayed to God the world wouldn't explode or blow itself up into flaming ashes before he had the chance to see this moment through. His body ached. His hands twitched involuntarily at his sides. *Wanting her. Wanting her.* Every muscle, every fiber, every cell, that had ever been or ever would be a part of him seemed to throb with the same message.

Her skirt dropped to the ground, and his heart forgot to beat. Oh, Lord! he thought. She was so beautiful. Long, slim legs, small curved hips. A silken scrap of beige lace panties, nearly the same tawny shade as her skin, dipped below her navel, revealing above their elastic band the soft, flat contour of her abdomen and a section of midriff not covered by her camisole.

In a bounding sprint, Seth's heart surged to life again. He raised his gaze to her face and thought suddenly that she looked like a wild, tempting siren with her dark hair flowing down around her shoulders and her hazel eyes glowing emeralds in the fading light.

He was dreaming, he thought. Dreaming as he watched her step back...and back, her body easing slowly into the water. And then, when she was not quite waist-deep, she lifted her arm and stretched out her hand to him.

How he got out of his clothes was a mystery. In the last fiery rays of the sun a steam had begun to rise from the lake, blurring reality in a scarlet haze. Warm. The water was warm, caressing his naked skin. But Seth hardly felt it. All that he wanted was within the reach of his hand.

His fingers touched hers, and a staggering jolt of sensation electrified Tess's body. "Seth," she whispered, drawing him closer, until they were face-to-face. "I've wanted you, too." Her voice thickened. Trembling, she lifted her hands to his face.

In all her life Tess had never known that touching a man could be so erotic. But when she touched Seth, when she slid her hands from the square of his jaw to his powerful neck her palms flattening as she slicked them over the broad mounds of his chest, a thousand fires ignited a sensual burning inside her. It was almost as if the feel of his flesh, sleek and wet and warm against her seeking hands, had somehow become the direct nerve-link to the very core of her womanhood.

Tess knew what it was like to be aroused. As a once-married woman, she knew the sensations of having her body caressed and made love to. But never, never had she experienced this fevered throbbing that made her arch and ache just because she put her hands on someone else's body.

But this was Seth. ''Seth.'' She wasn't aware that she had cried his name aloud until his arms went around her and he crushed her against him, one hand driving into her hair.

''Kiss me,'' he demanded, his voice ragged with passion. Her arms curled around his neck as she tipped back her head, giving her mouth to him willingly.

He bent his head, and his firm, wet lips took control of hers.

Oh, sweet heaven, she thought, her mind whirling with the feel and the taste of him. How could any man's mouth be so soft? How could any man kiss as if his heart, his soul, the very essence of his being, were wholly concentrated in the potent force of his lips? Seth had kissed her before, but never like this. Never with such consuming intent. His tongue ravaged and seduced, burrowing into the velvet of her mouth, bringing heat and drawing fire from every point of contact.

And suddenly Tess knew, in the way one knows without conscious thought, that though she might have experienced desire in her lifetime she was only beginning to know passion.

Abandoning her mouth in a gliding motion that came without a pause for breath, Seth nuzzled his lips into the hollow behind her ear. The fragrance of her hair drugged him, and he moaned, urging her closer, pressing her to the hardness of him. His heart contracted with a surge of blood. ''Tess... Oh, Tess, I knew it would be like this. You feel so good next to me. I love your scent, I love your skin.''

Under the water, his hands sought and found the heat of her flesh beneath her clinging top. When Seth touched her breasts, his fingers spread, moving restlessly over their fullness. Tess groaned and arched her back, pressing into his callused palms.

Drunk with the pulsating drive of his own need, Seth roughly shoved at the fabric of her blouse until her breast swung free. He caught his breath, and for a moment he could only stare at the beauty of her.

Siren? he thought. Yes, she was a siren. As she stood there, hip-deep in the water, the soft mounds of her breasts were exposed, tiny nipples turgid and tempting, luring him beyond reason. One arm encircling her waist, Seth gazed down into her eyes, watching her face as his other hand slid downward, over her belly. Gently, then, he slipped his fingers into her panties.

Liquid fire surged from her toes to her head, and she fell against him, her hands clutching at his back.

"It's all right, baby," he whispered. "You know I won't hurt you. Just let me touch you. Yes, baby...here." As he spoke, his hand moved to the tiny parting between her legs, and his fingers began to rub gently, slowly, back and forth, touching her.

Sensation claimed Tess in a delirium of arousal, and she whimpered, too dazed to speak, too weak to stand. But Seth held her with the strength of his own body and the power of his mind-robbing touch. His mouth sought hers again, and she clung to him, hardly aware of the words he murmured against her lips. She didn't know how she managed to do as he urged her, lifting her knee and freeing herself of her panties.

She was too far gone, lost in the molten, mindless waves of emotion that shuddered through her, taking her breath, as his body penetrated hers.

"Tess... Oh, I need you. I need you," Seth rasped, clutching her to him, rocking against her.

Warm water swirled around them, and Tess instinctively found the rhythm of his hips. With each bold stroke, her body sizzled and surged to greater heights.

His hands caressed her, coaxed her, while his lips drank the moisture from her face and her throat. Her skin flamed with the urgent burning in her body, and then, in a sudden rush, there was no holding back.

"Seth . . . Seth." She cried out his name, and he drove himself into her, touching off a wild explosion that carried them both to the peak of human emotion.

For long moments afterward, they stood, weakened and drained, still holding each other. And, as darkness encroached, Tess's heart gloried in the feel of him. Seth. Her lover, inside her and in her arms.

THEY DROVE HOME in the dark. Tess felt like a teenager who'd just stepped over the threshold of awareness, never to know the peace of ignorance again. It was impossible to get close enough to Seth, so she snuggled close in the seat next to him. His arm draped over the seat around her shoulder, enveloping her in a languid tranquillity she hadn't known before. One hand she nestled warmly, intimately, against his lower thigh. The taut shifting of his muscles as he drove reminded her of the way his bare muscles had rippled beneath her touch. She had imagined making love to Seth many times, in many different ways. But now she knew those dreams hadn't come close to the elation of reality.

A rare hush ribboned through her soul, calming all the doubts and fears and regrets she'd carried like an albatross for as long as she could remember. She laid her head on his shoulder. The engine's low drone had almost lulled her to sleep when Seth pulled her car into his driveway. He stroked her cheek with a knuckle. "It's been a long day," he whispered, a sleepy smile crescenting his lips.

"Why don't you leave your car and let me drive you home?"

Tess breathed an unobtrusive sigh. "Uh-uh. It would be too hard to let you come back home. No, I think we should say goodbye here."

He leaned his head back on the seat and traced the moonlight's lines on her face. "I'm crazy about you. You know that, don't you?"

A smile tiptoed across her lips. "You made that pretty clear today."

He kissed her again, drawing her back into an oblivion that was as potent as any drug. "Are we going to sit in the car and neck all night?" she whispered.

"It's a tough job," he teased, "but somebody has to do it."

Tess sat up straight, then smoothed out her clothes. "If I stay any longer, Eden is going to have the sheriff out looking for me." She glanced toward the house and saw that Jason's light was on. "I thought you said Jason was sleeping over at Tony's tonight."

"Guess he changed his mind," Seth said, frowning. "Kids. You never know what they're going to do."

He got out, pulling her with him. "You sure you won't come inside for a while?"

"No," she said. "It's getting late."

"Will I see you tomorrow?" They had already agreed that Jason should have a few days off after the weeks of work and testing they had done, and, in truth, Tess had made no plans concerning her further tutoring of Jason.

She feathered a finger down his shirt collar. "Do you want to?"

He pressed his lips to her forehead. "You know I do."

"Will you . . . call me?" she asked.

"Nothing could keep me from it."

His arms slid around her back, crushing her against him as he dragged his lips across hers again. Her senses quivered like tight violin strings. It was the most harmonious sound on the planet—the sound of being in love.

INSIDE THE HOUSE, Tony Spier was sitting beside the window when the flash of headlights caught his attention. "Looks like your dad's home," he remarked, idly drawing back the curtains to have a look.

"Well, it's about time." Jason sauntered over and threw an absent glance out over his friend's shoulder, then went back to the rusty starter they'd found for the go-cart. "I didn't think he'd be gone so long. He was going to take some stuff to the preacher's house. Tess was gonna ride with him to visit with her sister. I think they wanted to talk about me."

Tony gave Jason a wry sidelong glance. "Yeah? Well, I don't wanna insult you, pal, but it looks like you turned out to be a short topic."

"What d'ya mean?"

Tony shrugged. "See for yourself."

Jason snatched back the curtain and peered out just in time to see his father kissing Tess like a man who'd been deprived of a woman's touch for too long. Blood-red heat suffused Jason's cheeks like hot coals.

"I told you," Tony said, unaware of Jason's brewing temper. "Didn't I tell you? Daddy and teacher. Pretty convenient, huh? Hey, maybe that's why she's been so nice to you. She's after your old man. And the next thing you know she'll be moving in and you'll be—"

"Shut up!" Jason grabbed Tony's shirt and slammed the other boy against the wall with the strength of an older man twice his size. "You just shut up! She's nothing to him! Nothing! You got that?"

Tony only stared at him, stunned into defensive silence, and Jason whirled around and ran from the room.

Seconds later, Seth shoved open the front door and stepped into the living room. "Jason? I'm home."

But Jason didn't hear him. Locked in the bathroom, he slammed his fist again and again against the wall, until the pain shooting up his arm was greater than the fear building inside him. If his dad fell for Tess, where would that put him? Damn! his shredded heart cried out. Wasn't anybody ever true? Wasn't he good enough for anybody? Why couldn't they just love *him* for a change?

Seth went to Jason's bedroom and saw Tony sitting on the floor. "If I'd known you guys were sleeping over here tonight," he said, "I'd have gotten home sooner. Where's Jason?"

Tony shrugged. "In the bathroom, I think."

Seth noticed the lines of tension on Tony's face. "Is everything okay?"

"Yeah," the boy replied. "My parents were kind of fighting, so we decided to hang out here tonight. It's okay, ain't it?"

"Of course," Seth said. He left the bedroom and knocked on the bathroom door.

"What?" The word was delivered in a belligerent tone, but Seth told himself it was just one of Jason's moods—exactly the kind of thing he and Tess had discussed earlier.

"I'm home," he said. "Everything all right?"

"Everything's great," Jason shouted through the door.

Unable to see Jason's raging face, Seth missed the sarcasm in his son's voice. "Okay," he said. "I guess I'll turn in, then. It's been a long day."

In the bathroom, Jason sat on the edge of the bathtub, tears glistening in his eyes. "I'll just bet it was," he whispered.

But his father didn't hear.

MORNING RAYS OF SUNLIGHT slashed through the mini-blinds in the Calloway kitchen the next morning. Tess sat at the breakfast table in her robe, unaware of the smile curving her lips as she gazed into her coffee.

Eden set her elbow on the table and propped her chin on her hand. "All right," she said with a perceptive grin. "Out with it, or so help me, I'll sic Jo and Mariah on you."

Tess looked up at her sister, who still wore the soft pink nightgown that accented the natural blush of her cheeks. "Out with what?"

"Whatever it is that's got you grinning like a devil and humming that love song."

Tess's smile inched across her face, and she asked herself what the purpose was in keeping the good news to herself. All her life she'd made a game out of holding things in, of keeping her secret feelings as if they were the only things she'd ever had that were her own. But that game was getting old. She wanted to talk about Seth, wanted to shout to the world that life was beautiful and she wasn't really such a failure after all. She hadn't disappointed him, and he certainly hadn't disappointed her.

She swallowed and struggled with the confession. "Seth," she whispered, as if that one word explained everything. "We were together all of yesterday. It was nice."

"No kidding," Eden said, her eyes dancing. She took Tess's hand, made her sister meet her eyes. "I hope you fall irrevocably and thoughtlessly in love and live happily ever after," she said softly. "Nobody deserves it more."

Tess squeezed Eden's hand. "Nobody except you."

Eden's smile faded a degree, and she sighed. "I think my sisters found the last three good men ever to grace Calloway Corners," she said. "But if there's one out there for me, he'll come in his own good time. Meanwhile..." Her eyes lit up with excitement at Tess's newfound happiness. "It's your turn. Enjoy, it kiddo."

The phone rang, startling them out of their intimacy, and Eden gave Tess a wink and answered it.

"It's for you," she said in a singsong voice. "Sounds like Seth."

Tess's smile was laced with threads of fragility as she took the phone from her sister.

"Good morning," she said, casting a glance at Eden, who smiled secretively as she poured Tess another cup of coffee.

"Good morning." His voice was low and sleepy. "I miss you."

"I miss you, too." Their words were simple, the subtext was complex.

"Let's go somewhere today," he said. "Or tonight. Or both."

Tess laughed, and for a moment she mused that if they bottled the potent feeling she had right now it would have to be sold by prescription. "What did you have in mind?"

"Oh, I don't know. I was kinda thinking of a quiet, secluded spot somewhere, nothing special. Just you and me alone... with nature."

"Nature, huh?" Tess whispered, hoping Eden wouldn't hear and make the association. "It can get awfully hot out in nature this time of year."

"No problem," he said. "Just wear something light and easy to get off. You never know when the temperature might rise beyond control."

A warm, stirring heat rose to color Tess's cheeks. "What time?" she asked.

"Three o'clock?" he asked. "It's when most of the beasts are napping, so you won't have to be afraid," he teased.

Tess laughed. "I'll bet all of the beasts won't be napping," she said, thinking he could be the most dangerous one of all. "I'll meet you at your house. What can I bring?"

There was a long pause, and then he whispered huskily into the receiver, "That gorgeous little birthday suit. And a smile."

Her cheeks stung hot with anticipation when she hung up the phone and saw that Eden was leaning against the doorway, watching her and grinning.

SETH HUNG UP the phone and stood silently, anticipating how she would look later that day.

"Who was that?" Jason stood in the doorway of the kitchen, his face hard-set, his eyes glittering.

Seth turned around and regarded his son. "That was your teacher," he answered. "I called to see if she'd like to come over and spend the afternoon with us."

Jason's eyes narrowed. "Why? This is Saturday. I thought I wasn't going to have to work today."

"You don't. This is a social call. I thought maybe we'd load up the fishing poles and head over to Lake Bisteneau. If the fish are biting, we just might catch a mess to fry up for supper. How would you like that?"

Jason's face had an unyielding quality. "You said you would help us work on the go-cart today. That's one reason Tony slept over."

Seth grimaced. "Oh, Jase. I'm sorry. I just forgot. Well...I've already asked her. We'll just have to postpone the go-cart until tomorrow. Wouldn't you rather go fishing, anyway?"

Jason had wheeled around and started out of the kitchen. "I hate fishing," he mumbled. "Just count me out. Tony and I will stay here and work on the go-cart alone. After all, we did it all day yesterday, too."

"Now, wait a minute," Seth said, stopping him. Reluctantly Jason turned back, fixing his father with a grudging look. "I thought you liked Tess. You two seemed friendly enough the other night at supper."

"Yeah," Jason said. "Maybe I changed my mind."

Seth drew his brows together and took a step toward his son. Had he missed something? Had something happened to change Jason's mind? "Why would you do that?"

Jason shrugged. It was the gesture of a jealous four-year-old rather than a thirteen-year-old.

A vague thought formed in the back of Seth's mind, a thought that perhaps there was jealousy involved, that perhaps Jason sensed how close Seth and Tess were becoming. Quickly he discounted the possibility. That was silly. Tess had helped bring *them* closer. Why would Jason be jealous of the woman who had done that?

Still... A niggling doubt convinced him to change his plans, just in case. "All right," Seth said. "I'll tell you what. I'll just call her back, and we'll save the fishing trip for another time."

Jason regarded his father suspiciously. "You mean it? You'd do that?"

Seth smiled easily and chuckled at Jason's surprise. "Sure. A promise is a promise, right? And I promised to help with the go-cart."

"Yeah, right." His expression was still dubious and he looked almost a bit guilty.

Seth picked up the phone and started to dial Tess's number. "I'm sure she'll understand. She's a fair person."

"Meaning I'm not a fair person?" Jason asked defensively. "Is that what you're trying to say?"

Seth sighed with frustration and set the phone back in its cradle. "Jason, what's the matter with you? Why are you analyzing my words? I think you've been in this house long enough that we can be honest and communicate with each other. If there's a problem, we can sit down and talk it out."

Jason shook his head and gave another, more exaggerated, shrug. "There's nothing to talk about. You made a promise. I just wondered if you were gonna keep it. That's all."

"All right," Seth said. "I am. Now you know."

Jason hung there uncertainly, as if he were waiting for a catch, and Seth realized that they were reaching a turning point in their relationship.

"Well, what are you waiting for?" Seth asked. "Go wake Tony up, and let's go see if we can even get that old motor to spark a plug!"

A genuine smile tore across Jason's face. "All right!" He spun around and headed for his room.

Seth couldn't help smiling. It took so little to make Jason happy. But this little sacrifice was going to hurt more than he wanted to admit.

Tony rolled over as Jason dashed back into his room, humming the theme from *Rocky*. "What's with you, man? Did you win the lottery or something?"

Jason grinned. "Yeah. As a matter of fact, it looks like I did."

IN THE KITCHEN, Seth stared at the phone, debating whether to call Tess now and cancel or see how the morning went. Maybe if they got the go-cart running by noon he wouldn't have to cancel his date with her. Then he could keep both promises.

I have a life to lead, too, you know. Celia's words came tumbling into his mind.

It wasn't that way with him, he justified himself, quickly. Not the way Celia had meant it, as if Jason were a burden that hampered her social life. It was just that he couldn't let a thirteen-year-old boy dictate how he spent his time....

The fact that there was almost no difference in their words hit him with the force of a sledgehammer. Seth sighed and leaned his head back against the wall. The truth was, he wanted them both. Jason and Tess. If he let his son down now, the moment Celia decided to take Jason back—probably the same moment her father expressed disgust that she'd surrendered him to Seth—Jason would leave him willingly. As it stood now, he had a chance to make Jason *want* to stay. And if it was his choice to stay with Seth, then nothing Celia did would make a difference.

But time was running out with Tess. He was trying—slowly but surely—to help her make up her mind to stay in Calloway Corners. He didn't want her to go back to Dallas, leaving him as just a stepping-stone in her transition from her divorce back into the mainstream of life.

He cared about her...he always had. Hell, after yesterday, he had to admit that there was a strong possibility that he might even love her. But he was afraid to think about that just yet. If he was in love with her, then he'd have to do something...make some kind of commitment....

Asking her to move in with him was out of the question, and not only because of Jason. It was a small town, and she hadn't been raised that way. Besides, he'd never submit a woman he loved to the kind of humiliation his mother had suffered for most of her life. No, if he had the chance to make a commitment to Tess, marriage was the only choice.

Marriage. He smiled, thinking of waking up to her in the morning, seeing the smile that did more to brighten his house than the morning sunlight through the windows. He could picture her puttering in the kitchen, right beside him... And, of course, Jason was as dominant a character in that fantasy as Tess. He could picture him sitting at the breakfast table, smiling and animated, talking about what he was going to do at school that day.

Maybe he could make that fantasy come true, he thought. It wasn't such an unattainable dream, was it? Tess was coming around, and Jason...well, Jason would come to like her more with time. He couldn't imagine anyone being around her for any length of time without adoring her.

TESS GLANCED AT her watch and asked herself if she'd made a mistake. He had said three o'clock, but she had been sitting on his porch for ten minutes now and there was still no sign of Seth. She knocked again and waited and finally looked back to the driveway, where Seth's truck was still parked. They were here, she thought. Seth wouldn't forget she was coming....

Stepping off the porch, she started around the house. The backyard was more like a close-cropped meadow that sloped toward a wooded area. To the left was the tractor he used to cut the grass, and to the right was a small work shed. Still, there was no sign of Seth.

Disappointed, she was just about to give up and go home when she heard the cranking of a small motor, followed by a victorious shout in the direction of the shed. She started toward the sound and peered inside the shed.

There stood Seth and Jason, laughing like little boys, with grease smeared from head to toe. "Is this a private party?" she asked, grinning.

Both father and son wheeled around. "Tess!" Seth said. "What time is it?" He dropped the tools in his hand, wiped his hands on his pants and stepped over the go-cart toward her.

Tess saw the excitement drain from Jason's eyes. "I thought she wasn't coming," he said. The statement sounded strangely like an accusation. "You said you were going to call her." He jammed his hands into his pockets and leaned back sullenly against the wall.

"I meant to," Seth told Jason. He caught Tess's inquisitive expression. "To tell you that I might be a little late," he explained. He gestured toward the small device they'd been working on. "We're looking at a motor that may or may not eventually power a go-cart. Tony was helping, but he had to go home."

Tess smiled and examined the engine, thankful she had only worn a pair of shorts and a T-shirt. "If that means you're short a hand, I'll be glad to fill in. But I have to admit I don't know an Allen key from a ratchet. I've heard the terms, so I guess that's a start."

Jason threw down the rag he'd been holding. Without uttering a word, he started for the house.

"Jason?" Seth called behind him. "Where are you going?"

"It's hot," Jason muttered. "I'm going in."

Preoccupied with the way his heart hammered at Tess's presence, Seth didn't hear the dejection in his son's voice. "All right," he said with a smile. "Guess I'll just clean this up then, and we can work on it tomorrow."

"Yeah," Jason said. "Tomorrow."

JASON WATCHED FROM his bedroom window as his father's truck pulled out of the driveway. He had stayed in his room the whole time his father was washing up, and when Seth had finally stopped in to coax him into going with them Jason had refused, saying he was going to meet Tony later.

The feeling of utter loneliness crept up inside him, making him feel that he was seeing the end of something.... He wasn't sure what it was...something that had barely had time to get started.

Don't be a baby, Jason told himself sternly. *He spent the whole morning with you. Almost got the go-cart running.* But it wasn't enough, Jason thought, when they had so little time before Tess would steal his father away once and for all.

Jason got off his bed and pulled on his sneakers, deciding that he had to get out of this house before he got any more depressed. Maybe he could find Tony and they could go somewhere and talk, he thought. Maybe things wouldn't turn out as badly as he expected.

"WHERE DO YOU WANT to go?" Seth took his eyes from the road long enough to slip his arm around Tess's shoulders, urging her closer.

She went willingly, tipping her head back and gazing up at him, her eyes dark and dreamy. "It doesn't matter. I just want to be with you."

At the sweetness of her admission, Seth's heart swelled, and his arm tightened around her. His lips brushed her hair. "You know, if you keep saying things like that, I just might be tempted to pull over on the side of the road and drag you into the woods."

Tess stared at him, a saucy smile teasing her lips. "I think you did that already."

He grinned down at her. "Practice makes perfect."

That grin! He had the most beautiful face in the world when he looked at her like that. Her heart soared, and she turned in the seat, nestling her cheek to the curve of his neck, her hand resting on his chest.

Seth. Tess didn't say his name aloud, but it was as if every nerve, every cell of her being sang with his nearness. Never in her life had she felt this closeness, this sense of spiritual connection with another person, and the sensation was at once wonderful and terrifying. Where was it going to lead? Tess didn't want to think about it. She couldn't bear to consider where this relationship might take them. Or when it would eventually end.

Seth lifted his hand and skimmed his knuckles lightly over her cheek as he shifted his foot from accelerator to brake. "We're here," he said softly, and Tess raised her head from his shoulder, straightening to peer out the windshield. To her left she saw a small frame house, apparently still under construction, sitting a fair distance off the road amid a sparse grove of wild cottonwood and pine. The architecture was subtle in its wildness, for it blended well into the backdrop of trees and brush growing up around it. The outer part of the house was finished. Ladders, paint cans and stacks of lumber on the ground testified that the inside had work still to be done.

Tess turned to Seth, her brows lifted in question. "One of the houses you're building?"

Seth nodded. "In fact, this is the one Mariah and Ford picked out."

"Oh, it's lovely," she said on a long sigh as she swept her gaze over the house again. Images of children playing on the lawn, climbing the trees, playing hide and seek passed through her mind like a preview at a matinee. And she could almost picture Ford and Mariah working in a garden together, growing healthy things for their children to eat.

But that was *her* dream, Tess realized. Not necessarily Mariah's. It was her own family she saw there, her children, herself raising things with her hands. But what was it Eden used to always tell her about envying other people? It was a waste of time, Eden had said. And wasted time was about the worst thing Eden could have imagined.

"Come on," Seth said, cutting into her thoughts. He took her hand as he opened the door. "I'll give you the grand tour."

They went around to the back and Seth pulled the key from his pocket and slid it into the lock on the cedar and glass door. "The house is almost finished," he told her. "I'm just waiting for Mariah to decide on the wallpaper and carpet she wants for the bedrooms."

Tess was quiet as she stepped inside her sister's future home, and she caught her breath at the space in the great room, where kitchen, dining room and living room all blended together to create the bottom floor. "Mariah's going to get lost in here," she said, her eyes shimmering with pride for the baby sister who'd never really had much space she could call her own. "She's never in her life had so much room."

"The square footage isn't that much," Seth told her. "But the floor plan makes use of every bit of it."

Tess stepped to the center of the floor and breathed in the scent of fresh pine and sawdust. A massive stone fireplace provided the centerpiece for the room, creating the image of expense and sophisticated taste, though the house was modestly decorated elsewhere.

"If it were my house, I'd get a huge sofa to go right here," Tess said. "And a fat recliner, and..."

Seth's eyes were softly resting on her back when she spun around. "I could build you a house just like this one, you know," he said quietly. "Or even a bigger one. Or a different kind. Anything you want."

Tess stopped imagining the house was hers, and focused, instead, on the man who wanted it to be. "I...I'm sure you could. I mean—" She laughed uncomfortably, then berated herself for the weak sound. "I'm sure you could build any kind of house you set your mind to. But I don't...I don't need a house."

Seth's eyes grew even more serious as he stepped across the bare concrete floor. "Maybe not now," he said with a hint of hope in his voice. "But you might if you decide to stay in Calloway Corners. You might not want to go on living with Eden indefinitely."

Tess's gaze dropped to the floor, where bits of broken lumber lay scattered over the foundation. "I don't plan to," she said. "School starts soon, and I really have to think about my job..."

"You could keep tutoring Jason," Seth said carefully. "He needs you. I need you."

Suddenly Tess felt cold in the empty house, though it was August and the temperature outside suited the season. "I don't know, Seth. I have to support myself, and tutoring one child just wouldn't be enough."

"I can pay more," Seth said.

She turned to him, saw the hopeful offering in his eyes. "Oh, no. That's not what I mean."

"Well, what then?"

She threw up her hands, dropped them to her sides. "I need something permanent."

"You could get a teaching job here, at the high school. Or at one of the bigger schools in Bossier City or Shreveport."

Tess went to the kitchen, peered out the window over the sink. It all seemed so tempting, and yet she didn't want to fall back into her old pattern of depending again. Not on Seth or anyone. "I've thought about it. But, of course, I'd have to apply for a license to teach in Louisiana. And it seems a little silly to go through all that red tape when I already have a good job in Dallas."

She looked over her shoulder and saw the tightness of Seth's face, the hard lines from hard lessons that he hadn't stopped learning. "Then what you're saying is that you've already made up your mind."

"No," she said, turning around, wishing to heaven she could wipe that look off his face and bring back the one that made her heart sing. "I'm just trying to be practical. I—"

"What if I were to ask you to stay?" he ventured, his voice shaking. "Would that make a difference?"

She felt tears spring to her eyes, and her heart swelled.

"Don't." The word came out on a raspy sob, and she tried to stop her lips from shaking. "Don't ask me to stay, Seth."

"Stay," he whispered, narrowing the space between them and pulling her into his arms. "Stay, Tess. Stay, please."

Hot tears rolled down her face, and he kissed them from her cheeks. She closed her eyes and told herself that she deserved Seth's love. But her heart had barely healed from her last episode with love, and she wasn't sure it could survive another. "I've loved twice," she whispered, her voice hoarse and agonizing against Seth's ear. "Both times, I've been left completely alone."

"I won't leave you this time," he said. "I swear, Tess. You don't have to be alone anymore."

His lips found hers, soft and moist with her tears, and he kissed her in a way that pulled her fears right out of her soul, and replaced them with a peace that she never would have expected from the reckless Seth Taylor she had known so long ago.

Fate, Mariah had said. Fate didn't give up. It kept trying until it got things right. That was the tragedy of it all.

More tears escaped her eyes, and Tess felt her body shaking in despair as the kiss grew deeper, more melding, more giving. If she made a clean break, went back to her life in Dallas, she would never forget him. This time she'd had a taste of his love. She knew what it was like to feel his bare skin against hers, to experience his need inside her, to fly to heights she'd never dreamed existed before today. How could she turn away from that now?

He lifted her in his arms. Then, still kissing her with the urgency of someone about to lose his most precious hope, Seth carried her to a bedroom where a pile of drop cloths lay crinkled on the floor. He dropped her legs, letting them slide against his to the floor.

Tears still trekked down her cheeks, and with a hand callused and rough, but more gentle than the softest fabric Tess had ever felt, he wiped those tears from her cheeks. "Don't cry, Tess," he whispered. "Please don't cry."

She took his hand, then, and nuzzled her face into his palm, memorizing the texture of every hardened blister, every crack and callus, every line of his seasoned hand. Her shimmering eyes met his, soft and so full of love that she could feel it in her soul.

Slowly, she moved his hand down her face, over her neck and over the front of her T-shirt.

Seth moved with the gentleness of a man afraid he'd break the only light that showed him the way. He pulled her T-shirt over her head and let it drop to the floor. Then, with a tender touch, he slid his hands around to her back and unclasped her bra.

A deep, shivering sigh tore out of his lungs at the sight of her, standing before him, so much his for the moment, yet so elusive the moment their lovemaking ended. And so he vowed to make it last this time, make the moment stretch to the threshold of eternity, so that he'd never have to let her go.

The vulnerable expression she wore crushed his heart, tearing at the obsessiveness in his soul. Sweet agony stole through him as he slipped his shirt over his head and pulled her against him, holding her so tightly that for a moment, he almost believed he could erase all the wasted years that had passed between them.

His lips found hers, and she sank into the depths of his passion, allowing herself to drown in oblivion with no thought of yesterday or tomorrow...only here and now.

With frenzied abandon, her hands began to move over the smooth, muscled ridges of his back, down to his ribs, around to his smooth, bare chest, hammering with mad desire.

His eyes glittered with feverish passion as he broke the kiss, breathing in gasps as his face dipped to the luscious mound of her breast. His mouth cherished her with the force of all the loneliness he'd experienced in his life, making up for the lost time with every swirl of his tongue, every nip of his teeth. Tess shuddered in his arms, and a low, barely audible moan escaped like a whimper from her throat.

His hands tugged impatiently at her shorts, and quickly, with trembling hands, she released the zipper, allowing the waistband to fall to her hips. Seth dragged the garment off her, along with the lacy bikini panties covering her, letting them both puddle around her feet. Then he assaulted her lips again with fiery intent, and lifted her.

She felt him lowering her to the bed of drop cloths smelling of paint and sawdust, felt him anchoring her with his hard weight, felt his denim pants chafing her as he moved against her. And then, with the hurry of a man afraid the moment would be snatched away, he discarded his jeans and returned to her.

His lips made a sweet journey over her eyelids, her cheeks, her throat. His hands molded her thighs and hips, then found the throbbing center of her. Ripples of pleasure stroked through her, making her writhe in near ecstasy.

"Don't leave me," he whispered against her ear as she clung and shuddered at his ministrations. "Don't leave me, Tess."

"Seth," she cried, desperate for the completeness with which he had teased her.

And finally he entered her, escalating her ecstasy to explosive heights, where hearts thundered and bolts of lightning illuminated their souls. Where marks of permanency etched themselves on memories...memories that would never be enough again.

"I love you, Tess," he cried at the moment of his release. "Please...I love you...so much..."

The emotion bursting in her heart created a sweet agony that in itself contained a healing power. A power that she could neither fight nor run from. A power that made her whole, and right, and perfect. A power that only Seth could give her.

CHAPTER THIRTEEN

MILES AWAY, near the old Olin Mills Industries plant. Jason Taylor and Tony Spier sat in the shade of an abandoned railroad car. Less than twenty yards ahead, the tracks ran parallel to the highway leading out of Calloway Corners.

"I mean it, Jase," Tony said, as the boy beside him picked up another rock and tossed it idly, aiming between the rails. "I just can't stand it anymore. Their screaming and yelling all the time is bad enough, but this time, he hit her—I've never seen him hit her before—I don't know what happened. I just went crazy."

"You tried to stop him. Sounds like you did the only thing you could do."

"But, Jason, if you could have seen his *face*, man. I thought for a minute he was gonna kill me. But then he just went into his room and slammed the door, and she was crying and everything. Not just because he hit her, but because she was afraid he was gonna hurt me. And I..." Tony ran a shaking hand over his face. "I gotta get out of there. I'm tellin' ya, I can't stand the way they live."

Jason looked at his friend, youthful admiration settling on his features. "But where will you go? You don't have any money and you're not old enough to get a job. How do you expect to eat? And where you gonna live?"

Tony drew a deep breath. "I've got it worked out."

"Oh, yeah? How? You gonna stick up a bank or something?"

"I got a letter from my older brother once—about a year ago. He said he had a place in El Paso and was working for some oil rig outfit, and making good money, too. So I figure if I can make it down there, maybe I can get him to put me up until..." His words trailed off and he laughed a little, a dead-end, hopeless sound. "I don't know. Just until."

Jason shook his head and stood up, shoving his hands into the depths of his pockets. A frown cut between his brows. "I don't think this is a very good idea. How do you know your brother's still living in El Paso? He could've moved in a year. My mother dated a guy once that worked off-shore, and he was always going off somewhere. What if you can't find him? What then?"

Tony sighed. "Then I'll just cross the border and live in the streets."

Jason gasped. "Glory, man! Are you crazy? You can't do that."

"Sure I can. I've been reading all about it. El Paso is right on the Mexican border, and a lot of those little kids down there—some of them even younger than me—can support their whole families just by doing things like washing car windows or carrying stuff for the tourists."

"Man..." Jason shook his head, amazed at the extent to which his friend had thought things out. "This all sounds pretty risky to me. You know, you could get kidnapped or hurt or something down there."

"Aw, man. Nothing like that's going to happen to me. I just wanna get out of here. And this is the only way I can see to do it. I'm going to catch that train, Jason. Soon as I get up my nerve."

Jason turned to the tracks and gazed off in the distance, imagining all the places a train could take him. "Well, I hope you give me a call before you go trying to jump a moving train," he said quietly.

"Sure, man. I'll call to say goodbye, and maybe you might even want to come out and see me off." Tony laughed and got to his feet, then tossed a rock over the tracks.

Jason's expression was dark and troubled. "You just make sure you call."

"Yeah." Tony slid his hands into his back pockets.

They stood for a moment longer looking at each other. But there didn't seem to be much else to say. "Well, I guess I'll see you, then."

Tony nodded and Jason turned to go, but his steps had only carried him a short distance when his friend's parting words slowed him for an instant. "You know, Jase, you could go with me."

AT DUSK, the skies grew cloudy and a slow drizzle began to fall. Tess and Seth drove home in silence, only the rasp of wipers against a gritty windshield to keep them from their thoughts.

Don't leave me, Tess. The words seemed to resound in her mind, making her heart ache, and as if the very atmosphere echoed that thought, she seemed to hear the words in the rhythm of the wipers. *Don't leave me...don't leave me...*

Seth took her hand and pulled it to his lips, pressing a kiss onto a soft knuckle. The worry in his eyes told her that he sensed the end was coming. She could stop it, she told herself. With a simple declaration, she could wipe the pain from his face—from her own soul—and set her life straight.

But fear still held a reigning place in her heart. Fear of failure, of humiliation, of loneliness... Twice she'd loved and lost to someone else. Twice she'd suffered the devastation of wondering just where she hadn't measured up. Twice she'd realized how dependent she had become on a man who could betray her.

They drove back to his house, and instead of leaving the truck idling, he cut the engine. "I want you to come in," he said. "We need to talk."

Knowing the moment of confrontation was nearing, she nodded her head. "I know," she whispered.

The rain pounded hard against them as they dashed into the house, and once they were inside, she shook the dampness from her hair and brushed it from her clothes.

"I'll get some coffee," he said.

"Shouldn't you let Jason know we're back?" she asked, looking around for a sign of the teenager.

A soft smile tilted his lips. "Yeah. You know, you'd almost think you were the parent here, instead of me. I'm still trying to get used to having someone else around here to think about."

She smiled faintly and lowered herself to the couch as he started down the hall to Jason's room. If only she were his parent, she fantasized. If she and Seth could both be Jason's parents, and they could be a family, a happy family...

She stopped her thoughts in midstream and shook herself. What was she doing? Planning out a nice little happy future that couldn't be less likely? No, she told herself. There was no time for wishing and daydreaming. No time for envying the families other people had. She'd learned that long ago, when she realized that other girls had mothers to fix their hair, patch up their skinned knees, dry the tears that came from wounded feelings, that her family was different. She'd had to settle for what she had, and Eden had told her so many times that what they had was good.

So why had she never stopped feeling that she'd simply settled for too little? That she'd been shortchanged? That she'd never had the chance to know what a complete family was like?

She looked down the hall, thinking how good and patient Seth was with Jason, how he strived to give Jason that normal kind of life she had craved as a child. She only wished Jason could see how truly lucky he was.

Seth stepped into the dark hall and leaned against the wall before knocking on Jason's door. She was going to leave him, and soon, if he didn't do something about it, he thought. He had to stop her. Had to convince her that she needed him as much as he needed her. He couldn't lose her again.

He pulled himself together and knocked on Jason's door, then stuck his head into the cluttered room. "Hi, Jase," he said wearily. "We're back."

Jason was lying on his bed with his headphones on, and if he saw his father, he made no response.

"Jason!" Seth called.

Jason noticed his father then and sat up, shoving his headphones around his neck. He glared at his father without saying a word.

"I said we're back," Seth said, growing impatient.

"You were gone an awful long time," Jason said, his lips compressed with hostility. Then, with ardent sarcasm, he asked, "Did you catch any *fish*?"

Seth felt a strange ripple of apprehension inside him, and he frowned deeply. "We didn't go fishing. I took Tess to show her some of the houses I'm building."

"I guess she'll be spending the night, huh?" Jason bit out.

Seth stepped all the way into the room and set his hands on his hips. Was Jason calling him down like a kid who'd been caught at something? The idea made him angry. "No, Jason. She's not spending the night. It's raining and I invited her in for a cup of coffee. And when she leaves, you and I are going to have a little talk about your attitude."

Jason's mouth curled up in a snarl. "What's wrong with my *attitude*?"

Seth felt all the weeks of working with his son, building his trust, diminishing in one afternoon. He was losing him, just like he was losing Tess. "I'm going to give you a while to think about it, and then you can answer that question for me," he said.

He left Jason sitting there, amid album covers and clothes lying on the floor, and stepped into the hall. What was happening to him? he thought. Was it something about him that made people turn away? Was it so hard to love him or to accept his love?

He took a deep breath and started back into the living room, but Tess wasn't there. *Oh, hell,* he thought. *She's left. What if she'd heard what Jason said?*

But then he heard Tess in the kitchen and he rushed for the door.

There she stood, in the kitchen that had known only a man's awkward hands, pouring his coffee in a soft glow of light. Rain pattered against the window beside her, creating a low, seductive music that seemed oddly right with her. She looked so at home there, in the kitchen, in his house, in his life...

And suddenly he didn't care what it took. He wouldn't let her walk away.

Tess glanced at him and smiled. "Coffee's ready."

Seth leaned against the door frame, tilting his head in silent awe. "Do you have any idea how beautiful you look, standing there?"

He could have sworn he saw a blush feather across her cheeks. "No. Why don't you tell me?"

He shoved away from the doorjamb and crossed the kitchen to stand directly in front of her. "Better yet," he whispered, cupping the nape of her neck and coaxing her face up to his, "let me show you how much I appreciate such beauty in my kitchen."

She set down the cup of coffee and went willingly into his arms, letting his kiss sweep her away on a gale of hope and trust, a fresh breeze of love.

"Oh, Tess," he whispered against her lips. "You don't know what you do to me. I need you so much." He drove his fingers through her hair and pressed his forehead against her lips. "I love you. I want you to be my wife. Marry me, Tess."

He felt her stiffen in his arms as surely as he felt the wrenching of his heart when she pulled away from him. He let her go, watching the way she whirled around, running her hand through her hair. She halted at the table, gripping the back of a chair as if she needed it for support. And in that moment, he would have gladly bargained his soul to the devil for the power to read her thoughts.

Tess spun around to face him, rubbing her head with a trembling hand. "Oh, Seth. It's too soon. It would never work."

"Why?" he demanded. "Give me a reason." He caught her shoulders and pulled her around to face him. "Is it because you don't love me? Is that it?"

"No! It's because I'm afraid! I'm scared, Seth. I've made that commitment before, and I failed! I'm *tired* of failing!" She shook free of his arms and stepped back across the kitchen, putting some distance between them. "I've only been divorced six months! Six months! I haven't even dated anyone. We've been seeing each other for a few weeks, and suddenly you ask me to *marry* you? What do you want me to say?"

"Say yes," Seth entreated. "It's as simple as that."

"No," Tess said. "It's too much . . . too fast . . ."

A look of pain crossed Seth's face. "But you will have an affair with me?"

"No, that's not what I mean . . . I want . . ."

"Answer me," he said. "I'm good enough to sleep with, but not good enough to marry? Is that what you're trying to say?"

"No!" she shouted. "Of course not. Please understand. It's not you, it's me. *My* problem. Try and think back to when you were first divorced. Weren't you afraid about getting involved right away? Surely you can understand how I feel."

Seth's eyes glimmered with a fine mist that broke Tess's heart. "The truth?" he asked. "You want me to tell you how I felt after my divorce? I'll tell you. If I could have found you and thought for one second that you would've been willing, I'd have married you within the hour. I love you, Tess. I've loved you since I was seventeen years old."

Seth's voice cracked on the last word, and his mouth trembled as he continued. "I don't want to go on hiding in the woods or in vacant houses to be with you. I don't want to worry and wonder if this is just a summer fling with you, or if I'll be remembered at some future point in your life as the guy who helped you back into circulation after your divorce.''

"I could never think of you that way," Tess said, tears falling over her lashes and dropping like raindrops onto her damp blouse. ''I wouldn't.'' She reached out to touch his face, but he stepped away from her touch.

"It's got to be all or nothing, Tess. And you're going to have to decide which way it's going to be."

She covered her mouth with her hand and stared at him with all the yearning she had ever felt in her life. "Oh, Seth. I just need some time. Just give me some time."

"Take all the time you need," he said coldly. "But don't wait for me to change my mind."

Miserable at the ultimatum he'd laid out before her, Tess pushed past him, leaving him standing alone in the kitchen, a tortured mass of pain and regret.

Tess ran through the drizzling rain, letting it douse her clothes and soak her hair, but she didn't care. She stood at the car door and dropped her face against the Audi's metal roof.

All or nothing... The words reverberated through her soul. What's wrong with all, a voice inside asked. Why can't you accept what Seth has offered?

She opened the car door and slipped in behind the wheel, shivering in her wet clothes. Her hand trembled too much to get the key in the ignition, so she merely sat there for a minute, asking herself what would happen if she started the engine and drove away. Would she keep driving until she was in Dallas, in the apartment that was a poor facsimile of a home? Would she be happy there, going on as if she'd never had a second chance with Seth?

She looked at the front door of the house and saw that Seth was standing there, watching her with torment raging on his face. And suddenly all she wanted was to wipe that pain away and give him the answer he wanted. The answer *she* wanted. She only hoped he could help her with the fear.

ALONE IN HIS ROOM, Jason eased back his curtains and watched, stony-faced, as Tess sat in her car. She was crying, he saw, and his father hadn't followed her outside. Jason had seen her run out as fast as she could, but now she only sat there, a blur behind the rain-soaked windshield.

They'd had a fight, he told himself. Maybe it was over, and he and his dad could go back to being a family. No one would come between them. No one would push him out.

But then he saw Tess get out of the car, and his father bolted across the lawn. He saw Seth embrace her with the force of a man who hadn't seen his love in a decade of turmoil, saw him kiss her as if she were all in the world he ever needed ...

In the distance, a train whistle wailed.

Jason dropped the curtain and stood with his fists clenched at his sides. Then, very slowly, he turned from the window, picked up the phone and dialed his mother.

SETH WOULDN'T ALLOW TESS to leave him for the rest of the evening, and when Jason—still in a somber mood— left to "sleep over" at Tony's, he pulled her into his arms.

"I want to set a date," he said, his feverish lips trailing kisses over her face. "And I want us to decide when we can tell Jason. He needs to know."

"Soon," she said burying her face against his shoulder.

"Soon what?" he asked. "Soon the wedding, or soon we'll tell Jason?"

"Both," she said. "I just have to get used to it myself first." She looked up at him, framing his face with an adoring hand. "Oh, Seth. What if you wake up one morning and decide you don't want me anymore? I don't think I could take another—"

"Shh." He brushed his lips against her forehead. "That would never happen. I could never stop wanting or loving you. And if it's time you want, I'll give it to you. But please, Tess, just promise you won't go away and fall in love with someone else."

"I promise. As long as you want me, I'll be here."

He tipped back her head, and she gave herself up to the sweet demand of his lips. *All or nothing,* he'd said. And now, basking in his joy and love, she knew that all was a long way from nothing. How could she go wrong, now that she'd made the decision to spend the rest of her life as Seth's wife?

When at last he dragged his mouth from hers, she sagged against him, her heart pounding against his chest. His hands roamed urgently over her back and cupped her hips, molding her to him. She swayed unsteadily, and he gathered her closer.

"Are you sure Jason isn't coming back tonight?" she asked, realizing Seth had every intention of making love to her within the next five minutes, and that once he started, she'd have no will to stop him, regardless of discretion or propriety.

Understanding her concern, Seth smiled and brushed his lips against her hair. "He won't be back," he assured her. "The house is all ours." But in truth, both had thoughts of only one room in particular, and half a minute later, carrying Tess in his arms, Seth pushed open the door to his bedroom.

He didn't enter immediately, but turned his gaze to Tess, the luminous flame of his eyes blazing into hers. Slowly, he eased her feet to the floor and stood her to face him. His hands caressed her upper arms as he lowered his head, bringing his face on a level with hers. "I want you to sleep with me," he admitted, his voice thick with emotion. "In my house. In my bed. I want you to stay the night with me. Will you do that? Will you give me a chance to show you how wonderful it'll be, waking up beside each other, sleeping together all night long? Will you promise you won't leave?"

Tess looked into the bedroom, the intimate chamber that belonged only to Seth, the room she had never seen before. It was so tempting, the idea of sliding between the sheets with him, loving him the whole night through, with no interruptions and no rushing home. But what would Eden say?

Suddenly, it didn't matter to her what Eden thought, or Mariah, or Jo. It didn't matter that she wasn't perfectly perfect, or that she be above reproach. What mattered now was having Seth love her with all his heart and soul. All night.

"I won't leave," she whispered.

Her clothes were the same ones Seth had removed earlier that day, and so he knew where all the buttons, clasps and zippers were and wasted no time getting her out of them. He yanked his shirt over his head and kissed her with a blaze of searing passion just before ridding himself of his jeans.

But suddenly there was a knock at the front door, startling them both.

"Jason?" Tess whispered, grabbing her shorts and holding them up to hide herself.

"He wouldn't knock," Seth said. "Not unless he forgot his key."

The knock came again, and Tess began frantically grabbing the rest of her clothes. Dear heaven, she thought. What if it *was* Jason? What if he had walked in on them? Panic and guilt swept over her, and she found herself praying that it was anyone but Seth's son.

The insistent pounding grew louder as Seth stalked to the front door. He could hardly imagine Jason returning home so early, and yet who else could it be? Seconds later, his question was answered. When Seth drew open the door, he found himself staring at the one person he least wanted or expected to see.

"Oh, Seth! You've got to help me!" With a wail and a force that nearly knocked the breath from his lungs, Celia McKinsey launched herself into her ex-husband's arms.

He stumbled, catching her by the shoulders, prying her off him. "Celia! What are you doing here?"

She whimpered and slumped against his chest. "It's Ray. He's left me," she choked out. "He took all my money and used it to fix his stupid car, and now Daddy won't pay my rent. I got evicted, and it's all your fault...and Jason's!" she charged irrationally, then lapsed into a round of sobs.

Gritting his teeth, Seth kicked the door shut and half dragged Celia to the couch, where he deposited her, none too gently, glad to be free of her clinging weight. "Dammit! What do you want me to do?" he demanded angrily. Why in the hell did she always have to come running to him? Why couldn't she just steer clear of him and Jason?

Tossing back her head, Celia glared at him. "You've got to put me up, Seth. You owe me that for ruining my life when I still had a future."

Seth glowered down at her, his face suffused with the strain of suppressed rage. "And you want to make sure I keep on payin', like I have been for thirteen years. Isn't that right, Celia? To make sure I'm miserable... Isn't that why you're really here?"

She got to her feet, her mouth open, no doubt ready to spout a bitter retort. But Seth saw her face pale suddenly as her gaze strayed past him. Her eyes widened for an instant. She wiped the tears from her face, as if she had no further use for them.

"Well, well, well." Celia folded her arms across her breast, one pencil-thin brow arching to an arrogant degree. "You didn't tell me you had company, *lover*. I could've waited till you were through."

Seth swung around and saw Tess standing at the edge of the hallway, her face flushed, her hair hanging in tangles around her shoulders. That she had just come from the bedroom was a truth too blatant to deny. Not that Seth cared in the least what Celia thought, but he didn't want Tess to be hurt or embarrassed. Especially not for the amusement of his ex-wife.

Though he wanted only to go to her and protect her, Seth shifted his gaze away from Tess. His eyes were bleak and threatening as storm clouds when he turned his attention to Celia once more. "I think you'd better go." His tone said there was no thinking about it.

Celia lowered her lashes and smiled at him sardonically, her dark eyes glittering. "So you finally got a piece of that cheesecake you've been hungering for all these years. Was it as good as you expected, Seth?" she taunted. "As good as you imagined all those times you were thinking of her when you were making love to me?"

Tess knew the exact moment Seth lost the battle with his self-control. She could almost feel the gusting force of his rage as he grasped Celia's shoulders, looking, for a moment, as if he might physically throw her out of the house. Even Celia looked stunned, almost afraid.

"No, Seth!" Tess managed to shout. Momentarily forgetting her embarrassment and the humiliation at having Celia walk in on them, she knew only that she didn't want to be the cause of their fight.

It was at that moment that Jason came bounding through the front door.

One glimpse of his father holding his mother in barely controlled rage, and Jason screeched to a halt. "You!" he cried, and three startled gazes swung to meet his. But Jason's eyes were locked on Tess, bitter rage and accusation surging through him with a force that made him tremble. "You ruined everything. I wanted them to be alone!"

Tess stared at Jason, torn between confusion and guilt.

"What do you mean you wanted us to be alone?" Seth demanded. Blue eyes narrowed with dark, scrutinizing intent as they moved from Jason to glare at Celia.

As if he didn't hear, Jason turned to face his mother. "You came too early. I told you to wait until later, so she'd be gone!"

Celia blushed hotly and lifted her eyebrows like a little girl afraid she'd be punished. "It...it was Jason's idea," she stammered, looking at her son guiltily. The boy stared at her, his face ashen.

"He had this crazy idea about you and me getting back together," she went on, her voice dropping. "And since I'm flat broke and needed a place to stay for a while, I thought . . ." Her voice trailed off. She glanced down at her hands and shrugged, but it seemed obvious to the other three exactly what she had thought.

Seth's face went granite hard. "You mean you came here wanting Jason to believe we might get back together, when all you really wanted was a place to crash and some money?"

It was a statement, not an accusation. But tears came to Celia's eyes again. "He was upset!" she cried. "I really thought he'd feel better if I came. It wasn't some malicious scheme, Seth. He called *me*, remember?"

Jason stared at his mother, daring her to face him, to deny that the gesture had been only to appease him and that there was any selfish motive involved. But she would not, and suddenly he was seized with the pain of betrayal. It erupted from him in an angry gush, which he unleashed on Tess. "This is all your fault!"

He turned on her, all but sobbing with rage. "Why can't you just go away and leave our family alone!"

He spun on his heel then, and Tess tried to intercept him. "Jason, wait!" she cried, but all she received in answer was a crushing blow to the shoulder as he fled past her. Seconds later, the slamming of his bedroom door reverberated like a shot through the house.

Tess turned to Seth, who stood staring at her like a man who'd been slugged in the jaw completely unexpectedly, and to Celia, who stared at her with an expression of grim satisfaction at the things Jason had said to her.

"I think I should go," Tess said, her voice cracking. She went for her purse, but Seth stopped her.

"No, Tess. Don't go. Please. He didn't mean it. He was just—"

Tess shook free of him and backed toward the door. "I'm going, Seth. This is between you and . . . your family."

And then she gathered her dignity around her like a warm coat to protect her from the cold blowing through her, and walked to the car, desperate not to start crying until she was out of Seth's sight.

She drove more than a mile before the tears reached her eyes, but still she managed to keep from breaking down completely. Just because the man she had finally agreed to marry had a son who hated her and a dependent ex-wife who wanted to break them up for the second time, it wasn't the end of the world.

Fleetingly, her relationship with Vance crossed her mind, and Tess wondered what might have happened if they'd had a child. It would have forced her into a certain dependence on her ex-husband, she thought. And perhaps that would have made it more difficult to grow...more difficult to keep the bitterness and self-pity at bay.

But she *had* broken free, and she was still growing. As easy as it might have been to follow Celia's path, she had achieved a certain independence. She had even learned to take risks.

Risks, she thought. Where had that gotten her?

Only a person who risks is free, Seth had said to her long ago, before either of them knew the directions their lives would take. *The person who doesn't risk will live in bondage all his life, trapped inside himself instead of being a part of the world.*

He'd told her that just before she'd admitted that the thing she wanted most in life was a husband and family of her own. It was so funny how life repeated itself. Love, surrender, devastation. Only this time she wasn't going to give up. Not until she had to.

She pulled her car into Eden's driveway and sat still for a moment, watching the rain still drizzling over her windshield. She forced her tears back and dried her face. She had cried so much that day that she couldn't believe it, and yet she'd also faced such ecstasy, such pure joy with the man she loved.

It wasn't over yet, she told herself. She would win Jason over, if it took the rest of her life. And the prize would be his dad.

CHAPTER FOURTEEN

SETH SAT AT THE KITCHEN TABLE the next morning, staring at a lukewarm cup of too-black coffee. Celia had gone to the guest room last night and hadn't come out since. She was probably dead to the world, he thought, but he hadn't slept a wink and he was willing to bet Tess hadn't, either.

He glanced at the phone and thought of calling her, but decided to wait a little longer, in case she *was* asleep. There really wasn't anything he could say to her now that might help. He knew how hurt and awkward she must have felt, caught in the middle between him and Celia last night. And the ordeal with Jason had been the worst. Seth had tried to talk to his son last night after Tess had left, but Jason had been far too upset to be reasoned with. Celia's presence in the house hadn't helped matters, either. But somehow, Seth knew, he was going to have to find the right moment, the right words, to reach his son.

Somehow, he had to make Jason understand that love was not an exclusive commodity, automatically diminished through division; that his love for Tess in no way lessened his love for his son.

JASON CLOSED THE ZIPPER on his backpack and picked up his bedroll. Standing back, he let his gaze roam over his bedroom: the stacks of records, the postered walls, the stereo equipment his father had given him for his birthday a year ago. He tried to think of his room at his mother's house in Shreveport, but he was tired, and the image did not come readily to mind. Only the faces of a few of his friends, and the memory of the night his mother had let her boyfriend haul him in to juvenile hall.

A knot twisted in his stomach. Jason sighed and turned toward the door. His bedroll in one hand, he slung his backpack over his shoulder. He cast one final glance at the poster of E.Z. Ellis, carefully tacked to his closet door. "Another broken promise," he whispered to himself, then opened the door and stalked out.

Seth had just risen from the table and was in the process of refilling his coffee cup when he caught a glimpse of his son slipping out through the front door. "Jason!" he called, whirling around and sloshing hot coffee on his hand at the moment the door slammed shut.

Celia stuck her head out of the guest room. "Was that Jason?" she asked groggily.

Seth cast her a flickering glance before his eyes moved to the closed door. "Yeah," he mumbled. "I guess he's headed over to Tony's. *Seeking refuge from the war zone, no doubt.*

"Oh." She stepped into the hall, crossing her arms in front of the silk lounging robe she wore. "Do you think he's going to be all right?"

Seth poured his coffee into the sink and watched it whirl down the drain. "I don't know, Celia," he said. "I just don't know."

"So, HOW MUCH DO WE HAVE all together?" Jason watched as Tony recounted the bills and small change they had scraped up between them.

"Eighteen dollars and sixteen cents."

Jason sighed and shook his head, frowning. "Oh, man, that's not enough. We've got to eat! How long does it take to get to El Paso, anyway?"

Tony shrugged. "A couple of days, maybe—or three. I'm not sure. I guess it'll depend on which train we catch at the rail yard in Shreveport. Like I told you, we've got to travel south at first."

Jason nodded, and the two boys began to shove canned goods, taken from Tony's mother's pantry, into their already overstuffed backpacks. While they worked, they discussed their plan to hop the train where it normally slowed near the old mill plant. And after that, there was nothing to do but wait.

AT TWO O'CLOCK in the afternoon, the torrential rain that had been predicted for days due to the coastal disturbance of Hurricane Berle moved sluggishly over the northern portion of Louisiana. Tess stood at the kitchen window, watching the clouds roll in.

She was alone in the house; Eden had taken the children to see a Disney movie at the Eastgate Cinema in Shreveport. Tess had been invited to traipse along, but considering the mood she was in, she'd decided the shooting of Bambi's mother might be more than she could stand.

Several times throughout the morning she had gone to the phone and stood there, staring at it, willing the infernal thing to ring. Once or twice, she had gone so far as to imagine herself picking it up and swiftly dialing Seth's number. But imagining was as far as she'd taken it.

He would call *her*, she told herself firmly, when things had smoothed over and he had had a chance to talk to Jason. In the meantime, she would not allow herself to create more complications, more problems between father and son, by calling the house while Celia was there.

I wanted them to be alone together. Jason's admission tormented her now, just as it had all last night. She wasn't jealous, surprisingly, not of Celia. At least, not as far as Seth was concerned. She knew Seth loved her and that he had no interest in reconciliation with his ex-wife.

But in a way, Tess supposed, that was the saddest thing about it. After all these years, she felt almost certain that Jason had known there was no hope of his parents ever getting back together. His call to Celia had simply been his way of telling his father he didn't want Tess intruding into their lives.

Niggling doubts crept into her mind, doubts about her marriage to Seth. Could she really go through with it now, knowing how Jason felt? Could she really marry him in spite of Jason?

She honestly didn't know.

The peal of the telephone jarred Tess from her dismal thoughts. Turning from the window, she hurried to pick up the phone. Answering on the second ring, she was rewarded with the sound of the voice she had been hoping to hear all morning.

"I'm sorry." It was the first thing Seth said, his deep voice sounding husky and tired. "I'd have done anything to keep from involving you in that ordeal last night. Are you all right?"

Tess smiled, and her heart ached with loving him. "Yes," she whispered. "What about you and Jason?"

She heard him draw a deep breath. "Jason took off this morning before I could talk to him."

"Took off?" Her tone was full of concern, and for a moment she was afraid that Jason had gone back to the city with Celia.

"He's over at Tony's," Seth explained, and she breathed a sigh of relief. "He took his sleeping bag, and I guess he plans on sleeping over there tonight. But I'm going to swing by and pick him up after work. We've still got a lot of things to sort through."

"Don't lose your temper with him," Tess said. "He's hurting right now. Try to remember what it was like to be his age."

"I know that, but he can't go on with this fantasy that Celia and I are going to get back together. I want him to know that I love you and that we're getting married. He needs to know so he can have time to get used to it."

Tess was quiet for a moment. She ran her finger down the ornate carving of the old, rickety telephone table. "Seth, I think that would be a mistake."

"A mistake?" he asked. "Why?"

"Because he's not ready. I don't want to be the cause of problems between you and Jason."

"Why don't you let me worry about that?" he said.

"It concerns all of us, Seth. For most of his life, Jason hasn't really felt like he belongs anywhere. I think he's just started to feel settled with you. I can't go in there and ruin all that. His insecurities would multiply, and his self-image is bad enough already."

She heard Seth moan, then heard him swear softly. "Please, Tess. Tell me you're not trying to say that the marriage is off."

"I don't know," she whispered. "I think we should think about Jason's state of mind, right now."

His voice sank to a barely audible level. "What about my state of mind, Tess? I need you."

"I need you, too," she whispered. "But Jason needs both of us. Let's just get him through this, okay? Then we'll talk more about marriage."

Seth was quiet for a long moment, and finally he expelled a heavy sigh. "Look, I have to go to work. I'll call
you tonight, okay?"

"Okay," Tess said, not missing the pain dragging his
voice down, as it weighed down her heart. "I'll talk to
you later."

LATER, SETH THOUGHT as he set the phone mouthpiece
back in its cradle. Damn that word. That one word that
kept coming between him and Tess. Later.

He left the phone and went to get his keys and wallet
off the dresser. He wasn't going to let her back out of this
marriage. It was too important to him . . . too important
to Jason. If only Jason could see how good she could be
for them, how she had already drawn them together into
some semblance of a family. He had to make Jason see
that they would actually be closer with Tess in their
home, not farther apart.

Maybe this afternoon, after his son had time to cool
off, he could pick him up from Tony's and get through
to him. Then he and Tess could go on with their plans.
Then they could all be happy.

IT WAS TOO DARK to work. By four-thirty the skies over
Calloway Corners were cloud-swollen and discolored
with the noxious blue-black of a festering wound. The
wind moaned eerily, and the treetops whirled, branches
swishing like women's skirts in a storm.

From the unfinished porch of the Acadian-style
house—one of two he was building on speculation—Seth
stood watching the clouds gather.

"What do you think?" Jim Spier asked. Lowering his
gaze from the darkened skies, he directed his attention to
the man beside him.

Seth shifted his weight, pulling back and letting his arm drop from the support post where he'd been leaning. "Looks like tornado weather," he answered grimly. "Better tell the guys to knock off for the rest of the day."

The older man nodded, understanding the danger and the impossibility of working a construction crew in the rain. He disappeared inside the house. Then, minutes later, half a dozen men—some carrying small toolboxes, others wearing wide utility belts strung with various electrical gear—emerged from the house and began to disperse in the direction of their cars.

The storm had yet to break, but to the south, a spear of lightning lanced jaggedly through the clouds, indicating that it wouldn't be long now. Idly, Seth noticed his truck was the only vehicle to be seen.

With a half smile, he turned to Jim. "Where's your car, old man? Or did you ride in on your thumb today?"

Jim grinned and tugged his baseball cap, spearing his fingers through thinning hair before slipping it back on. "Naw," he answered. "I had Gloria drop me off. She needed the car to go visit her sister in town."

"Well, come on. I'll give you a lift," Seth offered as he locked the door of the house, then started down the steps. "I need to run by your house anyway and pick up Jason. I'd really prefer he didn't sleep over at your place tonight."

"My place?" The two men had already crossed the lot and were just approaching Seth's pickup when Jim's steps slowed. He glanced at his friend with a frown. "I thought Tony was staying at your house. At least, that's what he told me. Did Jason say their plans had changed since this morning?"

Seth halted abruptly. An uneasy feeling quivered in the pit of his stomach. His heartbeat quickened, and his skin felt suddenly clammy. Cautiously, he turned to stare at the other man over the bed of the truck. "I haven't talked to Jason," he confessed. "But when he left this morning, he had his clothes and camping stuff with him. And I just assumed... Since he didn't stay home last night..."

Seth's voice trailed off. The wind rose, flapping his shirt sleeves against his arms, and he thought Jim Spier's face paled in the chill.

"Maybe..." The man swallowed visibly, then licked his lips. "Maybe we'd better find out what those kids are up to."

"WHAT TIME IS IT?"

Jason glanced at his leather-banded wrist watch. "Five-ten. You just asked me that five minutes ago."

Sighing, Tony shifted restlessly against the steel wheel of the abandoned tank car. "I can't help it, man. I wish that train would hurry up. I don't like the looks of those clouds. Did you see that lightning strike over there a while ago?"

"Yeah," Jason said, huddling his arms a little tighter against his chest. The skies growled, and the sound of the wind was like the low-throated moan of a wounded animal.

Tony shivered. "Jase?" He watched as his friend turned to look at him. "Do you think your mom and dad will be sorry when you're gone? Think they might miss you, I mean? Maybe even wish they'd have listened to you more?"

For one brief moment, youthful eyes lost their prideful shield of cynicism and softened with a child's despair. "I don't know," he murmured. "But I wish."

THE STORM BROKE with an ear-shattering explosion of thunder that burst the clouds apart as if they were made of glass. The rain slashed down in cutting pellets, attacking the earth with the violence of a crazed knife man. Tess shivered and rubbed her hands over her arms.

Eden stood beside her, also staring out at the rain. "You know," she mused, "if I'd been twenty minutes later I would've been caught in the middle of this and would have had to pull over somewhere. How can anyone see to drive in this weather?"

Tess's smile was one of commiseration and understanding. "Well, I'm glad you made it. All the children got home okay?"

Eden laughed and answered that the kids weren't quite as dry when she dropped them off as when she'd picked them up, but none of them seemed worse for the weather. "Unfortunately, however..." Eden's gaze leveled with concern on Tess. "It doesn't look as if I can say the same for you."

Tess glanced down at her hands, avoiding the tender scrutiny in her sister's eyes. "Bad things always seem to happen in stormy weather," she murmured. Then, realizing how ridiculous that statement sounded, she laughed nervously and shrugged it off. "A minor phobia from childhood, I guess. I don't mind the rain at night. But dark skies when it should be daylight..." Tess laughed again. "I don't know. It's a crazy thing."

"It was raining the day Momma died," Eden said, surprising her sister with this bit of information. Tess had been too young to recall. "You were just over three years old," Eden continued. "It was raining when Dad came home from the hospital, and I remember that you went outside and got all muddy, and he was so angry he spanked you."

Tess's eyes widened. She didn't recall her father ever having lain a hand on her. A firm word, the slightest look of disapproval from him, had always been more than enough to keep her in line when she was growing up. Now Tess stared at Eden, her expression one of faint disbelief. "I didn't remember that," she marveled softly. "He actually spanked me? Only hours after Momma died?"

Eden smiled, her own eyes misting with the memory. "Yes," she whispered. "And then he held you. For a long time, he just held you in the rain and cried."

Tess's heart ached with the vaguest weight of remembrance, and though she knew it was impossible, she felt she could almost recall the broken sounds of her father's weeping, and her own voice—the small, sobbing voice of a child—promising Daddy, if he just wouldn't cry, she would never be bad again.

A loud clap of thunder boomed over the house, causing both women to jump. Realizing what they'd done, they looked at each other and laughed. Memories were once more forgotten.

"How about some coffee?" Eden suggested.

"Sounds good." Tess had just turned to follow her sister into the kitchen when someone pounded on the front door. Frowning, she glanced at Eden. "Were you expecting company?"

"In this weather?"

Feeling the nagging beginning of apprehension, Tess rushed to the door and opened it.

Seth stood before her, soaking wet from the downpour outside. Behind him, his truck idled.

"Seth," Tess said, seeing instantly that something was wrong. "What is it?"

"Jason," he said breathlessly. "I think he's run away."

THE TRAIN WHISTLE'S WAIL could hardly be heard above
the roar of the wind. Thunder crashed, and the rain drove
down in blinding, wall-like sheets, from which there
seemed no escape or shelter. Jason cupped his hands to
his mouth and nose to breathe.

"I can't! I don't think I can make it!" Tony screamed
frantically, gasping for breath.

As the faint, sweeping light of the train grew closer,
they crouched, waiting in the muddy weeds off the bank
of the tracks.

"You can! You've got to!" Jason shouted back, but
the wind tore the words from his lips.

Blinking furiously, the rain lashing against his face, he
peered down the tracks, struggling to judge the length
and speed of the approaching train.

"We could get killed!" Tony cried. "Guys have lost
their legs doing this. Jase, I'm scared, man. Damn this
rain! We can't even see!"

But Jason was beyond hearing. "Get ready!" he
shouted, and then the train was upon them. "Now!" he
screamed.

Launching to his feet, Jason ran, his heart pounding,
the rain driving like nails into his back. His clothes were
soaked. His bedroll banged against his thigh, twisting his
arm, the soddenness of it dragging against his body like
lead. Beside him, the train roared on, plowing over the
flooded tracks and heaping water in his face and against
his legs.

He stumbled; the mud sloshed up, splattering his chest
and his arms. But he caught himself and kept on running. His arm outstretched, he reached for, and briefly
grazed, the cold metal of a vertical handrail on the outside of an open boxcar. The lightning flashed, and the
sight of the handrail obliterated all other thoughts from

Jason's mind. Charged with his second wind, he had almost forgotten Tony's presence behind him until he heard the boy cry out.

"Jaaason!" The wail of the train seemed to drag his name on forever. He glanced over his shoulder just in time to see the other boy fall.

THIS IS ALL YOUR FAULT. Time after time, throughout that long and painful night, Jason Taylor's angry, recriminating words returned to plague Tess's conscience and tear mercilessly at her heart.

Why can't you just leave our family alone?

She asked herself the same question over and over, wondering how this could have happened. How could she have fallen so terribly and blindly in love with Seth that she had let her desire for him make her forget his son's problems, his insecurities, his desperate need for his father's wholehearted attention? His mother had, long ago, abandoned him emotionally. And now, Tess thought, surely it must have appeared to Jason that his father was about to do the same thing.

Because of her. Because she had intruded into their family, Jason had felt betrayed and rejected, and now he was gone. What if he was hurt? Or worse? Dear heaven! She couldn't bear to think of it. How could she live with herself? How could Seth ever forgive her if anything happened to his son?

They searched for hours—she and Seth, Eden, Tony's parents—in the darkness and the drowning rain. They found nothing. Seth blamed himself, and Celia blamed him also... But Tess reminded them both that blame wouldn't bring Jason back any sooner.

In that peculiar way the mind has of focusing only in hindsight upon the ironies of a situation, Tess thought of the conversation she'd had with Mariah just days ago. As she stood beside Seth—watching his face, her heart aching unbearably for the torment she saw in his eyes and heard in his voice—she listened as he phoned the police and gave the parish authorities a description of his missing son.

Fate. Tess remembered how Mariah had insisted it had to be fate, in the improbable form of a thirteen-year-old boy, that had brought Seth and Tess together again after all these years. Fate, the trickster, the three mythical daughters of night who were supposed to control human destiny with a sleight of obscuring hands.

Tess shook her head. Her mind was rambling. She turned from Seth's living-room window where she had been standing for the past half hour, waiting, looking out at the rain and praying for a miracle.

Seth didn't glance up. Even when she crossed the room and came to sit beside him on the edge of the sofa, he made no move to shift himself. He had held the same position for hours, it seemed, slumped forward with his face buried in his hands, his elbows propped on trembling knees.

Tess's eyes filled with tears as she lifted her hand, lightly stroking the tense muscles that stood out across his back, visible even beneath the stretch of his shirt. A tremor ran through him, and suddenly it was as if her touch had been the proverbial straw whose weight proved a final burden, too great to bear.

"Tess!" Seth cried, and her name seemed wrenched from the utter depths of him as he whirled around and caught her, crushing her against him. Her arms went around his back, and he dropped his head on her shoulder. Anguish racked his body with a force that shook them both. Celia regarded them from across the room with a numb and listless expression.

"What will I do? How can I live if something has happened to him? He's my son. My only son. He's all I have," Seth cried, and Tess cried with him.

No, she thought. She didn't believe in fate. But oh, Lord! How she believed in consequences.

By TEN O'CLOCK, the worst of the storm had blown over, but the rain continued to fall in a dismally steady drizzle. The wind had died, and the heated ground smoldered like doused ashes, sending up wisps of steamy fog into the rain.

Jason Taylor sat with his back against the corrugated tin of a small, doorless shed on the side of the McKinley road. The crude shelter—erected to serve as a bus stop for rural schoolchildren and left unattended during the summer—was smelly and nested with wasps and spiders and heaven only knew what else. But at least it was dry. And at the moment, that was certainly more than he could say for himself.

"Jase, you gotta do something," Tony moaned from the opposite corner, rubbing laboriously at the lower calf of his leg. "My ankle is killing me. I think I might've broken it. Look how swollen it is, man. I can't stand this. We've got to get somewhere. Home or somewhere."

Sighing, Jason lifted his head from the wall and opened his eyes with effort. He was so tired he thought he could easily go to sleep just as he was, soaking wet and sitting on a hard rail bench with barely a roof over his head, if only Tony would shut up.

He'd been so scared earlier, when he'd looked back to see the older boy fall beside the train. And then all that screaming—he'd thought for sure the wheels had caught

Tony. Now, however, in the aftermath of receding panic, Jason felt numb with fatigue and irrationally irritated with his friend.

"Tony, what do you want me to do? I'm sorry you stepped in a hole and bummed up your foot. But I sure can't carry you no place else. You're too dang heavy! And besides, you think we can just go strolling back like nothin's happened? Don't you know what they do with runaways? Detention center, man. Reformatory. It's like prison. And my mother's boyfriend would just love to see me there."

Tony sucked in a breath and leaned back against the metal wall. "I'm thirsty," he said miserably, as if Jason's words had gone in one ear and out the other without even registering. "If I could stand up, I'd hitch a ride up to the store, and get me a soda and a pack of aspirin."

Jason said nothing. Tony bent forward and began massaging his throbbing ankle again.

"You know, you're right about one thing, though," he said, his voice trembling slightly. "We can't stay here too much longer. Come daylight, there'll be no hiding in this tin can. But if I move anywhere, I'm gonna have to have something for this pain. What do ya say, Jase?" Tony looked up at his friend. "You think you might at least go get me some aspirin, since you got the money, and I can't walk?"

Jason tightened his lips, and for several long seconds he simply stared at Tony. It was still raining. He didn't feel like getting out in the rain again. His clothes and his hair were just now starting to dry. And he didn't want to take a chance on being seen—of being picked up and hauled in to juvenile hall again.

But, as he looked at Tony, Jason remembered how scared and white his face had been when the train was coming and it was raining so hard they couldn't see. He remembered, too, how sick *he* had almost gotten—like he might throw up—when he'd thought Tony had been hurt. It was this last thought that finally settled the issue.

"All right, I'll do it," Jason relented. "But let's don't talk about going home anymore, okay? Because I can't. My mother doesn't want me, and now my dad's got somebody, too. But I don't need them. As long as you and me stick together, we don't need anybody else."

"Naw, man. Nobody," Tony agreed, but Jason thought he didn't look as convinced as he sounded.

Shoving his fists into his pockets, Jason stepped out of the shed and ducked his head against the rain. The road was long and dark, and he had no idea if there was even any place open in town this time of night.

Idly, he thought about the train he and Tony had failed to catch and wondered where it was right now. And then he found himself wondering what his dad was doing. Was he worried? Were they looking for him? Or had they even noticed he was gone? Well, it didn't matter, Jason told himself. He didn't need them. Tomorrow, he and Tony would head through the woods to the edge of the interstate, and then....

"That's far enough, kid."

Jason froze, then wheeled around suddenly to find that he had been so caught up in his thoughts he'd failed to notice the tan patrol car parked by the side of the road. The door swung open and a khaki-uniformed officer slid out, blinding him with the beam of his flashlight.

"I'll say this for you, boy..." The deputy sauntered forward, shaking his head. "You sure picked yourself one hell of a night to go on the lam."

WITHIN AN HOUR after Jason and Tony were picked up, they were politely escorted to the front doorsteps of their respective homes. Tess stood trembling, gripping the back of an armchair as Seth, his voice low and willfully controlled, gleaned the details of the night's events from the parish officer who had seen Jason home.

Across the room in the rocking chair, Celia sat ram-rod straight. Her legs were crossed and her arms folded so tightly it looked as if she might explode from the sheer effort of trying to keep quiet until the officer had time to leave.

Jason neither spoke nor raised his eyes to anyone. From the moment he'd stepped through the door, he'd stood with his body half turned from the room, his hands jammed in his pockets as he scowled at the floor. His stance, Tess knew, was meant to project a careless sense of defiance. But somehow—as he stood there, shivering in his mud-caked clothes, his blond hair matted and clumped like cornrows, trailing into his eyes—she thought he looked merely vulnerable and alone.

This is all your fault. The boy's words returned once more to twist Tess's insides with guilt. And almost as if Jason had known what was in her mind, he chose that very moment to lift his head, his eyes boring into hers with such contempt that she felt the blood rush, sting-ing, to her face.

Unable to bear it, Tess glanced away, her eyes filling with tears. Lord, she thought, what had she done to make this child despise her so?

It seemed like eons before the parish deputy finally left. And later, Tess thought it was as if the very closing of the door behind him acted like the striking of a match touched to the fuse of a powder keg.

In a vicious explosion of rage like none Tess had witnessed before in her life, Celia McKinsey leaped to her feet and tore into Jason.

"How could you do such a thing!" she screamed, grabbing him by the arm and digging her nails into his sleeve. "How could you deliberately hurt me that way, when everything I've done for the last thirteen years has been for you? Think! Think about the sacrifices I've made for you, Jason! Think about the things you've put me through!"

"Let him go." Seth's voice was guttural with barely contained fury. Tess swung around to stare at him and saw the lethal menace in his eyes as he glared at his ex-wife. His fists were clenched at his side, and only his face seemed whiter than his knuckles.

Celia didn't bother to glance at her ex-husband. Instead, she shook Jason, as if it would jar him into seeing his mistakes. "Don't you know my parents still have friends in this town?" she continued, screaming wildly. "Do you want everybody to know that I've lost complete control over you? Jason, any imbecile ought to know you can't catch a moving train!"

Jason's mouth trembled, and Tess feared that the reference to his being an imbecile had been one he'd heard often in his life, one that had contributed to his damaged self-image. She was afraid Jason would cry in front of all of them, humiliating him further, a fate worse than death to a thirteen-year-old boy. But at the moment, it was Seth's emotions she feared the most.

"Let him go, I said!" Seth took a step toward Celia, and Tess's heart began to race in pure terror. Never had she seen Seth so angry, and she knew how easily this situation could turn into a violent one.

"Celia, let him go!" Tess cried frantically, and the shrill pitch of her voice rang with such alarm, everyone in the room seemed to freeze for an instant. Slowly, she saw Celia's eyes darken with a new contempt.

"And just who are you, Miss High-and-Mighty, to tell me what to do with my own son?" Dropping Jason's arm, she turned on Tess, her lips twisting into a sneer. "This is a private discussion, anyway, and you have no business here. And don't start thinking that you do, just because you've played nanny to my son . . . and whore to my husband!"

It happened so fast, Tess couldn't remember later how Seth had managed to cross the room with such speed. In a lightning flash of a second, he was standing between Tess and Celia, and all she could see was the rigid wall of his back.

"If you were a man, I'd beat the hell out of you for that," Seth grated. "Get out of here, before I'm forced to throw you out."

"You can't throw me out of this house," Celia shot back at him. "I'm Jason's mother. And I'm going to take him back with me."

"The hell you are!" Seth exploded. He grasped her shoulder, but Celia jerked free of him.

"I'm warning you, Seth!" she screamed. "Keep your hands off me, or I'll take him so far that you'll never see him again! I'll—"

"Stop it!" Jason screamed, and suddenly the room went deathly still, only the ragged sound of his sobbing penetrating the gripping silence. "Why do you have to do this? Why? I should have gotten killed," he cried, his face twisting in agony. "Then maybe I'd be out of everybody's way!"

"Jason, no..." Seth's face went completely white with pain and shock. Celia pressed her hand to her throat, her eyes wide. They relaxed their battle stance and straightened, both stepping away from each other, guilt stamped on their faces.

Tess felt tears running down her cheeks, and she turned to Jason, her heart twisting and aching for him. "Jason, honey. Your parents love you. They're just upset and worried for you." She started to reach for him. "Can't you see that—"

"No!" She had been reaching for him, wanting to comfort him, but he jerked away from her touch. "See what you've done? I told you to leave us alone. To leave my family alone. This is all your fault. You're the reason I ran away—not them. Because I don't want you here. You don't belong."

With that, Jason rushed past her and ran down the hall. Seth stood paralyzed for a moment, watching his son disappear. On his tormented face was the look of a man who had just sustained a mortal wound. There was no thought for comforting Tess or turning on Celia again. Slowly, he started to Jason's room, intent on healing Jason's wounds instead.

Tess stood motionless for a breath-held span of seconds, watching the empty hall and the door that closed behind Seth. It occurred to her that this was the time to make her exit, to leave Seth's undivided attention to Jason, to allow the child to have the reassurances he'd needed all his life.

Pull yourself together, she told herself. *Then turn around and walk out of here. If you love Seth . . . if you love Jason . . . that's what you have to do.*

She heard a sob behind her and turned around to see Celia, hands hiding her face, shaking with the force of a woman who's just reached the limits of her emotional control. She sucked in a tattered breath, released it in a broken wail and bent over almost double, as if the effort to hold in her despair was physically beyond her capabilities.

For the flash of a second, Tess thought Celia would fall to her knees, and something...something like compassion...welled up inside her. Slowly, she went to the woman she had envied during their high-school years, the woman who'd had everything...even Seth. Now, she thought sadly, Celia had even less than Tess had. For she had lost her dignity.

Tess touched a hand to Celia's hair, then took her arm gently and led her to the couch. She sat beside her, letting Celia cry out great fragments of her misery. After a moment, Celia moved her hands from her crimson face and wiped at her swollen eyes. "He...he could have been killed," she said. "Or he could have made it...onto that train. I never would have...seen him again..."

Her shredded voice collapsed into a round of sobs again, and Tess closed her eyes. Celia loved Jason, she thought, though she'd never been taught the right way to show it. All her life, love had been a material thing, heaped upon her with cash values attached. Now that she was broke...and broken...love was an elusive dream she hadn't quite been able to realize.

"He'll be all right," Tess whispered. "Seth will talk to him. I know you resent him, but Celia, he's a good father to Jason. Jason loves him very much."

Celia flashed anguished eyes to Tess. "Don't you think I know that? Seth always had more control over him... He knew how to handle the things that came up that just sent me right over the edge. But what was I supposed to do? Just hand Jason over, because Seth was a better

parent than I was? Just say goodbye to my son like I'd
never had him?''

Tears filled Tess's eyes, and she reached for her purse,
lying on the couch, digging into it in search of a tissue.
She had stashed a pack of them there weeks ago, as security against the sudden outbursts of tears that kept as-
saulting her when she least expected them. She had come
a long way since then.

She handed a tissue to Celia now, and the woman took
it willingly. Tess watched her blot her eyes, her nose, then
wad the tissue and press it to her mouth, where muffled
sobs kept hiccuping in her throat.

"You know, Celia, it doesn't have to be either you *or*
Seth. Jason needs you both. Not to belittle and malign
each other, but to work together as his parents. All he
wants is your love. He needs that so much.''

Celia squeezed her eyes shut, swallowed back her tears,
but she didn't answer. Tess sat still for a moment longer,
let her eyes drift to the dark hallway and told herself
she'd done all she could do. It was time to go.

Slowly, she picked up her purse, clutched it against her
stomach and started for the door.

"Wh—where are you going?'' Celia asked.

"I'm going home,'' Tess said quietly, desperate to
control the quiver in her voice. "The three of you have a
lot to work out.''

"But ... won't Seth ... ? Shouldn't you ... ?''

The incipient tears welling in Tess's eyes spilled over,
and she wiped them away. "Tell Seth I said...goodbye.''

And then, without allowing herself to think just how
final that word really was, she slipped out the front door.

CHAPTER FIFTEEN

THE OPEN SUITCASE covered the surface of Tess's bed, and quietly, so as not to wake Eden, she gathered her things out of the drawers and packed them as neatly as if she were beginning a trip...not ending one.

A light flicked on in the hallway, signaling that Eden was up. Tess released a wilting breath and prayed that her sister wouldn't try to stop her. Already, the decision to leave had proved to be one of the most difficult of her life. She turned and saw Eden in the doorway, a fragile silhouette against the light at her back. Her groggy eyes traveled to Tess, then to the suitcases and back to Tess. A look of forlorn disappointment fell upon her features. "Tess? What's going on?" she asked.

"I'm going home," Tess whispered.

Eden stepped into the room, into the small dim circle of lamplight guiding Tess's progress, and took the blouse that Tess was folding out of her hands. "This is your home," she said.

Tess shook her head. "No, Eden. This is your home. I have to go back to Dallas."

Despair passed over Eden's eyes, but she tried to recover. "Tell me what happened," she demanded. "Is it Jason?"

"Yes," Tess said. "We found him. He's upset and scared and... Well, he needs to know that his parents love him...without any outsiders getting in the way."

Eden cupped Tess's chin, turning her face around. Tess tried to smile, but fresh tears emerged in her eyes, and Eden pulled her into her arms. "Oh, honey," she whispered. "I know how things must look right now. But don't make any quick decisions based on something Jason may have done or said when he was upset."

Tess pulled back and wiped her eyes. "It isn't a quick decision, Eden," she said. "I've been thinking about this ever since the first time Jason told me to leave his family alone. Do you think it was easy, deciding to step out of the picture? The plain, simple fact is, Jason needs Seth more than I do."

She took the blouse back and laid it carefully in the suitcase, then went back to the drawer. Eden watched her—the meticulous way Tess shook out each garment and refolded it—and it was a moment before Tess realized that her older sister was crying, too. She turned around and saw Eden half hugging the bed post.

"Tess, sometimes you can't just run away," she said. "Sometimes you have to stay and fight."

Tess looked at Eden, and this time the smile that came to her lips was genuine, even if it was laced with sadness. "Oh, Eden. Fight with whom? A thirteen-year-old boy?" She took a deep breath and spoke again. "Besides, I'm not running away this time. I've come too far for that."

"Then what's this?" Eden asked, gesturing helplessly toward the suitcases.

"This is a beginning," Tess said. "I'm running *to* something. A new life." She dropped the stack of folded blouses into the suitcase and regarded Eden honestly. "You see, in the long run, I think I've gained a lot more than I've lost. Seth showed me that I was worthy of being loved, and that's something that I haven't really believed since the day Momma died."

Eden caught her breath—as if she'd been struck in the stomach—and took a wavering step toward her sister. "How can you say that?" she whispered. "I always loved you. We all did."

"I know that," Tess said. "But you were my sisters. And sometimes I thought love among sisters was more a habit than an emotion. Dad never ever opened up to me, to any of us, after Momma died. And somewhere in my heart, I got all mixed up, and I guess it just seemed like I was supposed to be alone, all enclosed in a shell that no one could break through. Because if they ever did, they'd find out that there really wasn't that much there."

"Wasn't that much?" Eden asked softly, her eyes luminous with glossy tears. "Honey, you just never saw in yourself how much there really was. Mariah and Jo and I always knew, but we didn't know how to show you."

Tess wiped the last of her tears away and pulled Eden down to sit on the bed beside her. "It's okay," she said firmly. "Because I know now. Seth taught me that I can be loved...and somehow, he showed me how to love myself."

Eden slid her arms around Tess's shoulders, embracing her so hard that, for a moment, Tess almost wanted to stay here, in the warm cocoon of Eden's love. "I'll be so lonely without you," Eden said.

Tess clung to her sister for a space of time that seemed oddly suspended in the dying night, and they wept together in a way they'd never done in their lives. But finally Tess broke the embrace. "I have to go," she whispered. "Before Seth tries to stop me. It would just be too hard to go if I had to face him."

Eden wiped her face with a trembling hand. "I wish you'd wait until morning," she said. "I could make you some fresh cinnamon rolls, and fix you a bag of some things to take back with you—"

"I can't," Tess said firmly. "It's best that I go now."

Eden sat on the bed, gazing at her feet with eloquent defeat in her eyes. Finally, she got to her feet and opened one of Tess's drawers.

"I'll help you pack," she whispered.

IT WAS MORNING before Seth stirred from where he'd fallen asleep on Jason's bed. He opened his eyes, rubbed them and looked at Jason, sleeping soundly, peacefully, in spite of all that had happened last night.

Gently, he sat up, moved his feet to the floor and leaned over, grinding his elbows into his knees. He had tried to talk to Jason when he'd come in here last night, but the boy had been too upset. The way he'd lain clutching his pillow to his stomach with his knees drawn up to his chest, crying like someone who'd been holding it in for months...even years...it had all broken Seth's heart.

And so he had sat here on the bed next to his son, not saying a word, just stroking the boy's head until Jason's sobs had subsided and he lay still, staring with listless eyes at the wall beside his bed. Seth hadn't left him all night, and finally, at some point in the wee hours of the morning, Jason had fallen asleep. Seth had, too, soon after.

His mind drifted to the two women he'd left in the living room. What must Tess be thinking right now? he asked himself. Was she as upset as Jason was, beating herself up for the things the boy had said?

Slowly, he came to his feet, not waking the boy, and slipped out of his room. He saw Celia asleep on the couch, still dressed in the clothes she'd worn the night before, as if she'd kept from going into the guest room for fear that she'd lose her chance to talk to Jason as soon as Seth came out.

He looked around and saw that Tess was gone. *Damn,* he thought. *I should have told her good night. I should have reassured her that Jason would come around...* But strangely, he had no regrets about sitting with his son all night. Tess would understand, he thought. That was what made her so special.

Celia awoke at the sound of his footsteps and sat up on the couch. She rubbed her eyes and frowned at Seth. "How is he?"

"Sleeping," Seth said. "I fell asleep with him, or I would have come out sooner."

He stood before her, hands hanging at his sides, staring at the woman who had both used and tempted him years ago. But now, he had to admit, he had used her, as well. "We've really screwed up, haven't we?"

Celia nodded, for the first time not flying back with an accusation. "Tell me what to do, Seth," she whispered. "I'll do whatever it takes to make things right with him."

"Let him stay with me," Seth said without hesitation. "Let me give him a home."

Celia's eyes filled with despairing tears, but she kept them fixed on Seth. Her well-groomed hand—adorned with extravagant rings that had never quite replaced her father's love—moved to hide her quivering lips. A long moment stretched out between them, a moment in which he expected her to scream that there was no way she would let go of Jason again, that he was *her* son, that Jason loved her, and a million other irrelevant, irrational things. But instead, Celia took in a deep, ragged breath. "Just do me a favor, okay?" she asked. "Say something good about me every now and then?"

Seth turned his face away for a moment, wishing to heaven that he could change all of the past thirteen years, soften the hate, heal the sting of sharp words flung in anger, erase all the bitterness that had passed between them. Finally, he turned around and found a smile for the woman who had given birth to his son. "I think I can handle that," he said.

IT WAS A FEW HOURS before Jason woke up, giving Celia the opportunity to say goodbye for now. After she'd left, he had gone back to his room and had hidden in the refuge of his headphones.

Now that Seth had the chance, he went to the kitchen, picked up the phone and dialed Tess's number.

"Hello?" It was Eden's voice, weary and quiet, that answered.

"Eden, it's Seth. Can I speak to Tess, please?"

There was a long pause before Eden broke the news. "She's not here, Seth. She went back to Dallas last night."

"*What?*" The word shot like an arrow across the line as reality shot through Seth's already aching heart. "What do you mean, she went back last night? She was with me until after midnight!"

Eden cleared her throat. "I'm sorry, Seth. She left at about four this morning. I tried to talk her out of it, but she felt like it was the thing to do."

Seth rubbed a splayed hand through his hair and searched the counter for something to write with. "All right," he said, his breath coming too rapidly, hampering his speech. "All right. Just ... just give me her address. I'll go after her."

"No." Eden's tone was firm. "I can't. She asked me not to."

Seth slammed his hand onto the countertop and whirled around, gripping the phone with his fist. "Eden!" he cried. "I love her! Don't do this to me!"

Eden's voice broke, as if she were having as much trouble with her emotions as Seth had with his. "She loves you," she said. "And Jason. But she has this idea that the two of you need each other now—without her."

Seth whirled around, a look of pure misery on his face, and saw Jason standing in the doorway. He caught his despair, reined it back in and told himself to hold on...he'd figure something out. "Eden, you know she's wrong. Please. Just tell me a phone number. Something."

"I can't, Seth," she whispered. "I gave her my word."

Seth hung up the phone helplessly and felt his hands trembling as he brought them back to his face.

"What is it?" Jason asked, stepping up behind his father.

"She's gone," Seth said in a strained monotone. "Just like that."

Jason stood staring at his father for a few minutes, watching his shoulders slump and his hands tremble, watching the mist come and go from his eyes. "Are...are you going after her?" he asked.

Seth closed his eyes and took a deep breath. "No, son. Dallas is a big place. And Eden won't give me her address."

Jason looked at the floor for a moment, then back at his father, who had taken a cleansing breath and was trying to wipe the tears from his face. "She left because of me, didn't she?" he asked.

Seth bent over and set his elbows on his knees. "Yes," Seth admitted. "Because she loves you. And because she loves me."

Jason's face distorted in disbelief. "She don't love me," he argued. "She hardly even knows me."

"She knows you as well as anyone else does, Jason," Seth said. "As well as you'll let anyone know you."

Jason leaned against the counter opposite his father, his face pale and battle-weary from the long night. "Are you mad?" the boy asked. "Because I ran her off?"

Seth's eyes misted over again, and he slid off of the counter. He stood in front of his son and cupped his hand behind his head. "Jason, what does it take to get through to you? I'm not mad at you, because last night you said what you really thought. You were hurt and afraid that you were going to lose me to her." He messed up his son's hair, and Jason's eyes strayed to his bare feet.

"But, Jason. It's time you realized that I love you more than any person on this earth. Nothing you do, nothing you say, is ever going to change that. And if it takes me the rest of my life, somehow, I'm gonna get that through your head."

He pulled Jason into his arms then, and held him with all the love he had held back for so long for fear that Jason would pull away. But now Jason clung just as tightly to him as if he'd been waiting all his life to hear his father utter the simple words that changed everything.

THE TREES WERE BEGINNING to turn from green to purple to yellow weeks later when Jason strolled out to the work shed to crank up the go-cart he and his dad had finally finished working on. He sat in it for a moment, thinking how he wished the day would hurry up and end so that his father would come home. He hated these long afternoons after school, especially when he was having trouble with his homework. Seth always helped him after supper, supplementing the work that his new tutor started each day.

The go-cart's engine buzzed like that of a lawn mower, and he shifted the gear into first and drove slowly out of the shed. Idly, his mind drifted to a day when Tess had found him and his father working on it and had offered to help. He had been rude to her that day, as he had on many other occasions, and yet she had never stopped being nice to him.

She's trying to get to your dad through you. Tony's words came back to him, empty echoes in the chambers of his mind. The theory didn't work anymore, he thought. If Tess had been trying to use him to get to Seth, she never would have left. She'd have hung around in spite of Jason's attitude, for Seth was already in love with her.

He cut across the acres in the backyard, thinking how his father had tried to hide his dejection. He never spoke to Jason of Tess, never alluded to anything that had passed between them . . .

But sometimes Seth's eyes would cloud over, and he'd stare off into space. . . Jason knew that at those times Seth was thinking of her, and that none of the things they did to fill each other's time would make up for what his father had lost.

Guilt surged through him, but deep down he couldn't help feeling almost victorious. He had his dad to himself now, and that was something that he'd never thought possible.

He turned the go-cart around and headed toward the front of the house. He saw a blue Astro van pull into his driveway and he slowed, downshifting, and drove around the house.

He turned off the engine as the van's driver got out. Jason stood up, watching the man walk toward him. He was tall and wore a pair of tinted glasses, tight faded jeans and a red flannel shirt with the sleeves rolled up to just below his elbows. Jason was sure he'd never met the man before.

And yet . . . there was something familiar about him.

"Hi," the man said, starting across the yard toward him.

Jason lifted his hand in a half wave. "How's it goin'? If you're looking for my dad, he's not home from work yet."

The man grinned, his broad smile once again triggering some vague recognition in Jason's mind. "As a matter of fact, I'm not," the stranger replied. "I was looking for you, Jason."

Jason stiffened instantly, and his eyes widened. "Why? What did I do?"

The man laughed and slid his fingers into the pockets of his jeans. "Well, nothing that I know of . . . It's just that my sister-in-law told me she'd made you a promise a few weeks ago, and I thought I'd drop by to keep it for her."

"A promise?" Jason asked, understanding dawning on him. "Wait a minute . . ."

Just as his realization began to take concrete form in his mind, the man removed his glasses, revealing the famous face that adorned Jason's bedroom wall. "E.Z. Ellis!" Jason shouted. "I can't believe it! You're him. I mean, he's you!"

"We're one and the same," E.Z. said with a grin of pure amusement.

Jason clutched his head and stumbled back. "Oh, man, oh, man. Wait'll Tony hears!"

E.Z. laughed again and strolled over to the porch, where he sat on the steps, his glasses hanging idly from his hand. "Well, maybe you can invite this Tony to come with you to my next recording session. Tess asked me if I'd mind, and I told her I never mind having a genuine fan watching me work." He peered at Jason, still standing, dumbfounded, before him. "That is what you are, isn't it? A fan?"

"Oh, man," Jason said. "You better believe it. I have all your albums. Even the old ones." He stepped onto the porch, peering down at E.Z. "You're not just kidding about my sitting in on a session?"

E.Z. inclined his head and shaded his eyes from the sun. "No more than Tess was when she promised to introduce us."

Jason lowered himself to the step beside E.Z. "Yeah," he said, nodding. "She really held to it, didn't she? I thought she was just trying to—" He halted abruptly, tried to rephrase his words. "I mean, I didn't know if she was—"

"Sincere?" E.Z. asked, suddenly serious. "Is that what you mean?"

Jason met the star's blue eyes, the eyes that were full of such vivid life on his album covers. "Yeah, I guess."

E.Z. leaned his elbows on his knees and looked over the lawn. "If there's anything I can tell you about Tess, it's that she's one of the most sincere people I've ever met. It's something about those Calloway sisters, I think. They're honest and caring, and family is about the most important thing in their lives. Sometimes they don't even know it themselves."

Jason lowered his gaze to his feet, and with his finger traced the dirty white leather there. "My dad wanted to marry her. But I was...I said..." His voice faltered, and he shot E.Z. a guilty look. "She went back to Dallas because of me."

E.Z. nodded and offered Jason a smile. "I know," he said. "Those Calloways are pretty tight. Eden told us the whole story."

Jason looked away, suddenly ashamed of what E.Z. must have heard about him. "You must think I'm pretty terrible, huh?"

E.Z. gave him a surprised look, as if the thought had never crossed his mind. "Do you think you're the first person who's ever had a selfish thought? The main thing, Jason, is that Tess didn't go back because of what you said, but because of what you felt. And you couldn't have changed that for her."

"Yeah," Jason said. He shot E.Z. a sidelong look and knitted his brows together. "You mean you didn't come here to try to make me feel bad about her? Or to make me take back everything I said?"

E.Z. laughed and shrugged. "No. I came here because I'm a ham, and I like to talk to people who listen to my music." He cocked his head and studied the boy for a moment. "Do you feel bad about her?"

Jason stood, went down the steps and kicked a rock into the yard. "I don't know. I guess sometimes I wish that my dad was happier. He doesn't even know where she is. If Eden would just tell him, maybe he'd feel better."

"Hell," E.Z. said, lifting one hip and pulling his wallet out of his back pocket. "If it's her address you want, I'll give it to you. I may have married a Calloway, but I never took the vow of secrecy those women seem to keep between themselves." He pulled out a slip of paper with Tess's address written on it and handed it to the boy.

Jason took the paper grudgingly, looked at it and wadded it in his hand. "What makes you think I want it?" he asked E.Z.

E.Z. got to his feet. "I don't know," he said. "Maybe you don't. But if you ever decide you want to find her, maybe to make your dad happy or to thank her for the time and effort she spent on you, well, there it is."

Jason stuffed it into his jeans pocket and regarded E.Z. suspiciously. "Why'd you give it to me instead of my dad?"

"It's not up to your dad, Jason," E.Z. said. "It's up to you."

He looked at Jason for a moment, watching the words sink in. Finally, he nudged him gently with his elbow. "Now, are you gonna keep making me stand out in your yard, or do I get to come in and see that album collection for myself?"

A broad youthful smile slashed across Jason's face, and a sparkle returned to his eyes once again. "Aw right," he exclaimed and dashed up the steps. "Right in here, man. Aw, *nobody's* gonna believe this!"

NOBODY WOULD HAVE BELIEVED all that Tess had accomplished in the past few weeks, she thought, sitting at her desk in the second bedroom of her new apartment. A stack of papers to be graded cluttered her desktop, a reminder that she was needed, that there was work to be done, that there was no time for daydreaming.

Her eyes strayed to the manila envelope in one of her stacked trays, the envelope containing the final papers on the sale of her house. They had closed the deal yesterday, she and Vance, and each had walked away with a nice sum in their pockets. Somehow, as she'd shaken his hand, as if he'd been a business partner rather than her husband, she had realized, once and for all, that her ties to him had been completely severed. No longer did she harbor bitterness over his new wife and the child they were having. In truth, she found that she had exactly the same amount of interest in the situation as she would have in a divorce she read about in the newspaper. It had been easy to wish him well, and she was proud of that.

She owed it all to Seth.

Her eyes strayed to the greeting card she'd kept on her desk for the past two weeks, the card that had jumped out at her from its rack in the grocery store. The heading, "I miss you," had beckoned to her, because at that very moment she had been thinking of him. For some reason she couldn't fathom now, she had bought the card, carefully neglecting to pick up the envelope that went with it . . . as though she could tolerate the thought of sending it, but not the action itself.

She'd kept up with Seth through Eden, who'd told her that he had permanent custody of Jason, but that the boy saw his mother more now than he had when he'd lived with her. Things had a way of working out like that. At least, some things.

Tess closed her eyes and tried not to ache at the thought of him . . . but aching wasn't one of the things she had control over lately. She supposed that the ache would always be there . . . that she would have to learn to live with it. Nobody had said it would be easy.

The doorbell rang, and she heard a light knock follow. Stacking the test papers, she got up from her chair and went to the front door. Probably one of the other divorced teachers from school, she thought, who occasionally stopped by on weekends for companionship. She welcomed the diversion, thankful that the knock had come just as she was thinking of Seth.

She opened the door and caught her breath at the sight of Jason Taylor, standing, awkward and self-conscious, with his hands jammed into his jeans pockets, looking at her threshold as if he couldn't bring himself to look into her eyes. "Jason!" she said. "What are you doing here? How did you get to Dallas?"

A half grin tipped his lips at her surprise, and he peered up at her. "Well, I didn't jump a train, if that's what you mean," he said.

Tess stepped back from the door and motioned him in, flabbergasted. "How...how did you know where I was?"

"E.Z. told me," the boy admitted. "He came, just like you said he would."

Tess exhaled a long breath, thankful to Jo for seeing her promise through, even though it had been the last thing on her mind lately. "Well, I'm glad he told you," she said. "You may not believe this, but I've missed you."

Jason looked around the apartment, still avoiding her eyes. The overstuffed sofa, the antique rocker, the cherry-wood tables, all seemed to interest him. "Yeah, well... My new tutor is this old lady with bad breath. I mean, she's nice and everything, but she's not..." His voice dropped down until she had to strain to hear. "She's not you."

Tess's eyes filled with a fine mist, and she swallowed the emotion, the tentative hope, inching into her heart. "Well, thank you, Jason. I appreciate that."

Jason leaned back against a table, and Tess sat down, suddenly feeling light-headed and confused. What had he come here for? And where was Seth?

"My dad has missed you, too," he said, suddenly looking into her eyes, as if that admission were easier to make than his own. "He's been kinda miserable since you left."

Tess's gaze drifted to the floor. "I'm sorry. I didn't want him to be miserable."

"Neither did I," Jason confessed. "It was pretty stupid, what I said." He withdrew his gaze again and looked into the small kitchen. It was undecorated, as if her stay here wasn't a permanent one. "The thing is, I've thought a lot about it. Everybody says it's okay that I just said what I really felt. But I don't really think I meant it."

Those tears she struggled with dropped over her bottom lashes, and Tess nodded. "I know, Jason."

He went on as if he had to get it all out before he lost his nerve. "So... I came to tell you... that if you want to see my dad again, or marry him, or just... whatever... well, it'd be okay with me."

It was then that Tess lost her battle with her tears, and melting with the most profound relief she'd ever felt, she went to the boy and drew him into her arms. She held him close as she wept into his hair, silently thanking God that it had been Jason's choice to come to her... Jason's alone. "Where is he?" she whispered.

"Outside," Jason said. "Waiting."

Tess released Jason, dropped a kiss on his cheek and started for the door as fast as she could go. She flung it open...

Seth stood leaning against the doorjamb, as if he'd been listening, waiting anxiously for the moment that he could see her. Their embrace was immediate and intense, and the kisses that followed came with a broken stream of whispers and promises and questions and answers.

"Marry me?" Seth whispered.

"When?" Tess asked. "Just name the time."

"Tomorrow," Seth said, weaving his fingers through her hair as his lips made forays against her skin. "To-day. Yesterday."

Jason cleared his throat, and they both looked his way, seeing him leaning awkwardly against the table, a smile curving his lips. "You know, Dad, if you waited till Monday, I wouldn't mind skipping school and standing up for you."

They all laughed at that, and together Seth and Tess pulled Jason into their embrace. Together, they all stood hugging, laughing, crying, for a span of eternity.

Outside the door that still hung open, a slow, cool drizzle began to fall. But through the clouds cut a deep, sharp ray of sunshine, painting the day in yellow hues. And Tess knew for the first time in her life that brightness lay ahead, and that when there was rain Seth would be there to help her through it. And so would Jason.

For family was more than mere circumstance of birth. Family meant being chosen. Family meant knowing you were loved.

Harlequin Superromance

The elemental passions of *Spring Thunder*
come alive once again in the sequel....

SUMMER LIGHTNING

by

SANDRA JAMES

You enjoyed Maggie Howard's strong fiery nature
in *Spring Thunder*. Now she's back in *Summer
Lightning*, determined to fight against the resump-
tion of logging in her small Oregon town. McBride
Lumber has caused nothing but grief for her in the
past. But when Jared McBride returns to head the
operation, Maggie finds that her greatest struggle is
with her heart.

Summer Lightning is Maggie Howard's story of
love. Coming in April.

SR335-1

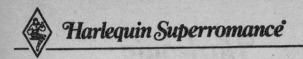
Harlequin Superromance

CALLOWAY CORNERS

Created by four outstanding Superromance authors, bonded by lifelong friendship and a love of their home state: Sandra Canfield, Tracy Hughes, Katherine Burton and Penny Richards.

CALLOWAY CORNERS

Home of four sisters as different as the seasons, as elusive as the elements; an undiscovered part of Louisiana where time stands still and passion lasts forever.

CALLOWAY CORNERS

Birthplace of the unforgettable Calloway women: *Mariah*, free as the wind, and untamed until she meets the preacher who claims her, body and soul; *Jo*, the fiery, feisty defender of lost causes who loses her heart to a rock and roll man; *Tess*, gentle as a placid lake but tormented by her longing for the town's bad boy and *Eden*, the earth mother who's been so busy giving love she doesn't know how much she needs it until she's awakened by a drifter's kiss . . .

CALLOWAY CORNERS

Coming from Superromance, in 1989:
Mariah, by Sandra Canfield, a January release
Jo, by Tracy Hughes, a February release
Tess, by Katherine Burton, a March release
Eden, by Penny Richards, an April release

Harlequin Superromance

COMING NEXT MONTH

#350 EDEN • Penny Richards
Eden Calloway was too much of a woman not to crave a man, and too proudly female not to wait a lifetime for the right one. When Nick Logan pulled into her driveway on a motorcycle, he seemed the least likely mate possible for Eden. But the heart has reasons that are inexplicable, and love has a magic that casts an unbreakable spell....

#351 ECHOES ON THE WIND • Tina Vasilos
In Greece to negotiate a deal, Joanna Paradises was surprised to run into legal eagle Alex Gregory. As teens in Vancouver, they'd shared adolescent kisses. Now, years later, the possibilities were endless ... if Joanna would allow Alex to breach her defenses.

#352 SUMMER LIGHTNING • Sandra James
Maggie Howard was furious when she discovered that Jared McBride was back in Silver Creek, preparing to reopen his family's logging business. McBride Lumber had caused Maggie nothing but grief in the past, and she was determined to stop him. But when it came to fighting Jared, Maggie's greatest struggle was with her heart....

#353 SPECIAL TREASURES • Sharon Brondos
When Colorado-based jeweler Maggie Wellington teamed up with Aussie opal miner Mick O'Shay to track down a killer, she wondered if she could get along with a man whose ideas about justice were so different from her own. But once in the outback she began to understand the elemental passions that drove Nick....